UNDERGROUND

UNDERGROUND

JUNE HUTTON

Cormorant Books

Canada Council   Conseil des Arts
for the Arts   du Canada

The publisher gratefully acknowledges the support of the Canada Council for the Arts and the
Ontario Arts Council for its publishing program. We acknowledge the
financial support of the Government of Canada through the Book Publishing
Industry Development Program (BPIDP) for our publishing activities.

Printed and bound in Canada

Library and Archives Canada Cataloguing in Publication

Hutton, June (Heather June Hutton)
Underground / June Hutton.

ISBN 978-1-896951-81-2

1. World War, 1914–1918--Fiction. I. Title.

PS8615.U88 U54 2009   C813'.6   C2009-900669-3

Cover image and design: Angel Guerra / Archetype
Text design: Tannice Goddard / Soul Oasis Networking
Printer: Friesens

CORMORANT BOOKS INC.
215 SPADINA AVENUE, STUDIO 230, TORONTO, ON CANADA M5T 2C7
www.cormorantbooks.com

for my mother, Ivy Kathleen

The story of war is told in the thousand and one things that mingle with the earth — equipment, bits of clothing almost unrecognizable, an old boot stuck up from a mound of filth, a remnant of sock inside ...

— FRED VARLEY

OFFICIAL WAR ARTIST FOR CANADA

FIRST WORLD WAR

The Somme, 1916

A MUD SKY CHURNS OVER a mud field broken by coils of barbed wire, a wheel severed from a cart, a tangle of brown limbs. He slides the barrel of the rifle over the dirt wall and nestles his cheek against cold metal and wood for one last sweep. No sign of movement. No spit in his mouth either. His own ragged breathing the only sound.

Relentless rain has collapsed the south wall and so they have spent the night digging. He, Kirk, Tubbs, another dozen of them up and down the trench, their helmets just skimming the top, a line of turtles along a ditch hoping their shells protect them. But approaching daylight is an oyster smear along the horizon. Attack is most likely now. They spear their shovels into their packs and fix bayonets to their rifles, take turns standing watch while the rest stamp their feet, blow on their fingertips to warm them and wait for the call to stand down.

He shoulders his rifle and jumps down from the fire step. Kirk takes his place. Tubbs shoves over to give him room, slaps him on the back.

He leans against the mud wall and drops the rifle upright. Holding the butt between his heels, he plucks a tin of bully beef from his pocket and jams it over the blade, twisting it around until the top gapes open. They were always waiting. For food, for orders, for action. Usually they fire blindly into the distance. Mostly they duck. He pulls the tin free, pries the lid off and scoops a spoonful.

A stray bullet zips right through the tin and sprays the contents. Freckles on top of his freckles. He blinks for a moment and they all laugh. *You're seeing action now!* He wipes his cheek with his sleeve, laughs too. Probably one of their own bullets. From one of their own clumsy bastards. But they grip their rifles all the same.

Within minutes they are marching back toward their bunks in the support trenches. Another tour done, reinforcements on the way. Soon, they can leave the front, get out of their filthy uniforms. A bath and a hot meal. Shelves of books and a carpet on the floor. Almost like home. Nothing like their dugout — a hole scooped out of the side of a trench, where the only decoration is a photograph pinned to the dirt wall. The four of them in the photographer's studio, Artie, sharp-featured and thin, Kirk, hairy-faced like a Scottie dog, Tubbs, plump-cheeked, all of them grinning into the camera except for him, helmet tucked under his arm, dark eyes caught off guard, looking down and off to the side. *Take it down, Tubbs*, he's begged. But Tubbs won't. He says, *One of us has to look like he gives a damn*. And in the end it's all they have of Artie. So it has stayed.

His boots squelch through brown water and mud. A square of brown sky above, the brown shoulders of the soldier in front of him, walls of brown dirt all around. Back home doesn't seem real any more — blue sky, green ocean. Trees.

There are no trees at the front, nothing to mark one trench from another. Yet they know exactly when to turn left, then right. Tubbs calls it their homing instinct. They turn left one last time and he knows without looking that they have reached their dugout. The mud is so thick it glues one boot to the ground. He has to grab his shin with two hands and pull and then quickly roll onto his bunk before getting stuck again.

He doesn't hear a sound, not a thing. His hands are still clutching his boot when the cold air becomes an oven, hot breath roars into his ears. A heavy hand clamps onto his skull and flings him up into folds of hot air, each layer hotter than the last. Upside down in that mud sky his guts jam against his lungs, his lungs crush into his throat, while the row of turtle shells below him bursts apart like a broken string of beads. The brown sky balloons and then collapses, hurtles him back to the ground. He falls through the air, past rocks and boots and shells that spin like tops, into the same brown dirt that has lifted him and now, instantly, buries him.

THE AFTERDAMP

One

IN THE SOUP GREEN CORRIDOR of an English hospital he sits on a wooden bench, his hands in his lap. To his left, another bench. Several others in bleached bedclothes wait their turns to be examined, bandaged, interviewed. To his right, the same. They haven't seen each other before this day, but each of them has been blown up somewhere. Belgium. France.

Already a doctor has told him, *We'll have you back in no time*. But he doesn't want to go back. He doesn't give a damn if the other side gains more ground — they can have it all. Every festering inch.

The others stare ahead like dead men. It's rotten luck, this whole mess. His throat burns but he leans forward, tries to catch an eye as he rasps, "Rot' luck," and waits for a response.

The radiators steam. A forgotten cart of dirty bandages stews beside him. Nothing.

He throws himself back against the hard bench and folds his arms.

"Albert Fraser?" The ruddy-faced matron rolls her *R*s slightly as she whisks along the row repeating his name, her veil of white cotton flowing from crown to shoulders, green eyes scanning the faces. Surely she can pick him out from this lot. But no, she doesn't remember him. She only stops when she nears the foul cart, nostrils flaring as she bellows, "Someone wheel this off!"

He gets to his feet, even though it pains him. She looks him up, down, then checks the chart. "Albert Fraser?"

He nods.

"Well, speak up."

He points to his throat, strains to say, "Sorry."

"Oh, yes. You. The doctor will see you tomorrow. Ten o'clock."

ALBERT REELS ALONG THE HALLWAY to his ward, past sacks of soiled bedding, carts of crusted dishes and a janitor with a string mop that cuts a wet figure eight on the floor and spreads the smell of piss from wall to wall. As he steps over the damp loops, Albert clamps his mouth shut and tries not to breathe in the stink.

Tomorrow. He knows what that could mean. He's seen for himself through a door left ajar. Just a flash of movement, but enough. Limbs jerking above a tangle of black wires. Strings of drool from a gaping mouth, the sound coming from it monstrous, a howl like a dog's, but deeper, more anguished, struggling to become a voice but failing miserably. The door had slammed shut, leaving Albert with the animal sound in his ears. And something else. A whiff of scorched hair in his nose and on his tongue. It fouled everything he tasted for the rest of that day. Yesterday.

He lifts his eyes to the walls. A former British boys' school set aside for the Canadians. The boys are gone, of course. They've gone to war, too. But their photographs are still up. Did no one think of that? Glowing, healthy boys with solid limbs and minds, looking down on the broken boy-men who've come back. Did no one think they might look up, see versions of what they had once been, what they had lost?

He runs a hand across his face, but still he feels the emotion that ripples under his skin like a live thing. He waits until his features smooth, then presses forward, a hand on the wall when his legs threaten to collapse.

But the unaccustomed movement of walking sends shock waves through his guts. He staggers to the lavatory, waving back the nurse who calls, "Do you need assistance?"

Christ, no. He's already suffered the indignity of the bedpan and the night shift's exclamations about the weight.

It's full of sand, one of them said. *The same thing happened to my sister's boy when he was teething. He ate the sand and it went straight through him into his nappies.*

Nappies! In the stark lavatory Albert's forehead beads in sweat as the sand rakes through him. He was all bound up after the explosion, the result of three days of no food or water. In the field hospital he lay under a white tent listening to the distant whump of guns. Bluebirds, that's what they called the nurses, fluttered in to feed him sips of water and broth. Every day the withered hands of a practised nurse pushed back her blue sleeves and kneaded the flesh of his belly, trying to coax his bowels back to life. They were stubbornly still until he reached England.

The sand began its slow grind yesterday, and now there seems to be no stopping it. When he pisses it stings like grains of glass, and when he coughs it comes up black grit into his handkerchief. Having scraped his throat going down, it scrapes again coming back up. It hurts to swallow.

As the cramps snake through him, he puts his elbows on his knees, buries his face in his hands, lets the darkness pull him back again to the shells thudding into the dirt, him falling toward the ground that rose to bury him, telling himself, *I'm going to die*, then everything going black.

He lifts his face into the harsh light glancing off white hospital tile. But that's just it: he didn't.

At the sink, he glares at his reflection in the warped mirror, distorted, inhuman. Nerves prickle down his back and he turns away from the sight.

When he reaches the doorway to his ward, he scans the two long rows of beds that flank the walls. The same bunch, no one new. There are four besides him who can sit up and move about. They're playing cards intently and don't notice him hobble in. As always, he veers near the faceless mummy with shrivelled air holes over mouth and nose, two vacant slots for eyes. How do the nurses even know there's anything alive in there? It can't speak, and how it eats he can't fathom. The sight of a nurse spooning sludge into it had Albert limping out the door fast as he was able.

Now, the dinner hour far off, he stands at the bedside and stares into the eye holes. He can feel sound travelling up his windpipe, teasing his tongue.

When he opens his mouth to speak, though, the only word he can manage is a clipped, "Al!" But soon, soon. And he likes the abbreviated name. Clean and crisp, easy to say. It makes a statement: here I am. To complete his introduction, he takes up the hand to shake it.

Fingertips flutter against his palm, the creep of lice along the scalp, the scuttle of rats over limbs. A death twitch. He drops the hand, horrified, and backs up, rubbing his palm against his thigh, seeking the roughness of fabric, the heat of friction. He wishes he could find a sheet of sandpaper, a fistful of jagged rocks, and scour the sensation from his skin.

He staggers to the window beside his bed, pulled by the sight of green hedges and lawn. Along a walkway, trees toss in the wind. He presses his palm against the cool glass, imagining ragged bark.

Behind him, the others continue playing cards.

His legs throb. He needs to rest. He sits on his bed, swings both legs up and over. Sweat greases his face. His legs, heavy as tree trunks.

He leans on one elbow and hikes up the cotton leggings, their coloured stripes bleached until they matched his pasty skin. The field doctor said the swelling in his legs was nothing serious. *Got a bit banged up, I imagine.* The nurses told him to walk as much as possible and elevate the legs when sitting or lying.

Al presses his thumb against the fat flesh and counts to ten before the thumbprint vanishes. No searing pain or pounding of blood, just a dull ache. The skin is stretched tight as a bandage. It feels as if it could burst open at any moment.

He wrestles open the drawer of the bedside table and fumbles inside for the book he borrowed from the second floor's collection. He rolls onto his right side so that he won't have to look at the mummy, and opens the book. A map just like a treasure map, but titled *Hardy's Wessex.* He flips through the pages, his attention snagged by the single word "naked." Back to the top of the page he begins reading the scene, but quickly discovers it's not that sort of book. It's about a woman named Tess who is captivated by the sounds of a harp as she walks in a wild garden. He reads and rereads the paragraph about her undulating among the weeds, branches and blades of grass tugging at her skirts and blouse, her naked arms stained by pollen and slug slime.

He snaps the book closed and a letter slides out — the latest from his brother, one he had hastily stuffed into the book. He unfolds the sheets and studies the words, again:

Dear Bertie,

How are you and did you get the tin of sweets we sent?

We are all in good health, not a sniffle amongst us this fall. Mum would have had a good crop of tomatoes but for the damage done by the rain. They were quite black with blight and we had to throw the works out. Did you know that the old bastard has an eye on some ranch land in the interior? He says there'll be no blight there it's so dry, and poor Mum, she believes him. Not about the blight, of course, but that they'll last long enough on the place to see a tomato grow. You and I know better.

The rest is about the union and the mine. Albert asked Jack to send him a world map that he could fold up into his pocket, so he could see where he was. But Jack wrote at the bottom of this letter, *P.S. You're in France!* Very funny. And anyway, he isn't, now. He's back in England, green England.

But Jack doesn't know that yet. None of them do.

He stuffs the letter back into the book and drops his arm. Damn the old man — he knows nothing about ranching. He knew nothing about running a farm in Manitoba, either, or a hotel in London before that, but that didn't stop him.

Albert stares at the ceiling. A ranch. Sagebrush and clouds of dust. Home is supposed to be blue mountains and green ocean.

A sweet voice calls down the ward, "Gentlemen, hello," and Albert wriggles up into a sitting position. A young nurse, all smiles and scrubbed, pink skin, has floated into the ward.

He opens his lips to accept the thermometer, holds up his arm to have his pulse taken and watches the blue sleeves of the pretty nurse move across the clipboard as she records the readings.

"Mar-ry," he says when she plucks the thermometer from his lips, his voice rough but clear.

"Well, listen to you," she says, smiling up from the chart. "Your throat is getting much better, Albert."

"Al," he says. Albert is a name she might give her brother.

"Al, is it, now?" She has a lilt to her voice. Eyes as blue as her dress. He noted that his first day here. His wrist throbs where she placed her finger and thumb. He pictures her hand in his, golden fields shimmering as they walk the evening hills toward home. He is seeing Manitoba and the soddie that had been his family's first house in Canada, not that coal-miner's shack in Nanaimo that was home before he ran off to enlist.

His eyes follow Mary as she leaves his bedside, stopping to check each of the men.

He was just fourteen years of age when he went into the ground. The other miners said he should go work with the Chinese, he was so short. And he had those narrow eyes. They got him drunk once, and tried to shove him into one of the Chinese tunnels, so cramped those workers had to crawl on their bellies. He saw their faces in the dark tunnel ahead. Monkey people, that's what the other miners called them. Thick-lipped and narrow-eyed. Monkey chatter that lifted the hair on his scalp. He fought back fiercely, arms swinging at his drinking partners as he burst out of the tunnel. They said, *What a soldier he'd make*. He threw up right at the pithead, right at their feet.

That was almost three years ago. He's grown half a foot since then.

He still has narrow eyes, though. Narrower.

Mary picks up the mummy's wrist and scratches something onto the chart. Then gently, she places the arm by its side. She waves to all of them before stepping into the corridor. Al watches until her blue dress rounds a corner, then he eases back against his pillow.

His thoughts swell and recede. His friend Joe, arms raised as he gestured at the raw dirt walls of Nanaimo's Newcastle Seam, blue eyes bugging out of a coal-blackened face, lips a surprising pink as they described the dangers. Explosions, drownings, cave-ins. All the things that can kill a man. *Mostly it's the fumes*, he told him. *There's an explosion far off and maybe even a cave-in, but there's not a mark on you. Then the fumes arrive. What they call the afterdamp. It forms after the explosions, but it kills you all the same.*

Albert survived two years chopping coal in the tunnels, though it felt like half his life. Joe gave him a lump of coal for good luck, and when he packed for overseas he tucked it between the rows of socks. *Bertie!* His mother cried. *What's this?* When he told her what it was for, she clapped a hand over her mouth and turned away.

Overnight, his legs continue to expand, until by morning the skin shines, and lumps form within the bloated flesh. There is no ten o'clock appointment for him. A relief, though he's alarmed at the sight of his legs, fat and mottled, a bluish grey that looks almost like bruises. His veins must be filling with dirt.

The nurses giggle when he tells them. Even Mary. He lets go of her hand and never again walks through glimmering fields with her.

He wants to pound the walls, tear his hair out, dig his nails into his skin to relieve the pressure. As he writhes on the bed, his mind fills with images of the land around Nanaimo's harbour, ink-veined like his legs, pockmarked by black holes, seething with the entrails of constantly moving coal.

Only the surgeon understands what's wrong. Later, he shows Al the hunks of metal that rattle around in a tray. There'll be no more marching for him, he says. He's removed enough shrapnel from Al's legs to get him a boat ride home.

Home. It's a word that has a shape, full and round, and he holds it close, even though he knows it has changed as surely as he has.

Two

DRAB WATER MEETING A GUNMETAL sky, rows of men in stretchers, the cheese stench of wounds gone sour and soft moans punctuated by sharp cries, eerie silence. That was the ocean crossing. Once on the train from Halifax to Montreal, and then across the prairies and mountains, civilians surround him. Days and days of their mindless chatter: the weather, greetings that don't need answering, praise for the Great War. Each time they say it he glares in silence. There is nothing great about it. But still they shout about victory, about king and country and the dirty Hun, as though they had been there with him. They wear reds and blues and bright, bright greens. They slam the train car doors.

He's the cadaver by the window. Numb from the back teeth down, six feet of shrapnel connected by the odd length of muscle or tissue.

Someone in the train car strikes a match. Smouldering meat. The stink of blood. A lipsticked mouth howls as the dog in her lap falls to the floor in a fit, legs jerking, pools of drool from its dangling tongue. *Stop it!* All the faces in the car turn and stare. The click-clack of iron wheels on the track. The shudder of doors and windows as the string of cars bends around a curve. Someone says, *There, there, son*, and Al turns back to the view outside, ears burning.

Patches of snow recede over rock. Spikes of trees push through crusts of ice. The train bores through the Rockies, each plummet into black a descent into the abyss of stinking mud and lurking thoughts.

He wakes up to find the train grinding into Princeton, the town's name swinging at him from a metal pole, then standing out boldly in black against a narrow white strip nailed to the barn red station house. The shriek of brakes fills his ears, iron biting into iron. The scream of the whistle filling the open mouths of the crowd that slides past, waving signs, *Welcome Home* and *Our Brave Boys*.

The mob in its Sunday best hugs and kisses and swarms the soldiers on the wooden platform, causing one to lose his balance. Idiot laughter as they bend to pull him up, silk arms sleek against his rough khaki.

Al hangs back, watching from the steps of the train. A brass band bleats on the platform, drawing civilians who place their hats over their hearts and sing along. "God Save the King."

All this noise and nonsense. If it were summer he could find a swimming hole somewhere, strip off this uniform and sink right up to his ears in heavenly silence.

He scans the nodding heads — their doffed hats replaced in one sweep at song's end, a couple of stetsons among the bowlers and feathered caps — looking for his brother and trying to get his bearings on the rise and dip of a constantly moving landscape. If he keeps to the edges he can skirt around unnoticed. He jumps down from the train and squeezes past a set of luggage, several figures lunge, the landscape ripples, and he reaches up to hold his helmet in place. The ground shakes, the thunder of hooves on the road, heels on the platform. Something grabs hold of him from behind. His rifle! He spins around, fist raised. Then looks down. A child. A bloody child in a sailor suit who lifts his arm and salutes. Al staggers back as though he's been struck.

A woman's voice beside him says, "You must be Albert."

His eyes shoot to the side. Hair like straw. Limbs like twigs. Pale lips crimped like an oyster shell. "He thinks you're a hero," she adds, nodding toward the child.

"Well, I'm not!" His anger surges, slackens. He slaps at the air half-heartedly and the satisfied child trots away. Then he faces her. "Who told you my name?"

She studies him with cool, navy eyes. "Jack said —"

"Oh, did he?" So, Jack won't be meeting the train, then. He's sent her instead. "Well, it's Al now."

"Agnes," she says, and reaches forward as a man would to shake hands. Hers is bony and chapped. He lets go as soon as good manners allow.

He looks away and sees plain wooden coffins being unloaded from the freight cars and stacked like firewood onto the platform. Why not shove them all into one big box and be done with it? Tie it up with one of those blasted banners? *Our boys!* He reaches for his bag and finds Agnes still there.

"He said you might need a ride."

Al wants to decline, but he doesn't know the way to the ranch. He wants to ask where Jack is, but that will draw further attention to the fact that Jack has contacted her and not him, his own brother.

"All right," he says. "Thank you."

He follows her to the wagon, people slapping him on the back and shouting things as if he's God himself walking along the platform. It's the uniform. But he's seen himself reflected in the train-car windows. A cadaver in a khaki suit.

Despite her skinny arms, Agnes handles the reins with ease. Her straw hat hangs behind her shoulders from a faded ribbon.

"Just feel that wind," she says.

Al glances to the side. Wind fills her shapeless dress, gives her substance. When the faded print falls she's left with nothing. He pictures breasts like winter potatoes and blinks rapidly to erase the image.

He turns to look at the scenery. They cross a wooden bridge and then veer onto Hedley Road. Mountains rise immediately to their left, leaving only a thin strip of benchland that stretches pleasantly to the river. Whenever the road curves toward the banks, he glimpses a shallow bed of rough water that foams over boulders and stones. On the far side of the river are more mountains, golden-grassed like the prairie and sparsely dotted with trees, some rugged-hilled and rocky under a blazing spring sun. Agnes says it was a dry winter with little snow. Other than that remark they drive in silence, which suits Al just fine. She must be connected to one of Jack's labour groups — and thinks Jack has told him so because she offers no explanation. And Al isn't about to ask.

A heavy scent of sun-cooked pine needles and bursting buds of poplar fills his lungs. He breathes deeply and feels his shoulders loosen.

When Agnes pulls on the reins he thinks there must be something blocking the road. She says, "Here you are. Home!"

A wind stirs over a lumpy landscape of dirt and patches of grass. A door that hangs by one rusted hinge to an old shed creaks loudly.

"It looks abandoned." The words are out before he can stop them.

"It was," she says. Her sharp chin dips as she attempts a smile. "But not now."

Is she making fun? He studies her calm eyes. No, he doesn't think so.

DUST LIFTS LIKE SMOKE AROUND his ankles as he turns left and passes through a gap in the barbed-wire fencing. It looks to be the gateway, though there is no sign of a gate. A few bricks or paving stones would put the road in order. Or boards they could mill from these trees — they'd keep the dust down in summer, the mud back when it rains. He tears his thoughts from the duckboard they laid in trenches.

The fence needs mending, too. The strings of barbed wire sag between each rotted fence post. Al breathes in sharply and the coils of barbed wire, the tangled limbs, disappear.

A few feet to his left, against a rising hillside, a shaggy-maned horse unfurls his prick like a length of fire hose, pointing at his own unshod hooves, mud-caked legs.

Jesus Christ.

Al pushes open the garden gate and it squawks accusingly. Overgrown bushes of some ragged plant mark the lopsided front porch of the house.

For almost two years he sent his army pay, a dollar a day. This is what the old man did with it.

Al gives the loose board a boot. *Stupid goddamn son of a bitch.*

"Freddie?" a voice calls. His mother's.

He tries for a bright reply. "It's me, Mum."

For a moment there is no sound at all. Then a rush of air as the screen door bursts open and his mother descends the three steps in a swoop. She stops at the bottom and clutches the unpainted railing as she regards him. "Bertie."

He steps forward and she lets go of the railing, throws her arms around him.

"You're nothing but skin and bones," she says, her voice buried in his collar.

"I'm taller, that's all." She has thickened, her dark hair grey now, and uncombed. "You look just the same," he tells her, and steps back.

"Oh," she says, and tucks a wild strand behind her ear before seizing his hand. "Let's get you inside. You can have Jack's room."

Al raises his head.

"The boys' room." She retucks the strand of hair as she corrects herself. "We didn't know when you'd be coming home, or —"

Al waits for her to continue, but she lets the words fade and leads him up the steps.

She stops to shake out her dirt-grimed skirts, then steps into the cabin. Al follows. A kitchen and sitting area on one side, two doors that must lead to bedrooms on the other. A back room has been built onto the kitchen end as a lean-to. A former chicken coop from the looks of it, with a small door leading to the outside, chicken wire across a long, narrow window. Only the presence of a small cot and a curtained doorway for privacy tell him this is the spare room, his brother's. His as well, now. They'll have to round up another bed.

"Where *is* Jack?"

"In the city. Union business."

Al ducks, too tall by several inches for the low roof. He fingers the flowered curtain. He remembers the dress it came from. Black with tiny, cream-coloured flowers. Grey now, with white splotches. She wore it when they left England — a third of his life ago. "You mean they got into another argument."

"I don't know why you boys give your father such a time." She leans against the doorframe, gazing at the chicken wire.

Neither Rose nor his father has come out to greet him. That's what he gets for arriving unannounced. Only Jack knew, and he hasn't bothered.

He tosses his rucksack onto the cot and sighs. "I'd like to lie down now, Mum."

Shavings of dried mud calve from the backs of her boot heels onto the floor as she walks away. Al stares at the flakes of dirt and then flops back onto the bed. Dirt.

He punches the pillow to plump it, thrashes against the lumpy mattress, pulls a jacket over a cold shoulder.

Brown walls. The whiplash lightning of a rat tail over his knuckles.

He sits up. Sleep is impossible. He swings his legs around and feels under the bed for his boots.

"SON!"

There he is at last, the little bantam rooster. That's what Jack calls the old man. Dark hair like a crown of feathers, a jaunty walk. He stops in the doorway between the kitchen and sitting area, snaps his suspenders and beams at Al.

"What do you think?"

"What —?"

"The place."

"For goodness sake, Freddie." His mother bangs pots onto the wood stove, preparing dinner. "Greet your boy first, he's been gone two years."

"Just a year and a bit." But Al notes her tone. She's angry. He hasn't expected that.

She slops gravy over plates of mashed potatoes, mutton and peas, turning a shoulder when he reaches out a hand to help.

"Bertie knows what's what." His father slaps him on the shoulder. "This will all be yours one day. Sit, sit."

Al sits and looks at his plate. Lamb and peas used to be his favourite. But the peas have been overcooked, no longer round, but many-sided, shrivelled hexagons. The meat is grey. He feels something leap inside his chest. Fear. Lack of air. Trapped. "This? Mine? I don't —"

His father crows, "Yours! Rose's, too, if she likes."

"What about Jack?" Al looks down at his father's small head, his hooked nose as he raises it up to eyeball him, the view straight down his nostrils. He's barely taller than their mother, standing or sitting.

"Do you see Jack here?" He snaps his suspenders again and humps his chair forward. "Where is my girl, mother?"

"Not feeling well. I said I'd take her a plate when we're done."

"I can do that," Al says, rising from his chair, too quickly, perhaps. As an afterthought he adds, "I ate on the train."

ROSE LIES SO STILL THAT at first he thinks she's asleep. Her hair falls
in pale strips over the white of her scalp. There are deep shadows
below her eyes and her face has turned a parchment yellow.

She tries to smile and he tries to smile back. No need to ask if
she's hungry. He slides the greasy plate onto the bureau behind
him, then pulls up a chair and leans over to kiss her.

Her hands rise from the covers and flap like startled birds. "No,
Albert!"

"It's okay, Rose." He grabs for one of her hands. "I won't catch
anything. Even the war couldn't kill me."

She doesn't laugh and he curses himself for mentioning death at
a sickbed. He is fumbling for more words when she presses her face
into the pillow, wheezing. Then she begins to choke, a gurgling
sound rising up from her lungs and into her throat.

Al stands bolt upright, sending the chair skidding into the
bureau. "Mum!" he shouts. "Quick!"

THE NEXT MORNING THEY WAIT for the doctor. Al paces from the
table to the stove and back. Finally, he asks his mother, "Where are
my clothes?"

She stares at the buttons of his uniform and turns, wiping her
hands on her apron as she crosses to the sitting area. "Somewhere
in here." She rummages in the trunk next to the chesterfield and
presents him with a large bundle wrapped in butcher paper and tied
with string. On it she has written:

Albert Lawrence Fraser
our Bertie.
1916

The paper crumples in his hands. Was she practising for his
tombstone? He yanks his head up but she has already turned away

to pull a large book from the trunk. A photograph album. She sits on the chesterfield and begins turning pages while he stands with his epitaph in his hands.

She points to a photograph of a family gathered at a picnic. Al cranes his neck to look. "That's my sister Ellen just before we left England, there, with that Spaniard of hers!" Anger again. She never used the man's name, never forgave him for taking her sister away, even though she herself moved to North America with her husband. But he was an Englishman. She shakes her head and recalls, "I used to feel sorry for her because she never had any boys, just the one girl. That's her there," she says, "little Maggie," and points at a tiny child with a mop of wild, dark hair.

Al remembers her. She tugged off her bloomers and threw them in the pond. Then she tumbled onto the blanket and upset a plate of cakes. That was probably icing in her hair. Rose, Jack and Al stand behind her, the taller adults behind them.

His mother sighs. "Ellen never had to worry about her sons going off to war and getting killed."

Al had been about to sit beside her. This was the aunt who sent them oranges and castanets one Christmas, and the three of them had leapt about the kitchen pretending to be flamenco dancers. He pulls himself up.

"I didn't get killed! Maybe I should have!" and then he turns on his heel.

In his room he tears the package open, chest heaving. Childish, childish, but still! Maybe she should worry about how it feels to hear that, how it feels to see his name written out like that.

He struggles into familiar, worn dungarees and hangs his uniform carelessly on a hook behind the door. Once the boots are laced up he stands tall and peers into an old, rusted mirror above the dresser. The boots pinch. The sleeves are too short, so most likely the trouser cuffs are, too. But that isn't it. The face that looks back at him doesn't look like his face at all, not from last year, and not from yesterday, either.

HE NAILS UP BROKEN BOARDS and sweeps out the barn but there is so much rusted equipment he doesn't know where to begin oiling and scraping. He gives up and focuses on forking hay down from the loft. Some ranch. There isn't as much as a cow on the place. They buy their milk in town.

Two hours later his father appears in the barn, hair like a crown of black feathers from running his hands through it. "What's this I hear about you taking off the uniform?"

Al holds out both arms to show his civilian wear, rake dangling from one hand. "I'm not in the army anymore."

"But you were. How's anyone supposed to know that if you don't wear it?"

Al can feel a fading grin twisting his mouth. If the old man had ever been in a war he'd know you don't get to keep the uniform.

His father jabs a pink finger at him. "You keep talking like that and people are going to wonder why you're back so soon."

Al lets the rake topple. "I was blown up." He folds his arms.

"Is that so?" His father eyes him up and down. "You look just fine to me!"

Fine? He'd been full of dirt and shrapnel. His legs thickened until he couldn't walk. He wanted to say to his father: *You try not breathing in while shells explode around you, sending all that muck into your lungs and guts! You try not carrying junk back in your legs!*

Instead, he says, "You'd prefer it if I was in that stack of boxes?" First his mother, and now his father.

The old man screws up his face. He has no idea what Al is talking about. Idiot! He never knew anything about anything. This isn't England where you can till your little plot of green and raise a few chickens. This is a big country. Acreage and livestock. Rust and rot and storms. It takes work and planning to run a place like this. An irrigation system. Fencing.

And now there he is strutting out the barn door with his black hair bouncing on top of his head. Like a stupid little windup toy. Al starts to laugh but the lump in his throat burns, his eyes burn. He grabs the side of the barn door to pull it shut but it sticks in its tracks. He hauls it back open and slams it so hard he feels the vibration right up into his back teeth.

THAT NIGHT HE LIES IN the narrow cot in Jack's chicken-coop bedroom, unable to sleep. The doctor felt Rose's forehead, listened to her chest, then wound up his stethoscope and stuffed it into his bag. *Her lungs*, he told them in the kitchen. *Her poor lungs*. He's never seen anything quite like it.

Al has. Men bursting through a golden green fog, their lungs filling with runny glue that gushed up to leak from their mouths. They staggered back through the lines, coughing and gagging, eyes rolling as they drowned in their own mucus.

He thrashes about in the cot as he pictures his sister's agony. He claws at his own throat.

It should have been him, not her.

Three

AT THE FAR END OF the dusty road, a black dot dances against the russet ball of the sun. Al sits back against the wooden seat, wondering, then slaps the reins to hurry the horse, churning up more dust from the spinning wheels of the wagon.

Surely that isn't Jack walking up ahead. Al called him from the hotel only yesterday. It was noisy in the lobby, so he wrapped his fingers around the candlestick base of the telephone and drew the mouthpiece close, shouting into it that, yes, he would meet his train. He even had Jack repeat it to make sure he heard him.

But even as he thinks this he sees black limbs unfurling from the dot like spider legs bouncing on a web, closer and closer, until those limbs swing in an easy stride that is unmistakably Jack's.

"I said I'd pick you up!" Al's raw voice scrapes at his own ears. He yards on the reins until the horse stops, then leaps down to the dirt just as his brother lopes to his side.

"That's a fine hello!" Jack claps his arms around Al, leaving the smells of engine oil, soap and tobacco on his shirt. "Bertie," he says, then stiffens his arms and stands back. "Two years. Look at you."

Al looks back. As much as he has grown, Jack is taller by at least two inches. Jack's brown eyes are lighter than his, and rounder. But the main difference is his hair, blond and lank.

Before Al can ask why he didn't wait at the station, Jack snatches up Al's old felt hat and rubs a hand in his hair. "It's as dark as the old man's."

Al swings a hand out and grabs the hat. It's lost its shape from years of wear, and if he thought it worth it, he'd get it blocked the next time he was in town. But it isn't, and he pretends to swat his brother with it.

"So how are you, Bertie?"

"I'm okay." Al climbs up onto the seat, grabs the reins and turns the horse around. "It's Rose we have to worry about."

Jack hoists his suitcase into the wagon, then pauses, a hand on the wooden side. "Is it consumption?"

"That or pneumonia. She's too sick to move or the doctor could do tests at the hospital."

Jack seems to consider that, his foot on the step. Then he boosts himself up. "Look at this piece of ancient history." He bounces on the seat. "I thought you might pick me up in the truck."

"Well, I thought you might've picked me up in the truck."

Jack leans forward, grinning. "I sent Agnes, though."

Al isn't quite sure what to make of the grin. "Well, she wasn't driving a truck, either."

"No, but everyone drives automobiles now. I'll show you. The old truck needs a little coaxing, but it runs."

He pauses to flip his hair back from his face, a habit that's as distinctively Jack as his loping walk. "So here I am, again. Seems I'm always running back and forth between here and Nanaimo. I'm thinking I might try for a spot at Lodestone."

"Never heard of it."

"At Coalmont. Just five miles the other side of town. They're hiring, if you're interested."

"I'm not."

The horse's hooves thud over the wooden bridge. The wagon wheels slice through grit on the other side, throwing up a rock that plonks against a tree trunk. Jack points to the river. "Let's pull over, here." Then he produces a flask from his jacket pocket.

"Where'd you get that?"

"From someone who knows someone. So — how bad is she?"

"It could go either way. Mum told the doctor Rose has never been strong."

Al guides the horse to a patch of shade. He reaches for the flask and takes a swig.

"I see you took off the uniform."

"That's exactly what the old man said!" Al tips the flask again and drinks hard, runs his rolled shirt sleeve over his mouth. "I suppose now you're going to tell me that you were right — I shouldn't have joined up?"

"Pass that over, will you? No," he says, "no, as a matter of fact, I'm not going to tell you that." Jack had been right, but he doesn't look happy about it. *He's just a child*. Jack shouted at their father, and he shouted back, *Well then war will make a man of him*.

Al had done the job of a man for two years. So had Jack. It was their work that put food on their mother's table. Al rests his wrists on his knees and stares at the water sliding over rounded rocks. He can hear the slosh of liquor as Jack tips back the flask.

"You went," Jack says at last, "because I didn't."

There. It's said now and at least Al hasn't done the saying.

The old man always accused Jack of being a coward for not enlisting. *It's not our war*. Jack replied. Al wasn't sure about that, and he worried that his father might call him a coward, too. He planned all along to enlist — to get out of the mine, climb above ground and breathe fresh air, see the world. But when he lit out that last day it was with one single thought: *I'll show him*. Now the old man treats Al the same way he treated Jack. What gave him the right in either case?

Al shifts in his seat to look at Jack, who flips back his hair. "Mom says you're still busy with that union —" he was going to say non-sense but thinks better of it. "Business?"

"That's right." He passes Al the flask again. "We might have won that strike if it hadn't been for the war."

Al remembers the strike, the blue light of night and the orange glow from the lamps, the men black cut-outs against the bonfires that kept them warm. Each evening their mother packed a dinner pail and Al carried it to the picket line for his brother. When war was declared, so many men left to enlist there was no one left to picket.

"I wasn't one of them," Al reminds him. "I didn't enlist for two more years."

"I remember. You weren't yet sixteen."

And there they are, back at the subject of war. Al takes one last sip before tugging on the reins. "I wasn't gone for two years like everyone seems to think. More like a year-and-a-half."

Once back on the road he loosens the reins and the horse plods homeward without guidance.

HEAT SHIMMERS OVER THE ROCKY hills that evening, unseasonably warm for spring. Even with both front and back doors left open, the cabin is stifling. They eat outdoors under the trees, the table draped in Irish linen and set with their mother's Waterford crystal and Blue Willow plates.

Inside, in her darkened room, Rose shivers with cold.

Each takes a turn looking in on her. When their mother leaves her chair, Jack claims, "This place is too much for her. She has her hands full with Rose as it is." He gestures at the rough cabin, the pretty table setting in stark contrast. "Sell it. Move back to the coast."

Their father sits upright. "I had little help from either of you. You were both away —"

"No help!" Jack blurts. Al wishes he hadn't. He wants to know what their father was going to say next, what accusations he would make. But Jack is livid. "Whose money bought the place?" He aims a thumb at Al. "Who's out here every holiday, working on it?" He jabs the thumb at his own chest.

But the mention of money triggers their father's usual explanation. "You need money for equipment, but how can you pay for equipment until you have a crop to sell, and how can you plant a crop —"

"Oh, stop it." Jack folds his arms.

Their father looks back and forth at both of them, seeking sympathy. "I might've let things go. But Rose got sick —"

"What did you say?" This time it's Al speaking, but the words seem to come from someone else. "You're nothing but a — a —" A rush of language churns in his head as he mutely accuses their father of never behaving responsibly, never owning up to what he has created, which is a family without a home that has been moved more times than any man has a right to expect. And now his daughter is sick and he's going to blame her.

Only Jack's hand on his shoulder stops Al from leaping from his chair.

THAT NIGHT THE HEAT INSIDE the house builds until they can't bear the warmth of thick mattresses beneath them and they lug them off, throwing just cotton sheets over the metal coils. In the first light of morning, their skins embossed with the rounds of the springs, the slats of the edges, and their backs aching, Al and Jack finally say to hell with it and sleep on the bare boards of the front porch.

Al rises at the first rattle of the teakettle being set on the stove. In the kitchen he hears the murmur of his mother's voice coming from Rose's room. He pours himself a mug and takes it outside, stepping over Jack and sitting heavily on the wooden steps. Eyes closed, he feels the sunlight on his skin. He breathes in the pine-fragrant air.

The dirt is back.

All night he's been feeling the familiar itch, aggravated by the heat. He scratched until his shins bled, could feel it even now, the sensation of sand sliding through him, coiling in his guts, filling his legs. He lifts a trouser leg, checks for lumps, but can't see any. The thought of them sickens him.

A bang splits the air and Al shoots to his feet.

"Bertie!" Jack thumps down the steps. "The door slammed. Sorry."

But he's already running, stumbling, sky hitting dirt hitting sky. *Bertie! Stop.* Boot heels crunching, the ground rolling and buckling. His legs stretch, leap, over the stubbly field, his breath coming in spasms until a force hits his back and the air turns black like the inside of a tunnel, the smell of damp dirt in his nose again, packing itself up into his nostrils, filling his mouth and his lungs and clogging his veins, choking him.

"Bertie!" Jack is sitting on him, needles of morning light exploding from around his head. He shakes Al by the shoulders. "Bertie."

THE SUN BAKES THEIR BACKS as they work. Flies rim the horses' eyes and gather on their flanks. Grey clouds of mosquitoes set them rearing back.

Each day he rises early and digs fence posts and forks hay and sweeps the barn floor. He works feverishly, sweat trickling under his collar, arms and legs tingling, the flesh stinging, that agonizing itching.

He runs his hands over the flanks of the horses, the doors of their stalls, the handle of the water pump, feeling everything around him. He shoves his hand under the strap of the brush and presses the bristles into the chestnut hide of the quarter horse, untangles and trims the mane and tail, carves the hooves free of stones and mud. He tells himself he feels no more alive than Rose, and yet the instant he thinks it, he knows what a liar he is to make such a comparison. Despite his discomfort, he grows stronger every day. She weakens.

In the barn, Jack kicks forward a stool and sits. "What was it like over there?"

Al nudges a bale of hay with his boot and drops onto it. "A rotten mess. It was all about sending over bodies to replace the fallen bodies. Bodies everywhere."

Jack unwraps egg sandwiches from folded sheets of newsprint. "And afterwards?"

Al takes up the uncut square of sandwich, half-smiling. "The paperwork," he says at last. "They didn't know what to do with us. All we did was make our beds and polish our boots and wait until they could arrange to send us home. We called ourselves the paper soldiers."

They eat in silence. Then Jack says, "Albert, I meant those — I don't know what to call them — nightmares. You were blown up —"

"Oh." Al stands quickly, brushes the crumbs from his legs. He shakes his head as he picks up the rake. "I don't know." He leans the rake back against the wall, but still he can't think of how to explain himself. Maybe if he keeps shaking his head all the loose thoughts will crystallize into something worth saying, like ice on a window that forms into a pattern. Maybe if he shakes his head long enough the thoughts will bang against each other until they break into tiny pieces, like dust, and float away. His mind will be clear of the dirt, and then he'll know.

AL STUDIES THE FRAIL BONES in Rose's hand. As she sleeps, he whispers to her, hoping the memories will force her to climb out of her stupor, maybe even join him in recollecting. "We used to dance." With their mother on the piano or their father cranking the gramophone, Rose led him over the polished oak floor. He loved the waltzes, loved to feel the music through his bones, though he was a terrible dancer.

"Remember the prairie and Mum in her black dress?" She stormed over to what she thought at first was the cow shed, an earthen hut set into a slope by the gate. *Freddie?* She cried, then sank right down into the dirt when she realized that soddie was their house. "We loved it, though, didn't we?"

That swoop of sky so big he lost his balance trying to look up and take it all in at once. But they moved, again, and everywhere they moved their mother dragged along that trunk. The Persian carpet and the precious china and silver that were her mother's. It all looked as silly in that soddie house as it did in the miner's shack, as it did here.

Poor Rose in this rough house without running water. Al pats her hand and stands, stretches.

She'll get better, though. He's seen death before, and it was nothing like this. It always rained, and there was mud. It was sudden and violent. One minute a man was talking to him and the next he was blown into the sky. A lingering death was one that lasted hours. The wounded ranted at the play of shadows along a wall, cried out for their mothers, a cry swiftly followed by silence. Rose has been ill for days. When pressed, the doctor said he had not expected her to last this long, and yes, he supposed it was possible that she might recover.

And yet, Al knows. Of course he knows.

One morning his mother's long, sharp cry reaches him halfway across the field. He keeps walking, pauses to nail up a section of sagging fence where the horses have been getting through to the road, then rolls up the hammer and wrench and screwdriver into a piece of burlap that he tucks under his arm. He has scraped the rust from each piece and rubbed them with oil until they gleam. The bag of nails he folds and pops into his side pocket. Then, slowly, he returns to the house.

There's no need to rush.

There'll be a funeral. Words will be read by a man who barely knows his sister. The family's been here less than a year. Townsfolk will attend the service out of a sense of duty or neighbourliness. And the Frasers will smile politely through it all. They'll even hurry home ahead of the crowd, spread the Persian carpet under the trees, set the table with the blasted Waterford and Blue Willow.

Al hopes a storm rolls up and rains all over it. The sandwiches and the cakes and the people, too, gorging to prove that they're alive and not the one in the casket.

He pulls the burlap roll from under his arm and flings it as far as he can. It unwinds and snaps in the warm wind like an angry serpent, spilling its metal guts in a cloud of dust onto the field. The sack of nails soon follows.

A GOOD NAME

Four

THEY SQUIRM FOR ROOM IN the back of the truck, hot breath on each other's necks, elbows jabbing ribs, pairs of legs wedged hip to knee. The tailgate has been removed and their feet hang over the end, boots knocking into each other's ankles.

Al clings to the very edge, an arm looped through the wooden slats, painting cap in his fist. Over the bridge with its green smell of ocean, up the slope under broadleafed trees. If he'd thought of it sooner he could have leapt onto the running board and had the wind full in his face. Instead, it comes at him from the side, lifting and yanking his hair and slapping black swatches of it across his eyes. To turn away from it is to face the rumpled crew and breathe the grease of hatbands, the tobacco stink of fingers.

Gears slip as the engines strain to haul the heavy loads of workers and equipment along the quiet streets. As each truck in the convoy passes through the wrought-iron gates, the workers lift their legs, and the low-riding bumpers strike the concrete drive, setting off orange sparks into the dark air. At the top of the circular drive the train of vehicles lurches to a crooked stop and the crew hits the pavement sprinting.

The back of each truck becomes a scrum of shoulders and arms jostling to reach the equipment. Al gets hold of his paintbox, drags it across the truck bed and clamps it safely under his arm. Then he shoves his way out, fresh air in his lungs, at last.

Above, soaring columns and tall, lead-glass windows, the cool blues and greys of the mansion's exterior. Glossy green branches of rhododendron, spiked sleeves of cedar. Another deep breath, and another.

"Michelangelo!"

Al pivots on one heel as Dom jams a shoulder into the same crush of workers, his big face turning red as he wrestles a stepladder over the tailgate.

"What are you looking at?" Dom asks him. "You planning to buy the place or something?"

"Maybe."

Al is known among the crew for his ability to paint ceilings with a sure hand — an *artista*, Dom claims. When the men aren't calling him Michelangelo, it's Albert-o. Another compliment, he realizes. It means he's one of them.

But he figures it would take two lifetimes of painting to buy a place like this. There were simpler houses on the Crescent, a street that was, in fact, a circle with a park in its centre and several side streets branching out like spokes on a wheel, forming several crescents around the park. There were larger ones, too, the finest of Vancouver's fine mansions. But this one, an Edwardian, has a quiet opulence. It also has a triangular yard that extends into a deep corner, promising hidden gardens and unexpected delights. An aviary, or so he's heard. The workers aren't allowed back there.

"Boss says one hour." Dom bends his squat legs and hoists the ladder onto his shoulder.

Al has been hurrying since he heard the horn braying beneath his window twenty minutes ago. Two splashes of water and two slaps of his suspenders and he leapt into his coveralls, still in a convenient pile on the floor. He didn't even use the stairs, but climbed out the window, the bricks serving as stepping stones down the corner of the building.

Now he shoves his cap into his back pocket and grabs the handle of a paint bucket. "Let's go," he says, and with his kit still under his arm, he strides down the side path.

Dom trudges behind him, past the service entrance, the neatly clipped boxwood hedge and raised bed of rose bushes, the buds still closed in the brightening morning air.

Al twists his head and talks as he walks. "He's crazy. We're in the middle of a job, and he throws a party?"

"A hustler," Dom huffs. "No wonder he's rich. She left because of our mess. He saw an opportunity, and bang!" Dom smacks a hand onto the side of the ladder. "He took it."

Al faces forward again. On the patio, two men drag the blue pool bottom for broken glass that glitters through the chop of water. Cleaning women with mops and brooms bustle in and out from the bank of open French doors. These doors form a wall of glass with panes that curve into a glazed ceiling. It's called an orangerie, and yesterday he was painting in the foyer when he heard a clear, high sound like music coming from this room. From the piano, or perhaps the gramophone. They were the only pieces of furniture left during the painting, but when he stepped inside, he saw that they were still draped in sheets.

He stood, alone, in the long, cool room, as a cloudburst of rain danced and chimed against the crystal panes above, and he thought: *So this is what it's like to be rich.*

Today is different.

He can hear the roar before he steps over the ledge and drops the bucket by the door.

Two workmen scuffle past carrying a gilded screen. Dom cuts to the right and disappears behind the panel. But when it pulls away, like a curtain drawn across a stage, a teeming scene springs in front of Al. Tarps unfurl and snap crisply in place, men trot past with buckets and wheeled vats, carpenters saw and hammer. The plasterer, Vito, balances a wooden tray on his fingertips like it's a pizza pie. With a trowel he works a wet, grey lump until it's smooth enough to spread. Matrons bustle by with arms filled with more of the party's evidence: long satin gloves, scarves, silken items with dangling ribbons and straps and even a single high-heeled shoe. Al's eyes follow the glossy leavings.

"On your right!"

He dodges and then ducks as men with two-by-fours on their shoulders swerve back and forth, seeking the place where they are supposed to drop them.

"Michelangelo! At last!" It's Rinaldo, who rises on his toes to slap him on the back. "Your expertise is needed." And he thrusts a thumb upward.

"My ceiling?"

Through the double doors he can see the scaffolding still looming in the foyer. Al pushes past his boss and angles across the floor until he is through the doors and standing below the rungs.

The damage appears to be minor. Al sets down the paintbox as he studies the ceiling. A champagne cork from an exploding bottle has lodged itself into a plaster rosette that hasn't set. Vito taught Al how to carve the simple flower with quick cuts of the putty knife. So, easily fixed.

Someone at the party must have climbed the scaffolding. Two people, he guesses, looking for a place to be alone. A man and a pretty woman with auburn curls, delicate heels that slip over the rungs, a shriek as her shoe falls to the floor — the shoe that just sailed by in the matron's arms — laughter as she shakes the bottle. He considers the waste of it, the glorious waste.

He drags his fingers through his hair, tugs on his cap. Then, paintbox back against his ribs, he scales the wooden slats.

Sprawled on his back at last, long legs dangling over the edge, his heartbeat gradually slows, the noise below fades. There's a smudge on the panel. A palm print, most likely. He'll take care of that first.

With the box opened by his side, he pops the lid to a small tin of paint, dips a long-handled brush and watches thick paint spread onto the ceiling like lemon frosting.

His family's house in England was beautiful, too — not quite this grand, but grand to him, and to Jack and Rose. The polished floor they danced across, the tall windows topped with stained glass. He can still see their suitcases and their mother's trunk by the door, their furniture and fine shirts sold for the cost of the crossing. He had just celebrated his twelfth birthday. 1912. He was born on the first day of the first month of the new century, and his mother assured him that meant he was destined for great things.

It's 1929 now, and greatness hasn't arrived. Back then he clung to the possibility as their parents fought bitterly over the contents of the trunk and what to leave behind to lower the cost of shipping. *Not the Spode*, their mother insisted, *and not the silver or the crystal*. It was bad enough their father lost the hotel business in Chelsea; if she had to leave England, she would at least take what her mother had left her. That was final. *Bertie!* she called. Then, *Jack! Rose! This way!* She never saw England again.

He saw it, though it was an England glimpsed from a hospital bed, and not that house, not ever again that house.

Late summer heat has already climbed the walls and begun to pool in the ceiling above the scaffolding. It beads on his forehead and raises a rash on his shin. Lifting a boot heel he digs at the spot through his coveralls. Beneath his shifting limbs the boards and bolts creak, a soothing sound.

Any kind of painting pleases him — the sight of fresh colour covering worn walls in great swaths from a wide brush, the mind-lessness of dipping a slender brush, drawing a bead line along a window pane, dipping again. He carries his equipment up six flights of stairs rather than step into a small, dark elevator. Has Dom noticed that? The first time Al climbed the scaffolding he felt himself surrounded by nothing but the purity of air, the glittering windows, the light. It was a sensation like floating, and Dom must have noticed because he called out that, up there, Al had the look of a man in love.

Al cares that the paint not smudge the window or harden in drips down the wall, that it cover the intricate whorls and leaves of the recessed ceiling without clumping, that bristles from the brush do not embed themselves in the fresh coat. He cares that when the owners or other painters see his work they might say: *Magnificent, who did this?* And whether the answer is Michelangelo or Alberto or just plain Al doesn't matter. His reputation grows. Without his work what is he? Who is he? Just a man who climbs six flights of stairs to avoid the cramped space of an elevator.

Reaching behind his head for the paintbox, Al's fingers spider-walk the neat slots containing putty knife, snub of sponge, jar of putty and lay each item by his side. Then he pulls out the cork.

It leaves a hole like a bullet wound, deep and ugly.

His guts climb toward his throat and his fingers fight to undo the buttons at his neck. Sweat courses down his ribs.

Outside. Fresh air.

He clatters down the rungs and angles across the orangerie toward the doors. Each step is a tug to peel the sole of his shoe from the sticky surface. The upturned backsides of cleaning women jiggle as they scrub the oak, the buckets beside them brimming in rinse water already dark with spilled food and drink. A wheeled cart rumbles to his right and a cook boy begins stacking it with dirty dishes and smeared glassware.

Every surface — chairs, ledges, even the top of the baby grand — is littered with discarded plates. He hasn't noticed till now.

Minton. That distinctive gold band around gleaming white, but encrusted with what appears to be shrivelled peas and congealed slices of glazed duck, with some sort of rice or potato, formed into the shape of oranges, turning brown. A cigar has been ground out into a platter of oysters on the half shell, and again nausea creeps across Al's belly as he imagines the rank scent of embers burning the flesh.

Rinaldo spins around as Al races past him. But there is no time to explain.

Through the doors, across the patio, down the brick path where at last he stops by the rose bushes, breathing deeply, mopping at his face with a handkerchief.

Then a sharp voice sounds. "What are they doing here?"

A woman with a large nose and thin mouth marches up the path toward him. Her eyes are wild, angry beneath a tight, black hat. A tall man in an elegant grey suit hurries across the driveway and up the path to take her elbow.

Al pulls off his cap.

So these are the Gordons, the people who live in this fine home. She should be using that grand entrance between the columns. But of course, she has seen the trucks parked haphazardly in her circular drive, with their signs proclaiming that *Rinaldo & Company Master Painters* are here on a Sunday.

"Who do you think you are?" she asks, her face close to Al's, unafraid.

He backs up. Surely his painting gear makes that clear. "I'm the one they call —"

"I don't care about your name!" Her teeth flash. "What are you doing here?" And then she calls behind her, "Stuart!"

Without waiting for an answer, she pushes past Al as though she were the only one on the brick path. Stuart Gordon shoves past too, his shoulder clipping Al's and throwing him off balance, off the path and into the rosebushes, where Al is swamped at once by the smells of compost mixing perversely with the dying blooms, a smell of funerals, a stench that grows stronger as the dark muck of the ground begins to swim up from under him, thorns clawing at his sleeves and wrapping around his legs like barbed wire.

A piece of memory breaks loose, then tumbles away.

Not here. Not now.

In one heave he tears himself free from the tangle of barbs and leaps back onto the bricks, skin stinging and fabric ripping with the effort.

He's made it.

One good lungful of air. Another.

He tugs his painting cap onto his head. Squares his shoulders. Just one minute more, and then back to work.

Five

ONLY RINALDO AND DOM ARE at the Gordon residence today. The rest of them have the day off to make up for yesterday. Each can do as he pleases.

Al drums his fingers on the window ledge. They still bear the marks of the week's work, butter, cream, lemon and Wedgwood blue, the colours of the wealthy. A good dousing with turpentine still leaves traces under his nails and in the creases of his knuckles, but he doesn't mind. It's clean dirt. Not dirt at all, really.

He pushes up the middle pane of the bay window and hangs out his head. Streetcars rattling, the soup scent of cafés, the mildly caustic stink of exhaust. Even as his lungs fill he's thinking of himself at work the day before, his reasoning fouled by odours and creeping thoughts, his limbs raked by thorns. If only he could take the moment back, if he could change events so that he saw only what was before his eyes, not behind them. A hole left by a cork, nothing more. But he recovered, and he returned to work. There was that.

A horse bows its head as it plods up Pender Street, hauling a cart with laundry heaped like dirty snow. Al pulls back in and swings around on the window seat. That's what he needs: something to do. He has extra linen for pickup today.

He leaps over the bedroll below the window where he spent the night.

A screen of gathered cotton separates the main room from the sleeping alcove. There, he set up a cot next to the narrow iron bed, one each for his overnight guests: Jack and Agnes. They already had their toast and tea, and said they were stopping at Woodward's to pick up a few things before the train trip home to Princeton. *Why didn't he join them*, they asked. Al couldn't imagine what a plain woman like Agnes needed from a department store. He pictured underthings, long, grey underthings that went all the way down to her knees.

He said his goodbyes on the stairs and watched them walk up Pender Street, their overnight things bundled like their lives into one simple bag that Jack carried over his shoulder.

When Al first heard his brother's plans to marry her, he said, *She's old enough to be your grandmother.* He should have said *mother*. The comparison was so ridiculous that Jack clapped his hands on his hips, leaned back and simply laughed.

That was five years ago, but still the difference amazes him. As he crosses the floor he calculates their ages once more. He's twenty-nine now, Jack seven years older, Agnes a dozen more on top of that. Almost fifty. What was the matter with him? They'll never have children.

Al shouldn't have been surprised. There had been hints enough, though it took Jack years to act on them. Al recalls the strange way Jack grinned about sending Agnes to meet him at the train station. He should have known right then.

Al steps behind the screen and sees immediately that Jack hasn't used the second cot, but instead shared the narrow iron bed with Agnes. He shoves his way between the beds to get a closer look, whirls around as though someone is playing a trick on him. But no, the cot hasn't been touched. The sheets and grey blanket are pulled flat, corners as tight as he'd been taught to make them in the army. He turns back to the iron bed with its mussed-up bedding and, arms extended, nose wrinkling, tugs at the sheets gingerly, afraid of what he might find. But there are no knife pleats of passion, linens twisted by a clenched fist, no evidence of ... marks ... he doesn't know how to even phrase the thought.

With the bedding balled up in his arms he pauses, ashamed at once for finding comfort in the way it fills them as a woman might, and for not knowing that there is such a kind of intimacy, that a man can want to lie with a woman, just lie with her.

And the cotton with that odour he can't quite place. Rosewater? That was Agnes. But the other smell: Jack, and something else. A smell of men, of engine oil and coal dust and metal. Guns. That was it. The hospital could smell like that. Bleached bedclothes and sheets and the surgeon behind a cotton mask, digging shrapnel from his legs. That familiar itch he felt yesterday — of course it wasn't the heat. A stinging burn, almost. It irritates him even now.

He edges past the bed and, through an open window, drops the bundle onto the veranda for pickup. Then he squeezes back around the bed and leans against the wall to dig a heel against his shin.

But scratching gives only temporary relief. He sits on the edge of the bed and rolls back the pant leg to look. Several lumps — and not the first of them since the hospital. The doctor removed enough to get him a boat ride home, all right, but he left plenty more inside. Al thought he'd got them all by now, but obviously he hadn't. He runs his fingertips over his shin and knee, then feels in his pockets for his penknife.

Using the dull edge, he presses, kneading a dark lump between thumbnail and blade. He can almost pinch it free, it's that close to the surface, just below and to the right of his kneecap.

With the blade's tip he pierces the lump and exposes, briefly, a black point of shrapnel. It slips back into the lump and so he probes with the blade, feeling gristle and flesh and bone. He digs until his stomach rises. With each jab he feels the sickness right down to his groin, a gnawing ache. Sweat soaks his neck as he pushes deeper, and at last a black pearl of shrapnel pops out, leaving a tiny hole soon covered by a matching pearl of blood.

He thought it would be a larger piece than that, and rougher, jagged. He pulls an old handkerchief from his hip pocket and dabs.

The bleeding stops right away. But the sight of the tiny wound still sickens him, because the other lumps have gone under again, the grey promise of their return revealed in a trail down his shin.

ON THE STREET AL STOPS to flex his knee. The throbbing eases, but the sensation is still there, like a swollen bug bite. He walks it out, striding past fruit and vegetable vendors who wheel wooden crates onto the sidewalks outside their shops, stacking full ones onto empty, tipping them just so until the contents are clearly displayed. Neat rows of orange, red, yellow and green.

Further down the block Al sees men trotting beside lumbering trucks, bamboo poles bending across their shoulders, baskets on each end weighed down with sacks of rice or pottery or bricks. Horns honk and voices shout.

He cuts across Main Street and ducks down an alley. Quiet descends. Steam drifts from the back doors of cafés. A cat twitches its tail from a windowsill. A foraging seagull hops among the trash cans.

Panic seized him the first time he saw this part of town.

He and Jack left the ranch — bolted from it, they admitted to each other — and headed straight for Vancouver. When they rounded the corner from Hastings onto Carrall Street and then up Pender, he blurted, *Christ!* at the sight of so many Chinese.

They were everywhere, it seemed, spilling over the edges of the street, jamming the sidewalks. His own narrow eyes narrowed further still at the painful pitch of their language, at their sidelong glances as they glided past him like fish, nudging him as though he didn't exist, the unmistakable odour of ocean rising from their cotton jackets, wafting out from open doorways, a part of the air itself, their air. Plucked chickens hung by their feet above baskets of shrivelled twigs and foul-smelling grasses. Live chickens screeched and flapped between the slats of their crates.

All along Pender Street he heard the same chatter he'd heard when the drunken miners shoved him into that tunnel, and he wanted to burst above ground as he had then, fists swinging at the bastards, at the enemy who seemed to come at him from every direction, from sidewalks and street corners and doorways.

Now, in the quiet of the alley, steam drifting about his ankles, he thinks of the year that had followed his return from war, the cramped city spaces that made him sweat, the loud noises that had him ducking.

The influenza outbreak marked the end of that year. He had loved the midnight feel to those empty midday streets. The rare pedestrian he passed wore a mask, making conversation wonderfully difficult. Only when the war ended, and people foolishly jammed the streets to celebrate, did Al have to worry about dodging crowds again. Despite this, neither he nor Jack fell ill.

With the din of Chinatown fading behind him, Al steps out from the alleys and begins angling toward Granville Street.

On this visit Jack wondered aloud if exposure to Rose's illness had somehow made them immune. It was a different illness, he agreed, but he couldn't think of any other reason for their continued good health. Even their parents survived both influenza outbreaks that fall and winter.

Al admitted this was true. They didn't die until years later, and when they did it was from heart attacks, one right after the other.

He'd missed their burials. While Rose's health had dwindled, their deaths were quick, their hearts old machinery, clogged with the grease and grime of life, that simply stopped. Jack said the bodies wouldn't keep in the heat. That was all right. Seeing Rose's coffin drop into the hot earth had been more than Al could bear. Each handful of dirt tossed into her grave made him wince, as though it was raining onto his own skin. He couldn't have gone through that again. But he arrived in time for a belated double reception with tea and sandwiches served on his mother's old china, and that seemed an appropriate farewell.

Al lifts his head, breathes the smell of smoke from burning leaves. It was good to see Jack and Agnes this weekend, to have company for a change. But Al was just as glad to see them go.

Now he can do as he likes. Take a streetcar. They aren't so bad if he sits near the exit or an open window. Or he can go for a long stroll. If nothing else, it will relieve the pressure in his leg and keep the blood from pooling around the small cut.

He removes his jacket, hooks it over his shoulder.

Sometimes the eye plays tricks. You pass a fine residence with lawn chairs and you see a young woman in pale grey or white step into the sunlight, testing the air for warmth, and you expect her to fetch a glass of lemonade and a book so she can read in the lingering warmth of a September day. But then she turns back for a moment, and when she returns it's with a rickety wicker chair on wheels, and a young man hunched like an old man with a blanket across his knees.

All right, all right. Look up. Blue sky. Golden leaves. Breathe. Just breathe.

BY NOON HE CROSSES THE park on the Crescent. A lone truck with *Rinaldo & Company Master Painters* on the side door is parked neatly, just inside the gates.

Rinaldo is leaning against the fender, thoughtfully fingering a sparse moustache, until he sees Al.

His arms fly up. "Here comes Michelangelo! Can't stay away even one day."

Dom jumps down from the truck bed with a basket in his hands that contains, Al knows, his lunch. "You need a woman to keep you home. Tell you what, you stay here and I'll go home to my Louisa."

Rinaldo walks to the back of the truck with his lunch and sits, legs swinging over the lowered tailgate.

From one of the upper windows comes a shrill voice and then the sound of slamming doors.

"Help us finish up so we can get out of here." Dom rolls his eyes toward the window.

Rinaldo's legs go still. "It's his day off!" He won't want to pay any more. He's already done the calculations for the day.

But Al doesn't need the money. Each member of the crew was given a bonus from Gordon for their Sunday work.

If he helps out for an hour or two, though, then walks a good portion of the way back, he'll have killed a day.

"I'll do it for some lunch," he says.

"Here. Sit. When a man has a woman like Louisa, she packs him a wonderful lunch. Enough for two men."

The incision point throbs when he puts all his weight on the one leg. He grits his teeth and hopes the cut won't tear as he climbs up and past Rinaldo. As soon as he sits on the side of the open pickup, the wound beats slowly, and then stops. Good. It won't bleed.

With the sun on his back he eats olives, prosciutto, cheese and bread. Dom pours him a tin mug of strong coffee.

He knows that at any moment Rinaldo will offer to introduce him to his beautiful unmarried niece. Then Dom will say she is beautiful, yes, but big, and to show how big, and just what a big woman such as her can do to a skinny man such as Al, he will grab up a couple of dried sticks and snap them in half.

What they'll say isn't all that different from what Agnes was saying to him the night before: how nice it would be, one day, to hear that he has met someone. Al appreciates the way Dom and

Rinaldo say it, as though the fault were in the women he's met so far, not in him. They turn it into something all of them can laugh about.

Al is already smiling when Rinaldo reaches for his flask and says, "Michelangelo. I have the perfect woman for you."

Six

HE'S HAD TOO MUCH TO drink, but tomorrow is Sunday, and this time he can sleep the whole day away. No overnight guests. No wild party at the Gordon residence. Mrs. Gordon has seen to that.

A flask of whisky sloshes inside his jacket pocket as he grabs the wooden railing to steady himself.

It was a satisfying week of work, painting scrollwork on the tops of the columns at yet another residence on the Crescent. He was quick to spend the bonus, one evening stopping in at the Chinese tailor's for a fitting and the promise of a completed outfit in just two days, then this afternoon, after his usual half Saturday at work, shopping for shoes along Hastings. Now, just a quick tug on the cuff of each black silk sleeve, a slight shake of each linen trouser leg, the knife pleat falling just so over the soft, tan leather — and he's ready.

The pier is wide enough to fit two automobiles parked side by side, and pedestrians spill around them as they head for the pavilion at the far end. Al pauses to run the back of his hand over the fenders and the cool, glossy paint. The occupants will never notice. The young men and women are dressed in white, gleaming white, their limbs draped over the edges, long fingers dangling drinks and cigarettes. Laughing. Flirting.

Al knows his automobiles. A 1927 Phantom. A 1921 Silver Ghost. And he knows which one he'd take. Not the deep red Phantom, though its colour pulses with life. No, he runs his sleeve along a strip of chrome on the side of the Silver Ghost. It's painted a white with just a hint of cream, but there is so much trim the paint takes on a silvery glow. The strip of chrome leads his arm right up to the hood ornament, The Flying Lady. He turns his hand so that the backs of his fingers can glide down her cheek, her shoulder and then her arms draped in fabric that becomes wings.

How he'd like to fly along the road with her leading the way. The only thing he's ever driven was that old truck on the ranch, his brother beside him telling him to feel his way through the gears, not to worry about the shriek and squawk of metal against metal, as they lurched down the dirt road, the sound an abomination to any automobile lover.

He'd practise on anything else before he ground the gears on a beauty like this.

With one last caress to the Lady's chrome cheek, he turns and continues down the pier. He tips his head back, holding onto his white straw boater with one hand, the railing with the other. A warm September night on English Bay. Chunks of stars, a slice of moon, and the ocean sliding beneath him. To his left is the Sylvia, a fine red-brick building of apartments. He could live there one day, with the beach and entire ocean his front yard. Why not? It's 1929, the last year of the decade. In the New Year he'll be thirty years of age. He's earned it. He's a painter of fine homes, dressed in fine attire for an evening out. A fine evening out.

Maybe he is drunk. He gulps mouthfuls of salty air.

At the far end of the pier the pavilion glitters with light and the movement of dancers drifting from the floor. For the moment the only sounds are distant laughter and the surge of water below the boards.

He pauses by the posts that mark the entrance, savouring the anticipation of the dance. When the music begins, he steps in, allowing his senses to be saturated.

The tune swirls in his head — the one-two-three of a waltz he recognizes from the phonograph in their parlour in Chelsea, where his sister taught him to dance. The same notes played on an accordion in a bar in Paris, a plump matron singing wearily on a smoke-filled stage, and then a violin joined in, Christ, a violin, and the boys in their clean uniforms all smiles and raising their glasses, only to be marching next day back to the mud. A dirty trick.

All right, then. All right.

A waltz. What can be better? A waltz in the open air, just a roof in case of rain, though for now he will watch. Young women with their small hands and feet, their pale summer dresses that float as they turn in their partners' arms. At the tables over there, giggles and a stirring of silk in the warm evening air, legs crossed and recrossed. God, how he loves it.

His eyes go immediately to a group of thin girls with bobbed hair. One of them.

He edges around the half-empty dance floor, removes his hat with a flourish and to a brunette in pearl grey silk, simply asks, "Dance?"

"My fiancé has just gone to get us drinks." She has aloof green eyes that avoid his.

He smiles. He wants a dance, nothing more, and perhaps the smile conveys that because she stands abruptly and takes his arm.

One grand swoop followed by two tight steps, swirling, round, round, round, they make several passes over the dance floor.

The heaviness in his limbs is gone, that persistent itch and even the knick where he removed the piece of metal, the grey track below it that throbbed. Gone. Now, he's flying. Twirling and dipping — better than running, better even than being up on the scaffolding. A rush of feeling as the room swirls past, joy and sadness both at once. Because now, right now, the violin sounding like Paris and this silken woman in his arms, he can almost believe that she is his woman, his wife perhaps, and when the dance is over they will cross the beach to their rooms at the Sylvia, holding hands like lovers, talking of what they will do on their Sunday off. They will read the papers in bed while drinking cups of hot chocolate. They will go for a swim, racing each other to the water's edge, where he'll pick her up and dump her, screaming and laughing, into the cold froth.

The violin sounds its last notes, and the waltz dies in his arms.

A singer leaps to the microphone and a trumpet player swoops forward, dips his horn, then raises it high and blasts out the opening chords of "Five Foot Two."

Couples swarm onto the dance floor as Al tries to lead the woman back to her table. She drops his hand and makes her own way. He follows, only so that he can fetch his hat. Her head is already bent in conversation with her fiancé.

The boards thrum against the pounding of heels, the corner poles buzz. Al has never seen the place like this. Hat in hand, he is swamped by the crowd as he tries to press along the edge of the dance floor to the pier, to fresh air. The throng slides as one mass and he has to turn a shoulder and muscle his way through. Shrieking voices ricochet about his head. He recoils only to be confronted by an aging woman who sways, then lifts a fleshy arm and offers a deep view into her withered armpit. A rim of sweat and powder looms around the black armhole as she tips back a high-heeled shoe of champagne. Who brought it? Those kids on the pier.

This is what the Gordon residence must have been like the other night. Reckless joy. A frantic need for pleasure.

The golden liquid gushes down the sides of her red mouth and pools in the puckered skin of her neck. Above him, a thin blond, her skirt wrenched above her knees, reels on the shoulders of two men who pretend to gnaw at her tangled limbs and then throw their heads back to sing out, *Has anybody seen my gal?*

The crowd continues to pulse, dragging him farther from his goal, the pier. With one big push Al squeezes past the twisting lot of them and nears the outer edge.

A hand grabs at his arm and a voice says, "Whoops."

He has just about knocked the girl to the floor. "My apologies," he says, and curls an arm around her back, noting at once the too-tight blouse, the rolls of flesh and the flounced skirt. The style is slimmer, now. The other women wear sheath dresses with fringes and beads. Even her hair looks out of place, pale strands pinned haphazardly instead of a clean cut at the chin.

But she keeps her arm on his and begins tapping her feet and swinging out her heavy legs, as though he has asked for a dance. He pulls on his hat and waves both hands, confesses, "I'm not fond of the Charleston."

Her round nose lifts in a manner that makes her seem pleased, as though his talking to her is more than she has hoped for. Flattered, Al smiles.

She's out of breath. "All right, then. A walk?" Her hand slides down his arm.

He uses his elbows and bursts through the clot of onlookers in the doorway, his feet finally touching the boards of the pier.

The Sylvia is lit up like a ship, drawing him, and he thinks of the woman in pearl grey silk, again, seated across from him at a table in the window, sipping from a cup and reading the papers.

He has forgotten all about the girl until a pull on his arm steers him the other way, toward the trees.

"There's a nice spot up here," she says.

Has she told him her name? She is chattering and he can't keep up. She talks about her job in an office, or maybe it's a warehouse, and the smocks they wear to keep ink or dust from their shirt fronts. No, not an office! She laughs when he asks. She wanted to work in an office, that was exactly what she has just been saying.

Her name is Bitsy. Wasn't he listening? What an odd-sounding voice he has, more like an old man's than a young man's, has anyone ever told him that? Before he can answer she has dropped to her knees and is tugging at his trousers.

"What?" He backs up. "Really — this is not —" He falters, picturing the silken straps left behind at the Gordon residence, the sort of girl who would leave them, who would let a man take them. Bitsy looks more like someone's sister or neighbour.

A quick glance down shows Al that she's already unbuttoned her blouse herself, and one of those white undergarments — sidelacers, he thinks they're called, things that woman use to bind their bosoms — has been loosened and yanked up under her armpits.

"Don't look," she says.

Too late. He pulls his gaze away from two breasts distended like gourds by the pressure of the twisted garment. She fumbles in his drawers, talking the whole while about her Scottish friend who told her about a trick called a diddy ride. A man can press himself between a girl's — she pauses, and the silence swells more wickedly than the word breasts might have — with no loss of virtue on her part. Since he's the man, though, he'll have to throw his jacket on the ground or she'll ruin her outfit. Take care he leans on his elbows so he doesn't crush her. And he agrees to take her out next weekend?

He blushes to hear her talk like this. She must have done this many times. And virtue — what's virtuous about it? His eyes are closed and he can feel his ears on fire, is thankful of the dark night that hides them from her. So why not just push her away? He's about to, is about to object to using his jacket. It's silk! New today! And this isn't what he's come here for.

And yet now, under her probing fingers, he wants exactly this: soaring pleasure, the promise of release.

He shrugs off his jacket and tosses it forward, telling her to mind the flask. Bitsy flops onto the jacket, grabs his arm and pulls him down on top of her.

"What's your name?" she asks, her voice muffled beneath his rib cage.

"Michelangelo," he says.

He feels her head twist upward. "Italian?"

He wants to laugh but closes his eyes again when he feels the warm flesh surround him. His elbows dig into a sandy patch of grass. Long blades tickle his chin.

He wishes she'd stop talking. If he could think of something else. Amiens. Yes, that. A gypsy wagon at the side of the road and an old woman in black who strutted beside them in the dark November rain, shouting coarsely, *Dix minutes!* A soldier behind him wondered aloud who could last as long as ten minutes? Another long line. Even for this they had to wait their turns.

Bitsy's voice below him rises and falls. He has to concentrate hard on Amiens to block out her incessant chatter.

He charged up the steps then stopped, the red velvet curtain limp in front of him. The old woman said, *Vite! Vite!* then clomped up the steps behind him and yanked the curtain back.

Stale perfume of sandalwood and spice. Peach satin and a single nipple sprung loose from the corset's rim. The tops of black stockings and pink skin bulging around the straps of garters. The stockinged legs zipped across the sheets, spreading wide, and a musky scent filled the room, a stink of low tide. He was on top of her before he even knew she'd unbuttoned his fly. She tore at his trousers, tugged them down, clamped her gartered legs around his naked waist and then his swollen prick plunged deep inside. He felt something — her red fingernail? — trace a line from rectum to scrotum and up the seam between his balls. And then a cry. His?

Deux minutes! a voice shouted from outside. *You're seeing action, now!*

Artie.

Bloody hell, don't think of him, not now.

Al had — what? Had stumbled back out through the velvet, blushing, tucking in his shirt. Gunfire boomed in the distance, but he'd barely heard. He'd been fucked — finally understood the rough sound of the word, its perfect, low pitch.

Atta boy, Artie said. *Ya took much longer, I'd a grabbed her*, and he bolted past the old crone who stuck her hand out for the coins.

Artie.

Beneath him Bitsy sighs heavily, "Now what's wrong?" She clamps a hand on either side of her breasts and presses them together.

The effect is instant, wrenching, all-consuming. Al gropes for his handkerchief but she beats him to it, whipping a hand into his pocket and then mopping at her cleavage.

He has worn his hat the whole time, which makes him feel ridiculous, and rude.

He rolls off her and fastens his buttons, then gets to his feet and brushes sand from his trousers. She stands, runs her fingers through her hair, tightens her laces and tucks in her blouse. Now he knows why she doesn't wear the more fashionable sheath dress. She'd have to remove the whole thing.

"Next Saturday at seven, then. Promise? The other girls will be green that I have a real date." And she walks back to the pier beside him, chatting about music or washing up, he isn't listening, grabbing his jacket instead and feeling for the flask, twisting this way and that to see if they have left anything behind.

Some girls know that all they have to do is appear on a fellow's arm and that's enough. And that's all he wanted this evening: to have fine things around him. Music, lights, pretty girls. He wanted to feel happy, to dance. But now? He's filled at once with a deep loathing for himself and for Bitsy that he never felt for the whore at Amiens.

OUTSIDE

Seven

IT'S BLACK AS NIGHT, THOUGH it's only midday. The sergeant's voice booms in his ears, *Which one of you idlers is going out there?*

Al doesn't want to but it's Artie who needs help. Artie who'd shouted just two days ago, *Atta boy!* Artie who's lying in the mud, wounded. So Al gets to his feet. *I'll go*, he says, climbing over the edge, sliding under the barbed wire.

It snags on his sleeves, tugs at his leggings as he slithers into the muck, wraps around his ankles. The reek of decay. Fear making him puke down his front as he humps forward. And then he finds Artie all right, twisting in pain, but Al feels joy rush through him.

Artie! he whispers. *Artie, it's me!*

They'll fix him up. He'll be all right. And Al grabs a leg to pull him back.

Something wriggles under his hand and he lets go, but not soon enough. Artie is dead, but his corpse is alive.

Rats slip out from his pockets and cuffs. They swarm over the ground, over Al's arms and legs and back, their claws like thorns piercing his skin, and he is alone, all alone out there in the foul mud surrounded by bodies and those brown buggers and he forgets himself and leaps to his feet, howling as he runs, bullets peppering the mud and scattering the rats, blowing some to bits, but somehow missing him, arms pumping, legs pounding, all the way back.

HIS EYES SNAP OPEN BUT images continue sliding behind them until he blinks. Once, twice, three times. The mud lifts, the rats scuttle to the edges and the small noises that roused him begin to settle on his brain. Wood clattering to the ground, the snap of a fire taking hold, the rattle of a pot put on to boil. Then coughs. Rustling of tent flaps. Yawns.

In his wakeful hours he chants, *don't drift, don't drift*. But in the unguarded moments between sleep and wakefulness, the memories slip in, unbidden. Even they are preferable to full sleep, when he is helpless against the shifting shapes that darken and swell into nightmares.

He puts his hands behind his head and studies the water stains on the canvas ceiling.

He always counted on his painting job to leave him exhausted and dreamless at night, to help occupy his thoughts in the day. But the job's gone now.

One month after completing their work at the Gordon residence, Al was getting his shoes shined in the basement of the Hotel Georgia. His raised position on the throne-like seat of oak and red leather made him feel that much more removed from the panic around him. Afterward, he would even indulge in a glass of whisky at the bar. In the meantime he read the papers while a balding man bent over his right shoe and then his left, and whipped each to a shine with a blackened rag. There'd been a series of stock-market crashes and the papers reported calamitous losses, particularly on Wall Street. There were repercussions in Canada, but the prime minister was saying that business was never better. So Al wasn't worried. Granted, for several days he saw grown men running in the streets, their voices shrill as boys', their faces gaunt and sickly. But unlike them, he never dabbled in stocks. He was a painter.

That was four years ago, and sure enough, for two of those years his skills were in demand. Hustlers like Gordon went on making money on booze and gambling, they continued throwing parties and receptions. Mansions still needed painting.

But then the work started to slow. Some of the mansions were turned into rooming houses. Many fell into disrepair. Shaughnessy Heights became known as Poverty Hill. The painting work dried up and, with it, any connection to Dom and Rinaldo. Al never saw them again.

There'd been a string of jobs long before he worked for Rinaldo — jobs that never satisfied the way painting had. He cleaned eaves-troughs of houses and stores. Washed windows. Swept out warehouses. Shovelled gravel. His nerves were raw and sometimes he lost his temper, told a roofer looking for help that he could shove it if he thought Al was going to hang from his kneecaps and hammer nails into shingles.

Go hire a Chinaman! he shouted.

He'd take any one of those jobs now.

Flipping back the coat that blanketed him all night, he lies flat another moment, listening. A breaking branch? Next to him another man snores then sputters and sits bolt upright.

"What was that?" the man asks.

Three more stir beneath their ragged coverings.

"Sh-h-h," Al says, and they wait. It was nothing.

The man beside him drops down again.

Al can't go back to sleep, not now. Once he starts thinking, his mind won't stop.

All winter he lined up at soup kitchens. He slept in flophouses, several beds to a room, four of five of them to a bed, complete strangers lying sideways on the mattress like intimates, knees drawn up so they'd fit. He kept to the outside edge, preferring to stare through the bars at the head or foot of the bed than to lie in the middle surrounded by the heat and smell of other men's bodies.

As he had the year before, he moved to this hobo camp once the weather warmed. Here, they slept several to one tent, but each had his own space, his own things. Barring any police raids they lived peacefully under two simple rules: any food brought into the camp must be shared and any man caught stealing must leave.

Behind his head are trousers he rolled up as a pillow. He reaches back and stands. The smell of leather from worn boots is strong in the tent. As he slings suspenders over his shoulders he thinks about the ranch. The leather bridles and saddles, the heaving sides of the great beasts, their soft noses nuzzling his pockets for lumps of sugar. Whenever he stepped into that barn, warm and ripe with hay and horse flesh, all the noise in his mind stopped. He roped and dug and forked and swept, and thought of nothing but the task before him.

In the tent the air is steamy and close, and the smell of leather boots gives way to the smell of feet, of hair, of unwashed skin. Al cinches his belt and finds he has to undo it and cinch it tighter by one more notch. He doesn't need a mirror to know what his face looks like. His hands are the colour of ashes. His cheeks will be, too.

He lifts an elbow, sniffs the sleeve of his undershirt — it reeks of campfire. So will his hair.

He steps through the tent flap and looks around. Ragged clumps of bushes with dusty leaves flash silver in the sunlight. Raw, open earth, gouged and tangled with blackberry vines. A clear stream running into the brine of False Creek. And in the midst of all that a fire and a circle of men, their shoulders hunched against the sharp morning air.

Crowning the hill across the water are the tall, stately buildings of downtown. Crouched before them, out of sight from this low vantage point, is Chinatown and his former rooms above Pender Street. In his entire life he's never lived in any one place as long as he lived there. Yet what dreams he had of living somewhere else, of silken women and cups of hot chocolate over the morning newspaper. He had no idea that one day he would long for the sleeping alcove and bay window that had been, if nothing else, his.

Now, as each man stumbles out of the tents and lean-tos — one fashioned from the hood of a Ford — the backs of those already at the fire stiffen, anticipating food that others might bring. Al fights hunger pangs until he can clean up. The longer he can delay eating, the longer the food will last. He has to consider how to share a half loaf of bread with so many men.

Al crouches and inside the tent flap feels around for his shaving gear, his folded shirt, his jacket, and carries them to the sorry apple tree where they've hung a cracked mirror. Only one side of the tree bears fruit, much of it misshapen and spotted. In a few weeks the fruit will ripen and the camp will smell of apples roasting by the fire. The tree won't look so bad then. Even the most cold-blunted apple still tastes deliciously of apple, and of all the things associated with it: family, home.

Al lays his shirt and jacket over the branches to air. The thinner branches snap under the weight and again he thinks of the sounds that awakened him. Probably that group at the fire. He strips to the waist and leaves the long sleeves of his undershirt dangling next to his suspenders. Then he drags out a pot of cold water he scooped from the creek the night before and dips a cupful to brush his teeth.

There are no women here.

Sometimes, he goes for days without seeing a woman, and when he spots one, often from a distance, he stands amazed, staring at the willowy shape bending down to a child, at the elegant heel that steps onto a streetcar. When he has five cents to spare he climbs aboard just to sit near a woman and smell the powder and lavender of normal life.

Now he squints at the houses across the tracks with the mark of a notch in their gates. In those homes the kindly housewives give food or supplies to men in return for yardwork or chopping wood. Yesterday Al chopped contentedly for an entire afternoon. His spot in the yard offered a direct view inside the house of fine hands kneading the dough that became his payment, a loaf of bread. He would have done the work for free just to be a part of her world for one afternoon. But she insisted he take it, wrapped in an old, striped tea towel.

With the remaining soapy water he soaks his close-cropped hair and scrubs his scalp. Then he splashes a handful under and over his arms, across his chest. There's no rush. He dresses slowly, squatting to rinse his razor with the last of the water in the pot. Bedraggled branches hang so low they block any curious eyes at the fire. He reaches behind the tree trunk, fingers scrabbling over the rocks, rolling back the largest that hides a hollow at the base of the tree.

It's gone. The bread and the striped cloth.

He looks up and thinks he sees at least one of the heads at the fire look down. From here, he can't tell whose. Is that the sound that woke him? Someone stealing?

Shaking water from the blade he wipes it clean on his shirttail, tucks the shaving gear back inside the tent flap. He walks over to the fire and squats, spreads his hands over the flames' warmth. Three sets of eyes meet his, but the open smiles fade when they see that, this morning, he has nothing to share with them. He can't detect anything from their faces. Older than their years, scarred, grim. The exception is the Ingram boy who stares hopefully at the fire.

This was Al's fourth month in the camp and he has learned by now not to bother with names. Men come and go every day. He and the boy are the only regulars.

"Tea?" one of them offers. "It's all we got." He doesn't look so good, skin almost as yellow as his hair. Al decides he wouldn't have the energy to steal. He holds out his mug and nods his appreciation.

The one with a head as thin as his neck picks up on a conversation interrupted by Al's arrival. "I'd be a postman."

That one again. Postmen wear uniforms and deliver letters, something any man in the camp feels qualified to do.

Normally, Al might have told them, *I had a good job. I used to paint mansions.* They could have laughed about that. Because here he is, Michelangelo, painter of magnificent ceilings, looking up at filthy canvas every morning.

But this is not a normal day, hasn't been from the moment he'd been awakened — by something, by someone sneaking around, stealing from him.

The yellow one adds, "The way I understand it, you have a wife, you get relief when a job falls through."

The man is an imbecile. Al leans forward and tells him, "That's exactly the problem. Don't you see? Who'd want to bring a family into a life like this? No woman's going to look at us. Without jobs we're nothing." He rears up and shakes the dregs of his tea into the dirt.

The others drain their mugs and get up slowly, the yellow one sighing deeply.

Each cleans his own dishes, an easy matter this day because they haven't used their plates. This week Al is responsible for cleaning the coffee pot they used for tea and the stew pot that had soaked all night. He gathers them up, banging them loudly as one by one the men drift away. Only the boy hangs back.

Al digs his boot heels into the gravel and slides down the bank. He wonders: *Would life with a woman like Agnes have been so bad?* Jack seems happy enough.

There'd been that girl named Bitsy. But no. Al shakes his head, as he does each time he thinks about her and her idea of virtue. He did as promised, took her to the pier the following Saturday. But he made sure they stayed on the dance floor.

There were other girls, of course, but after all those years this camp is all that Al has.

He crouches at the stream and grabs up a fistful of gravel to scrub the bottom of the stew pot, when he hears the boy's voice close beside him.

"Want some help?"

Al jerks his head to regard him — a boy whose hair still bears streaks of blond in the summer, who squats at the water's edge and in his haste forgets to roll back his sleeves, soaking himself to the elbows, who's never offered help before today.

He's also the only one who sat at the fire with his eyes downcast, a fact that occurs to Al only now. So much bitter disgust fills his mouth that he spits on the ground. "You took it, didn't you?"

"What?" The boy looks over, startled.

"The bread, that's what."

The water is achingly cold and Al can see the boy's teeth chattering.

"You know the rules," Al says. How old is the boy, sixteen years, eighteen? Old enough.

The boy gives a half-smile, uncertain if he's hearing right. Al wraps his fist around the handle of a fork to make his point. The Ingram boy dumps the lid he was washing and backs up.

Al stays crouched at the water's edge.

The boy can't seem to find the right words at first, just shakes his head. Finally he cries out, "I didn't go looking for it. Honest. But — once I saw it, I couldn't stop looking." He throws his hands up. "I'll make it up to you. I know what you've been through. I hear you. At night. Sometimes you yell —"

Al's face flames. "That's none of your business."

"Please. I'll do whatever you want. Don't send me away."

"There's nothing you could do! There's no paying this back! You took food."

But it's more than that. It's the woman who gave it to him, the magic of that afternoon, watching her hands, feeling included in her world. There is no replacing that.

Slowly, Al rises. The boy looks hopeful for an instant until he sees Al's face. He turns and runs.

Al goes straight to the tent and gathers up the boy's things.

"Hey," one of the men shouts.

Al rolls up the blankets, punching them tight. "He's not coming back," he says. "You need these?" and tosses them over. He shoves the striped towel inside his jacket.

He picks his way through pockets of mud and ragged debris that surround the hobo jungle, then tears his tweed cap from his head and slaps angrily at a hanging branch.

At times like these there has to be trust. What else did they have? You steal a man's food and you shorten his life. All the men agree. Damn that boy for putting him in this position.

He labours along the shore, heels sinking in the rocky soil.

Had the Ingram boy been older Al wouldn't care. But he can't shake the image of himself at that age. Sixteen or eighteen, it doesn't matter. Neither made Ingram a man any more than it had made Al a soldier back in France. The only reason the boy was in the camp was because his family couldn't get relief with him around. Al curls his lip thinking about it. The government figures he could just step out the door and find a job. So he wound up with the hobos and was too young and stupid to realize they were serious about the rules.

But had Al taken it seriously when he joined the army? They practised firing weapons, cleaning weapons, using bayonets. He must have thought he could march around all day in his new uniform while someone else got shot at.

Most days, now, he walks along the water like this and tries to figure a way out for himself. Jack was surprised when he wrote recently to say he'd take a job in the mine after all. But it runs only one day a week now. The company isn't hiring anyone.

A low whistle cuts through the air and Al lifts his head. It's the camp's warning signal. Cops.

Al runs back to the camp. The crack of branches, not the boy, not then. The snort of breath, not the sound of a man, but of horses. That's why he couldn't get the ranch out of his head. The smell of horses grows so strong he knows they are almost on top of him.

The loaf of bread is nothing now. He is about to lose everything precious to him. His bedroll, spare shirts, letters. The ground shakes from the drumming of hooves. Can he outrun them, get to his things in time?

No. He makes it as far as a slight rise above the camp. Waves slap the shore behind him, their tents and shelters lie immediately below in the shallow hollow.

The air fills with dust and then a burst of chestnut flesh and flaring nostrils through the breaking branches, snorts and squeals as the horses loop through the camp. The ground and everything before Al — tents, shacks, the very air — vibrates from the fury of the charge, the sudden sharp swerves, a continuous figure eight that, with each loop, crushes the shelters and the bushes sur-rounding them. The hood from the Ford truck is flattened under the hooves, the sound like the crackle of gunfire. Hard green apples bounce and roll across the campsite like falling rock.

The mounted cops lean down to swipe with clubs at whatever the horses miss. Scrambling men hold their heads, red streams between their fingers. Lean-tos and tents topple over with a rip of canvas and squawk of sheet metal pulling free of nails. Their pos-sessions, tucked under blankets, shelved in wooden crates, explode in the air and drift like ragged leaves over the ground. Books, let-ters, photographs, shoes.

Cops on foot march in after the horses, boot heels thudding in the soft dirt until they reach the centre of the clearing that was once the camp, and then branch out, chasing down and herding the remaining men, Al among them as the foot patrolmen stomp up the rise where he has been standing, and, for a moment, considered running from.

They are shoved into one clump, some of them barefoot, heads and elbows still bleeding. Army trucks pull up along the road.

"You want to eat?" A club jabs Al in the ribs. "In you get!"

Al climbs in. It seems a fitting end to the day. He kicked out the Ingram boy. Now he has to leave.

Eight

UNDER A GREY TRUCK CANOPY Al and the others are bounced and tossed from wooden benches. They've travelled all night, by truck, then train, then truck again. The canvas flaps hanging above the tailgate lift and slap to reveal workers on the roadbed knee-high in dirt, swinging picks and shovels. More hobos, most likely, rounded up from other camps in the city and from other towns.

The deep treads of the churning tires disgorge rocks and roots, the road a double trench of deep ruts that snake behind the truck like the earth's entrails, making his own guts cramp in sympathy.

Eventually the dirt itself dries and takes on a yellow pallor, coating the flaps he sways beside, hoping for fresh air despite the dust gritting his teeth and his tongue. The dark shadows of mountains pull back until they fall away altogether and the heavy capes of cedar and fir are replaced in one twist of road by the tortured limbs of the ponderosa pine. And sunlight, brilliant blue skies.

The point where the tires will finally plough to a stop might be five miles from Princeton or fifty. They've been told only that they will be working somewhere on the long stretch of the Hope-Princeton Road. This means he'll be somewhere near Jack, and the family's old ranch site. *Home*, he once called it. It was their last home together. It was the subject of one of Jack's letters, too, now trampled in the dirt of the hobo camp. But Al has read it so many times he knows every line:

Each day we dig in new fence posts and string up more barbed wire,
but there's a lot of work before we're done. You were right, Bertie. The
section by the Hedley Road is the worst.We have to sleep outside to keep
an eye on the cattle.

I never thought I could love it here, but at night with those stars
overhead and a fire going, I can almost see why the old man didn't
want to give it up. Agnes brings her border collie Ginger, he's good at
herding, and we sit up half the night talking.

It was dated June 1924 and was the clue that confirmed Al's
growing suspicion: his brother was courting Agnes. Jack had gone
back to Princeton to help their parents close up the ranch, and he
never came back. For years he talked about getting work at
Lodestone Mountain. He finally did, and then he married Agnes.
That was a decade ago. Al kept the letter all these years because it
seemed to sum up all that was good in Jack's life. They were not a
perfect couple, but they found their moment under those stars.
They bought a small place not far away from the ranch, off the
Tulameen Road. Even if the mine closed, they could scrape a living
from it.

Only after their parents' deaths could Al see what else the letter
showed: his father had found his dream, too. He was incapable of
keeping his cattle fenced in, but still, he'd put several head of them
on that ranch.

A note from his aunt was also among the letters lost in the police
raid. It had offered condolences over the death of their mother, her
sister. It included a likeness of her young daughter, Maggie: a wide
impish mouth and wild dark hair springing out from the bounds of
plaited braids. He hates to think of hooves landing on that image.

The truck engine whines up a steep hill and the men sitting
around Al begin to talk excitedly, rousing him from his thoughts.
He looks out through the flaps.

"Jesus Christ," he says, and flattens his back against the side of the truck.

There's nothing between them and a plunge into the deep valley but a jagged edge of road.

The truck brakes, the tailgate clanks down and they spill out onto a plateau of boulders and torn earth ringed by craggy mountaintops on three sides, a sheer drop-off on the fourth. The valley beyond stretches out clear and blue-green, and Al finds himself standing higher than any scaffolding ever placed him. And yet his feet are ankle-deep in dirt and its dank smell stirs up shadows and creeping thoughts.

He turns abruptly and joins the line of men winding past shacks that extend along the plateau. The larger buildings at the end include a mess hall, it seems, and a supply depot. Men come away from the line carrying army fatigues and boots.

Some of the khaki appears badly worn, but when Al reaches the front of the line a uniformed clerk hands him a shirt that looks almost new.

A man with hair the colour of rough lumber and a moustache to match is barking at a subordinate about shipment numbers.

"Who's that?" Al asks.

The clerk replies, "The foreman. Potts."

Al glances around. Not a gun in sight. So the men can leave if they want to — but in the middle of nowhere, where would they go? Above him, spikes of trees bristle like sentries along a cliff.

The clerk scans the lists of names until he finds Al's, then checks it off and points to his left. "Bunkhouse C-6. Next!"

The shacks. Wooden tents that sit low in the rocky dirt. Al shuffles in the door of C-6 along with about twenty others. Bunk beds line each of the two, long walls. At the far end is a wood stove, a table, a few chairs. Al chooses the bunk closest to the door, with a window between it and the next bunk. He tosses his fatigues onto the top bed and unbuttons his own shirt while a tall, skinny fellow scrabbles up the ladder onto the top bunk across from him.

In the corner cupboard between his bed and the door he hangs up his tattered city outfit and steps into army drab.

THE BREAKFAST BELL RINGS JUST after sun-up and Al leaps out of bed, hops on one foot to yank up his trousers and races out the door with his shirt unbuttoned. He sees men running from every direction for the mess hall.

They sit down to stacks of pancakes and toast, to saucers of butter and jam and heaps of fried potatoes. Only yesterday Al's breakfast was just a mug of tea. Today he has all this, and a choice between coffee and tea. He eats his fill and then they grab picks and shovels and march out to the roadbed.

By midmorning, though, he is hollow-bellied and light-headed. Back in the hobo jungle he ate a lot less but spent his days ambling along the streets. On this roadbed, among the ruptured hills and shattered boulders, he swings a pick, shovels, hacks at roots and hefts stones. He soon works off his breakfast.

The sight of the open earth sickens him. He is here, a raw swath of dirt winding like a filthy ribbon behind him, marking the path that he and the crew of hobos have cleared. And yet he is several other places at once, thoughts ricocheting from the mine to the mud to the six-foot pits that lay not far from here, each with a headstone bearing the name *Fraser*.

If he could choose an end for his own remains it would be fire. He has spent enough time below ground.

As the tip of his pick plunges into the hardpan, he considers how the grid work of mine tunnels weren't unlike the trenches that zig-zagged in the mud, except that they were two thousand feet below the ocean floor. He used to push his helmet back with a gloved thumb and try to imagine the black and white hulls of whales that must be gliding over him, the sun that must be shining. Instead, the only lights around him had been headlamps dim as dying embers. And he used to think, *Nothing could be darker than this.* But he'd been wrong.

AT NOON HE WORMS PAST the other men into the mess for platters of sausages that raise cheers of appreciation, heaps of potatoes with gravy such as the cop back at the hobo camp never hinted at. *You want to eat?* was all he'd said. And by God they're eating.

At supper, after a full day of shovelling and lifting leaves him ravenous, there is more meat — canned corned beef — and then fried potatoes and parsnips, greens, loganberries, bread with butter, cake, tea. A feast.

The next day presents pretty much the same meal, only roast beef instead of corned beef, which they get for lunch the following day.

By week two Al tells his tall bunkmate that even a diet of lobster and caviar would get tiresome after fourteen days in a row. The complaints from the rest are minimal, though. At the long tables Al glances up and down at men whose faces have been wind-burnt the red of dried blood. Their hands are worn like his, brown and dry with calloused palms, and knuckles like cracked walnut shells. The grub is routine all right but they are famished and eat quickly.

Not his bunkmate. Like Al, he is older than most of them, not as old as Jack, but he has the same long and lean look, though he is missing the forward section of his fair hair. He's also missing two side teeth, and his name whistles out the gaps when he introduces himself: "Hender-S-en."

Every other *S* sputters and chirps out the gap as he tells Al one evening, "I've been in a dozen different camps and I still haven't found one that's figured out how to put variety into the grub."

He's in no hurry to eat more of the same, he adds.

"At least we're eating," Al concedes. Then he squints at his shirt as he lifts it toward a hook above the window. The last rays of light pierce the room at a sharp angle, showing the shirt as he's never seen it before. He chucks it to the floor.

"What's the matter?"

Al points. "A bullet hole. They patched it right across the shoulders so I wouldn't notice." Even after it was washed it never quite felt right, but he put that down to its newness, a stiffness that would eventually soften with wear. But this evening he saw the hole clearly as he held the shirt up to the light.

Hendersen lifts his legs up onto the bunk across from Al and gives a sigh of exhaustion. "If it's another shirt you're after then you were smart to come here. That clerk has boxes of them."

Al knows he's trying to change the subject, calm him down. He grabs up the shirt and jams it onto the hook as he climbs up to his bed. "I was persuaded." He forces a smile and flops onto his bed.

"Ha." Hendersen shows the gaps in his teeth and lifts his chin at one of the boys in the bunkhouse. "The young ones were smart. Otherwise they'd end up bum boys in those hobo camps." Hendersen leans on one elbow. "Go ahead, look disgusted all you like. It's different for us. We had jobs before. We've known different times. But they think this is how it is, how it's always going to be. And some of them — well, for some of them it's just different. Some give up."

"There was a boy in our camp but I don't think —" Al hears the Ingram boy again. *Please! I'll do whatever you want. Don't send me away!* Is that what the boy meant? Al didn't want that. He wanted to breathe in the powder and lavender of normal life. Watch the hands of a woman kneading bread.

"I knew these two fellas," Hendersen says. "Skinny and Foot were their names. Foot lost his legs in a logging accident. Skinny always blamed himself. He was a big fella, opposite of his name. Both were." Hendersen chuckled. "He'd carry Foot through the door and set him down at the bar as tender as a parent with a child. Or he'd lift him into a truck and drive him places. They got themselves a cabin on the lake, because in a boat, Foot didn't need legs. I remember one time drinking with them in Nelson, that's where I'm from, and noticing how carefully Foot's trousers had been rolled and pinned. I got to wondering who did the rolling and who did the pinning and what that meant."

Al shifted to his side and looked evenly at Hendersen. "I don't know what to make of that."

"Well, that's just it. Your inference is exactly right. What you and I think doesn't really matter, does it? All that matters is what it meant to Foot and Skinny. So I left it at that."

"You two done gabbing?" A sour-faced man slams his shaving gear onto the rickety nightstand and throws himself onto the bottom bunk below Hendersen, thrashing around until he has his back to Al. "And you. You whistle like an old kettle. Get some sleep, Chrissakes."

The next morning Al sits up in bed and reaches for the shirt, clenches it in his fists and rips it down the middle. He'll be god-damned if he's going to walk around with a target trained on his back.

He takes it to the supply office.

"It got caught on a tree branch," he tells the clerk. He exchanges it for one that's well-worn and shows no sign of being patched. It slips on easily, doesn't scratch as the new material had. But the memory of it still drills him between the shoulder blades, especially at night.

SEVERAL MORE NIGHTS PASS BEFORE Hendersen tells all of them about the lack of meat in their first meals.

"At first you're too worn out to notice." His voice is soft, gentle, each *S* a mere sizzle. It's dark outside and Al lies in his bunk listening.

"That first crate of roast beef was tossed into a truck and on its way to Vancouver by nightfall. Remember that lunch of sausages? That was supposed to be breakfast along with the pancakes.

"The foreman doesn't keep it up for long. Knows you'll catch on soon enough. But it adds up. He makes a tidy profit, that Potts. And he's not alone."

It was the way of the world, he adds, and he's been everywhere — up to the Charlottes as a boy and then to Rupert. The Okanagan is a land of fruit and honey and soft, rolling hills. He's tramped all over Vancouver Island and sailed a boat down the length of Kootenay Lake. He's even sweated in the smelter at Trail. His sigh is a hiss between his teeth.

"Name me one place," he says, "and I'll bet I can tell you about it."

"Revelstoke," a voice calls out.

"Snow this high in winter." Hendersen holds his hand over his head for anyone who might be looking.

Ten feet, Al thinks.

"Kamloops," calls another.

"Cowboy country," he says.

"Lillooet."

"Hot as the hobs o' hell in summer."

Al smiles at his friend and his notion of what constitutes the world. At the rest of them, too. The place names stretch out into the night air, roaming from the coast to the Rockies, then up north and back again, until they fall asleep, weary with their travels.

HENDERSEN SNIFFS EACH MEAL BEFORE eating. Sticks his finger in the milk jug to the outcry of many. "Just checking," he says. "You get in the habit, too."

But one day when Hendersen declares the meat to be off, they shout him down.

"You said that last week, and it was fine." Al looks up to see who's speaking. It's the sour-faced man, who calls himself either Elmer or Elmore. Al doesn't care enough to ask which it is, and settles on the first. "Didn't we all feel fine after?" Elmer asks.

Al scans the table. Heads nod.

"This is worse," Hendersen counters.

Al raises his plate. It smells fine to him.

"Go to hell," someone calls out, and the men dig in. Al, too.

"Suit yourselves," Hendersen says and pushes his meat to the side, won't touch the gravy, either. He eats delicately around the parsnips and potatoes adorned with just a touch of butter; smiles as he samples the apple pie and concludes at the end that he's full enough.

By three o'clock in the afternoon Al and everyone around him begin to drop their picks and shovels and run to vomit their lunches onto the sides of the Hope-Princeton Road. Al swears he's dying.

Potts watches from a distance, his bull neck tensed.

Later, the men debate whether he knew the meat was tainted. Wouldn't their sickness put the project behind schedule? Why would he want that?

But Al thinks that whether he knew or not doesn't much matter as much as the fact that Potts is untouched by illness. It's clear he's not eating the same food.

Hendersen ducks his head shyly at the profusion of apologies from the men that night, acknowledges how food is a thing that can turn on you. He recalls how in one camp one skinny little lad arrived so malnourished that when the platters of food were set out, beef and gravy and mountains of mashed potatoes, he went crazy.

"Everyone told him to take it easy. But he had to be dragged away from the food. His guts grew like a dog's about to whelp its pups, and he died howling like one."

No one spoke. A few men shifted uneasily. Al pictured the Ingram

boy. If he could do it all over again, show the boy instead, teach him
— but how? It was too late.

"You gotta be cautious," Hendersen concludes. "That kid shoulda
et a little bit more at each meal until his shrunken insides could
take on a big supper."

The men mutter amongst themselves. Gradually they stand and
return to their bunks.

"Was he one of those boys?" Al asks. He sits on the edge of his
bed pressing his thumbnail against a speck of black that has pushed
up through the skin at his ankle.

Hendersen says, "I'm supposing that if he was, he wouldn't have
been so hungry." Then he pauses. "What's that you've got there?"

It's too complicated to explain, and explaining might make it
worse. "A thorn," Al says.

The sliver of shrapnel pops free, and he flicks it into the floorboards. His guts rise as they do each time he digs out another piece
of metal, one time the edge of a brass button, but he knows how to
talk himself down, doesn't he? He knows how to think of each
piece as no more than the slivers he got when he was a child. Easily
removed. Not half as painful.

That night Hendersen's story sifts into Al's dreams where the
bullet hole found him several nights in a row, lost in all-consuming
darkness, smelling the stink of mud and rotting limbs, of rats and
piss and madness. He's gagging on the dirt, crying for help, his legs
and arms fattened from the swallowed dirt, and then his belly. A
white-hot current of light rips open his grave and he sits up, clutching
his ruptured stomach, split wide open from too much dirt, the way
men's middles are disembowelled from shell fire.

He sees Hendersen's face pop up over the top of the bunk's railing,
checking on him and calling to the others, "Just a dream." Then in a
whispered whistle, Hendersen repeats to him, "Just a dream."

The next day as they head out to a new section of road, Hendersen remarks that he has never been to war. "I didn't volunteer and the war ended before they could conscript me. I guess you already figured that out. I don't have nightmares."

Al nods as they walked. "You were smart."

"Some called me a coward."

"I thought the same about my brother. But I was a fool."

In the sunlight the bad dream seems far away. They take their places along the roadbed and lift their picks. With each upward swing Hendersen belts out a line of song, *Oh, why don't you work like other men do?* Their picks punctuate the line's end with a thud into the dirt, *Well, I'd get a job if I didn't have so much to do!* Again their picks fall. Soon the men are singing, too. Hendersen says they sound like a chain gang. *Hallelujah, I'm a Bum!*

Their joined voices become a single, jubilant roar, though there's little to be happy about, is there? Yet as Al picks up more of the words and sings along, too, he realizes how happy he is to be one of them, to be working together. By the time they've sung through the verses twice over, they've broken up the surface of ground, a ragged stretch of roadbed that clings to one mountainside. And yet the sight of dirt hasn't set his mind reeling. He's barely sweating, and that's from exertion, not thinking.

Potts appears then over a hill of rubble. "C-6!" he shouts. "Cut the racket! Back to work!"

Now the only sound is the clang of shovels as they scoop up the debris of roots and rock and soil. The singing kept Al breathing evenly, kept the dark thoughts at bay. Now his eyes dart around him, trying to find something to focus on.

Has Hendersen noticed his sudden agitation? Gradually, quietly, Hendersen begins to hum. Others pick up the tune and then Al does, too, the sound as soothing as the stirring of pine boughs, the rushing of creek water, but a hum of defiance nonetheless.

Nine

AS THE WEATHER COOLS THEY reinforce the bunkhouse walls and fill cracks around windows with paper and rags. There is no electricity and night comes early. Individual candles and lamps are forbidden because of the threat of fire. There's just one oil lamp for the entire room, and it sits on the card table.

In the fading light of each afternoon Al thumbs through what passes for books from the camp library. All are used, most donated by organizations and churches. Several are children's Bible stories.

Eventually he settles on a tattered collection of magazines that he carries to his bunk to read. Some are missing covers, some have pictures clipped out. Most are plundered of anything he would have enjoyed reading. A *Redbook* cover promises Dashiell Hammett's *Thin Man*, but someone has yanked out the entire story. Al is left with recipes and tips on how to get your baby to eat. But there are pictures.

In *Canadian Homes and Gardens* one evening, he finds photographs of magnificent houses, both interiors and exteriors, all replicated in black and white. But Al has stood in such homes and can predict their colours. The grey is probably Wedgwood, the white a buttery cream. With equal certainty he decides that the luxurious gardens surrounding the homes are filled with the perfume of roses in summer and the tobacco scent of dried leaves in fall.

An advertisement for lamps includes an illustration of couples dancing, the men in tuxedos and the women in cocktail dresses, and it fills him with such longing for his old life he wants to throw the magazine across the bunkhouse. Instead he shakes it at Hendersen, who is backing down the wooden ladder.

"Proper lighting — a social necessity! Did you know that?"

Hendersen swivels his head, a grin already hinting of a comeback. "It is if you want to see your hand." He toes the floorboards with one grey-socked foot, then jumps down from the last rung. "C'mon. Join us for a game."

"Nah."

Al settles back into pulling magazines from the stack. He feels compelled by a need to see what he has lost, or what he might have had: a ticket on a Caledonia steamer leaving New York for the West Indies for just $275; an Overland automobile, $615; the roadster, only $595; a picnic dinner for two in just twenty minutes; a wife to share it.

Two *Chatelaine* covers offer distinctly different choices in women. He places the covers side by side. October 1930 pictures a woman in a full green dress with two children by her side, along with the heading: *The Ten Commandments of Marriage*. In direct contrast is February 1929, just a year and a half earlier, showing a colourful illustration of a flapper in a tight shift with a parrot perched on her shoulder. Between these two editions the stock market crashed and the parties stopped, the world grew serious. A man wants a wife who is a family sort, not a dancer. Al supposes that's true of him as well. Of course the magazines can't show life as it really is. Who'd buy a cover called, *Autumn 1934: Five Years into the Depression*, with an illustration of this bunkhouse, men with no wives at all, wearing army drab, their grizzled chins bent over the table as they play at cards, filling the hour until chow time?

He settles back against his pillow. A bunkhouse full of men gives off the peculiar scent of salt and fuel oil and hair tonic. But when

Al looks in the magazines he can imagine a world inhabited by lip-sticked mouths and perfumed skin. He pictures himself sitting at a table across from a woman with an indistinct face but a halo of curls — blond, maybe. She would smooth her apron and take his hand and each would talk about their day. Then she would rise to make their supper and the children would come running in, each racing to reach his arms first.

Once evening falls it's too dark to read any more. Later, he'll fall asleep dreaming up names for the children, and maybe a name for her, a pretty name like Violet, or Daphne, or Emily.

HEAVY EQUIPMENT IS BROUGHT IN to help carve out the new roadbed. Trucks haul them to and from the work sites when snow clogs the paths. Al still has to use a shovel to remove boulders and roots, but darkness, freezing temperatures and frequent snow-storms shorten the working day. By January small problems in food that the men might have overlooked earlier become sources of griping. A hair in the soup. A chipped cup or cracked plate. A smaller scoop of potatoes than the next guy. They don't need much prompting to get them angry, but there are agitators among them, communists, Al supposes. The smooth-handed newcomers have a manner of speaking that he recognizes from others who visited the hobo camp, a way of holding their heads as though they are doing important work instead of ditch digging. They speak as if they are reading from the pages of a book. They remind him of Jack.

It isn't just the general conditions, they press, *or the food. Why is the military here? Why are any of them?* Al knows. In the city he kept up with the news through discarded newspapers. The *News-Herald*, the *Vancouver Daily Province*, the *Vancouver Sun*. Keep them busy, the politicians were saying, and keep them fed. Just make sure you keep them out of the cities.

One night in the bunkhouse, one of the newcomers leans

forward, hands on the table, and, under thin, arched eyebrows, studies the gathering.

Chairs have been pushed back to make room. The men squat on their heels or lean against bunks and walls. The seams of the pot-bellied stove glow and flicker with red light. Men who have stepped in from outside join the huddle, steam rising from their still-damp jackets.

"No one cares if you're too sick to work. Am I right? No one expects the road to be finished. They brought in the machines only because of the snow, or you couldn't work at all. And then you'd be idle. This is all —" he waves his hand in the air "— busy work."

Al thinks of the tainted food. So it hadn't mattered to Potts one way or the other if they lost a day of work.

The newcomer spreads a map onto the table with his smooth hands. "Look," he says.

Al pulls his shoulder from the wall and marches over to look. Every province in the country is dotted with camps. The man tells them that British Columbia has the most and that the total number of men in such camps is over six thousand.

"A man needs a good, decent job — or what is he? What does he call himself?"

"A bum!" someone shouts.

The wooden bunkhouse rings with laughter.

Al lifts his head slowly. They call themselves bums, sing it out, in order to say it first, before Potts or anyone else can. It takes the sting from the remark and, somehow, makes them proud of who they are. And it galls men like Potts.

The newcomer continues, "A man with a job calls himself a fisher-man. A plumber. A logger. But you! You labour for twenty cents a day, wages that only a coolie would accept. It used to be two dol-lars a day. You don't sleep in real beds or in real houses." He gestures around the raw cabin. "You might as well be sleeping outside, like Indians. Is that what you are? Coolies? Indians?"

That gets the men talking.

WHEN THE SNOW BEGINS TO melt, Hendersen tells him, "There's talk of a strike."

"Here?" They've just finished their shift and lie back on their bunks, smoking.

"The Union of Relief Camp Workers' strike." Hendersen sticks the cigarette in the corner of his mouth, dangles his legs over his bed so he can face Al. "We want better wages for the work we do. Better conditions. Why not strike?"

"Because we get fed here —" Al pauses. "And we're in the middle of nowhere."

"Did you see those maps? Princeton is a Sunday stroll from here. But your choice. You can either join us or stay here. That sour puss Elmer's thinking of staying."

Hendersen is probably grinning when he says this but Al is studying his own weathered hands, picturing himself with no real company except his own miserable thoughts — wondering why and how and what next? No.

"You ever been to Princeton?" Hendersen asks him.

"I lived there. My brother's there now, and his wife."

"Then you know that its people are more uniongoing than church-going. I'll bet they're gathering blankets right now and cooking for us." He contemplates the rough ceiling boards. "Come to think of it, I'll bet the churchy ones are, too."

Hendersen boosts himself up and then drops to the floor. The rest of the men come bustling into the bunkhouse talking excitedly. News of a strike has spread quickly.

It's only April, barely spring in the mountains.

The next day they drop their tools and return to the bunk-houses, where they leave their fatigues in piles on the floor and step back into their own tired suits.

Potts is standing on the tailgate of a truck, scribbling numbers onto a clipboard, when the strikers swarm past, shouting insults.

He barely raises his voice above the clamour. "You go right ahead," he calls out. "There's another truckload of you on its way."

Another truckload. As Al squeezes by, he cranes his neck, trying to gauge the look in Potts's eyes. But the man keeps his head of rough, red hair down, and Al hopes that indicates some level of shame. Another truckload of men will mean another missing crate of roast beef, and more money in Potts's pockets. It also means that Al and the rest of them aren't even worth chasing after.

The strikers trudge past, then up into the hills and along dirt roads, Hendersen tipping his head back to sing the Hallelujah song. The others bawl along with him. Eventually Al sings, too. Why not? He's moving at last, arms swinging, legs striding. Each time his boot heels sink into soft pine needles and dirt he feels a sense of purpose that is new to him. Is this what Jack was on about all the time? He looks over at Hendersen and the others and thrills at the sight of them all, not just walking away, but marching.

As they reach the camps that are adjacent to Princeton and then the town itself, Al can hear shouts and laughter and more marching feet, phones ringing and then radios singing "Ain't She Sweet?" and finally the crackle and honk of a megaphone directing the strikers to the community hall for food. Above the streets hang banners that read, *Welcome!* and *Unite!*

On every corner people are gathering. Al looks for Jack in the fading light. He'd enjoy an event like this. There are men standing in clutches, their voices reaching an excited pitch. Women, too, some talking in groups, one looking out her window, another pulling wet laundry from a ringer set up on the back porch, then abandoning the soggy sheets to run to the lane to watch the strikers pass. Boys ride by and ring the bells on their bicycles, little girls stop mid-jump on hopscotch squares to wave.

A man honks a horn as he rolls past in a Model T pulled by a horse.

"Bennett Buggy," Hendersen calls out, "named in honour of our illustrious prime minister."

The men around him laugh and point. But Al looks away. It's hard to see once-sleek automobiles run dry of gas and be dragged along the streets by horses, the wheel treads mired in manure, the silver spokes clogged with it. Men like Gordon caused this. And if they can't hold onto their lives then what chance did the rest of them have? Still, this moment feels like a chance.

The town doesn't seem the same place that greeted the returning soldiers, but maybe it's Al who is different. He wants to follow the crowd this time, not run from it. He wants to hear what people are saying about the camps and the strike, and add his own opinion. Of all the issues, surely isolation is the worst, and this gathering, then, the perfect cure. He pushes his way into the community hall.

At long tables along one wall, townspeople are setting down kettles and trays of food next to stacks of plates and piles of cutlery for the men to help themselves. Al takes a plate and fills it with shepherd's pie and cabbage rolls and chicken casserole.

A couple of the camp men pull out harmonicas and begin to play and a local old-timer brings out a fiddle and joins in. It isn't long before the men are up and dancing. Al scrapes up the last of the casserole, puts down his plate and joins in.

He doesn't care what manner of dance it is or what manner of woman he dances with — someone's wife or mother, it's all the same. Silk dresses and crimped hair might still be seen in some parts of Vancouver, but here, five-and-a-half years of the Depression have ground down most women. Still, he loves the feel of their hands, the tapered fingers and thin wrists, the look of their plain, cotton-print dresses fancied up with a lace collar or shiny brooch. He could fall in love with any one of them as they reel around the room, faded skirts flying.

"Bertie!"

He spins around. "Jack!"

Al leaves his six-year-old dance partner abruptly, turning back to bow and apologize to a burst of giggles, before crossing the floor in long strides and throwing his arms around his brother.

The last time he'd seen him was the summer of '32. Three years ago.

In '32 Al was about to work his last job — though he didn't know it then — and arrived for a visit carrying a showy gift of champagne for Jack and Agnes's anniversary. It felt strange to see the last pieces of his mother's Blue Willow in Agnes's china cabinet and the Persian carpet on her floor. He fought a ridiculous urge to roll up the rug and run for the door. But what had he needed with such old things? He still planned to live in a fine suite of rooms one day, and fill it with shiny new possessions, like a modern telephone with a handset and dial. Until then he spent his money on showy gifts like the champagne, and on fancy threads for himself.

It was on that same visit that he and Jack argued about their father. Even dead, he had the ability to rile his sons. As Al recalls their words, he looks at Jack, balding now, though his face is the same, still freckled, still spirited.

Jack said, *You thought life meant a piano in the parlour and a closet full of white shirts. You never forgave him for taking that away.*

They had been drinking rye whisky at the kitchen table and Al shot back, *That's right. I had to chop coal in a mine. At fourteen. You want me to be a man, I told him, I'll show you a man.*

Jack said, *You showed him all right.*

Al replied, *What about you? You took to the union like you were born in the working class. You did it to rub his nose in it! After a while you even convinced yourself.*

Jack burst into laughter. Tipped his head back and hooted. *Aren't we a pair? You with your war and me with my union. D' you think the old man ever noticed?*

On that visit Al wore striped shirts and a white boater and tan shoes, soft as butter, to match a new pair of tan trousers. Of course it was a silly outfit to wear outside of the city. The Tulameen Road ruined his shoes. That struck him as funny now.

The tan trousers ripped long ago. This outfit is durable tweed, though gone in the knees and elbows from working and sleeping in it.

"Like my new dancing suit?" Al laughs. "Where's that wife of yours? I'll give her a spin, too, if she doesn't mind dancing with a bum."

"In the back room, come on." And Jack claps a hand on the back of his neck and shouts, "Aggie! Look who's here!"

Jack pushes open the door, triumphant.

"Albert!" She steps through the door, a stack of posters under her arm, a hammer in her hand.

Al wraps an arm around her neck and kisses her firmly on the cheek.

She wears her spectacles on the end of her nose, and his hug leaves them slightly crooked. "What a homecoming!" she says. "You've brought a few friends with you."

He bows slightly at the waist and indicates the dance floor.

"I have to post these," and she lifts an elbow, revealing a boldly lettered *Welcome*. "There's going to be more of you needing directions and food. Will you stay with us? We can dance in the kitchen."

Al raises his hand and touches the wire frame until her spectacles straighten. "I think we're all going to bunk down together. Part of the strike and all."

Jack grabs him around the shoulders, saying, "Here you are marching and protesting like a card-carrying member! We'll see you in the morning, then," and releases him.

Their first meeting in over three years — it had been too brief, but Al smiles as he watches them cross the floor, Jack's bald spot bouncing as he lopes, Agnes marching briskly beside him, the waltzing partners in their baggy trousers and worn dresses making room, spinning and circling around them. Agnes still looks more like someone's mother than a wife, though it seems Jack has aged to match her.

NEWS ARRIVES EARLY THE NEXT morning that relief camps across the province have emptied. The strikers are marching to Vancouver, where their protests over the camps will draw even more attention. Jack and Agnes step into the hall just as the crowd moves Al out the door.

"Join us!" Al calls to Jack.

But Jack squeezes forward only to force a couple of bills into Al's hand. Then he is gone and Al is marching with the others down the road and over to the tracks.

He does as they do, creeps at a run along the rail bed, and, at the same moment the cars slide past, he grabs a rusting handle. The movement of the train jerks his legs out from under him, yanks at his arms, but he swings himself up and into the boxcar, flops on his side, then rolls over and up, the smell of metal and sweat on his hands as he runs them over his hair, straightens his jacket. They slap backs and shake hands. There must be two hundred of them, and yet the railway crew pretends not to notice.

Al pushes forward to be near the open door and cool breezes. Hendersen stands beside him. "Watch those cars behind us," he says.

The wheels grind against the rails and the train slows at a spur line. Al leans forward to look. Arms bristle from open doors, fists raise. A signal? Yes. Voices ring out and shadows emerge between the fir and pine trees that line the tracks, and then from those shadows men, dressed in tatters like them, and then more men behind those men, dozens of them, run for the train, their arms outstretched. From the opened boxcars, hands reach for their hands, until they touch, grip, and with a grunt pull the men aboard, more hands grabbing at their belts, arms, legs, to hoist them up, cheers as each man lands safely. Over and over at each spur line and rail stop, men and then more men run out from trees and brush and rock piles and wooden sheds, huffing alongside the boxcars that shake with song, "Hallelujah, I'm a Bum!" It's as if the whole train has come alive as it snakes its way toward Vancouver.

Ten

THE FOLLOWING WEEK THEY ARE marching in twos down from the parade grounds on Cambie Street, afternoon sunlight glancing off the green top of the old World Building. Children recruited by the organizers run alongside the strikers with tin cans, collecting coins from observers lined up at the curbs.

As they reach the north side of Pender Street Al glances one last time over his right shoulder. He remembers when the dome had a spire that supported a world globe. Now it holds up a moving and storage sign. It ruins the lines of the tower. He's glad he's too far away to see its effect on the nine stone nudes shouldering the cornice ledge. If he were marching next to someone like Dom he might remark on it. But Hendersen is a practical man. He'll say what better spot for an advertisement than up there where it can be seen for miles? Certainly every man marching in front of them has turned to look.

Al is never alone. Not on the train, and not in the Ukrainian hall where they are billeted, their cots in rows two feet apart. His midnight mutterings increase in the cramped spaces, but Hendersen says he needn't worry. No one could possibly understand such gibberish.

Now, Hendersen reminds Al about the expected crowds just ahead. "If we get separated, you've got my friend's name."

"I won't need it. I'll be careful." Then he glances at Hendersen. "But I've got it."

They trudge down the hill alongside Victory Square, where other columns of men are gathering — so many Al can no longer see the triangular patch of green or the streets that surround it, just a streetcar slicing through the bumping shoulders and bobbing hats, eclipsing the Tip Top Tailors sign across Hastings Street. A handful of police watch from the side, but what can they do? There are thousands of men today. Al's group flows into their midst.

Hendersen salutes the steps across the street where the mayor read the riot act the day before.

To their left is the cenotaph, the empty tomb for the soldiers who never came back. Al can't see much of it from here, but he knows that each corner of the obelisk is crowned with a stone helmet, and he struggles against thoughts that would set them spinning in the air like tops.

"You okay there, friend?"

"Fine."

A whistle blows and at once the marchers strike out along Hastings, at first a knot of bodies pressing eastward, bumping and nudging each other, then gaining elbow room as they find their rhythm, soon passing under the light-bulb studded canopy of the Pantages Theatre, as though they're a parade of movie stars. Another whistle and they fall into formation, three and four abreast, and begin to weave back and forth across the sidewalk and then the street.

Hendersen gives Al his gap-toothed smile and Al grins back as they join in. He imagines moving cameras recording them, pausing for several seconds on his own face, and then he imagines Jack sitting in a Princeton labour hall watching the latest newsreel of the marches in Vancouver, feeling envy and joy at once.

Their division has been meeting daily to be drilled on the execution of this Snake Parade, an adaptation, they're told, of a Chinese dragon dance. Now the crowds rumble as the serpentine mass of men ripples and coils. It undulates from curb to curb until it chokes the streets, blocking streetcars, trucks, cars and police more effectively than any straight parade might have. The constant movement churns up a cloud of dust that rolls with them.

The crowds on the sidewalk continue to cheer. Each turn of the snake brings Al out of the mash of bodies and into sunlight, fresh air, curling so frequently he feels neither cramped nor panicked but part of a mighty, invincible beast.

Dust coats the collars in front of him. He can taste it, too. So many pedestrians have left the curbs to join them that the snake unwinds and straightens, a solid trunk of bodies that fills not just the streets but the sidewalks, too, pressing itself against shop windows and into doorways, becoming one with the brown clouds of dust rising from their feet.

Rounding a corner, he loses sight of Hendersen. The crush of bodies flattens one side of Al's face against a brick wall. He is the guts of the snake, its blood spilling. He can taste it on his lip where his teeth bite down. He can't see. Nothing in front of him but snot-streaked sleeves and twisting backs. He can smell the stench of panic, the sweat. Can taste it, the raw metal of adrenalin drying out his mouth. He has to burst out of this seething mass, escape the heat of other men's flesh, reach cool air again. Cops! What else would cause the snake to jam together and then to veer so suddenly?

Craning his neck, twisting and shoving to get his balance, he pushes through until he sees above the ornate balconies of Chinatown, then a door in an alley just ahead. As he nears it he lifts a shoulder and slams his weight against the wood. It's locked. He lifts a boot, leans back against the bumping, jostling crowd and kicks hard. The door gives way and he tumbles in while the rest of the snake spurts down the street.

Inside, for a moment, he feels the cool relief of a large, empty space. He's broken the rusted latch right off the wooden door frame. It lies on the ground, with the padlock still looped through the ring, and locked. He kicks it aside.

Then a voice calls out, "Police! Hands above your head."

A flashlight shines in his face, blinding him.

If he stayed in the snake he would have been fine. Now there's just him and the cop.

He must be in a warehouse. A dirt floor and a damp smell. Lettuce or spoiled celery.

He does as he's told, turning slightly from the glare, but the cop rushes up behind him and lowers a club against the back of his head. Pain fills his head, red hot, burning from his skull right through to his eyes.

"Don't move, I told you!"

When did he tell him? "I didn't —" Al begins and the cop shoves him up against a wall. His nose flattens against the wood. He can taste the iron of nails on his lips.

"What's your name?"

"Al."

"Al what?"

"Albert."

"Think that's funny, do you?"

"Can't breathe!" The cop loosens his hold slightly and Al turns his face, gulps air. "— Albert Fraser."

"Albert Fraser, huh? Got anything to prove that? Something with your address?"

His address? He has no home, that's why he was marching. The cop knows that. Christ. That also means Al could have given any name to the cop. He'd never know it wasn't real.

Al has done nothing wrong, nothing that other marchers hadn't done, too. There's the broken lock, but it would take nothing to replace it. Easier to arrest him, though, than the whole parade of men. He can be made an example.

His thoughts skitter up and down the length of the warehouse. Run! Or he will be hauled off to another relief camp just like before. He made his choice to leave. He can't go back now.

Al closes his eyes, breathes in, then tears free of the cop.

Heels thudding on the soft dirt floor, elbows slicing the air, he runs down the length of the dark warehouse, leaping over vegetable crates, kicking them into the path of the cop. But before he reaches the door the club lands on his ear, hot sticky liquid running from it. He puts his hand up. Blood.

Al reels around, blind with anger, and punches at the cop, missing. The cop strikes back and blood fills Al's eye, pain arcs across his face as he grabs one end of the club before it falls again, wrenches it from the cop's hand and smacks it down on the cop's head. Once, twice. He gets ready to hit again.

Then from behind him a thin hand shoots forward, surprising him, and snatches the club from his fist.

Al staggers back, turns, expecting to see another cop or perhaps one of the organizers, either delighted with him or infuriated at the trouble he might cause the strikers. Instead he sees the face of a young Chinese, mouth open from exertion, elbow raised to chin level as he throws the club to the opposite wall.

"This way," he calls, "quick!"

Eleven

AL'S LUNGS SQUEEZE AT THE sudden darkness. He races behind the slight figure, down a hallway and then a flight of stairs. They run across a basement to an old iron door that looks like the opening to a furnace. The young stranger slings it open.

Fear fills Al's throat and he wheezes as he folds his long limbs into the half-height doorway and follows at a slower trot, down a long black tunnel that bends to the left, to the right, like a trench in the mud, each bend presenting a doorway or opening into a crawlspace or cellar.

In the yellow-brown gloom of each entry, small men stand guard, stiff as dead soldiers, their faces identical, expressionless.

Al feels his scalp lift as though his body were trying to skin itself, leave his rack of bones to run along unimpeded by sensation, by dread. The stink of damp and mud still fills his nose, the back of his throat. Movement in the shadows, the sound of dried leaves scrabbling over stones. Rats! He snaps his head up, down, back and forth, and thoughts rattle like gravel in a bucket, gathering force until the bits churn into the muck of the mines. Him, scrambling backwards in that cramped tunnel, the drunken voices of the miners who'd shoved him in and chanted a mock death list for the Chinese, so many, so foreign, they were nameless: *Chinaman Number One, Chinaman Number Six ...*

Sweat slicks his face and his stomach pitches for a moment, then settles.

All right, then. All right.

He continues to run, but with his head yanked up, away from the sight of those dead-faced men.

The space is lit by the soft lilac glow of the glass bricks set into the sidewalks above them. How many times has he walked over these bricks on Pender, on Hastings, on all the connecting streets between, and never thought of what was below? Storage rooms, of course, a basement café on Hastings, dark places he has never ventured into. But neither has he imagined this intricate, disorienting maze of hallways and hidden rooms.

Feet slam black against the purple glass above him, ink blots that magically lift and disappear in the odd, other-worldly light of a movie theatre.

The young man comes to a stop where two hallways merge, forming a triangle, and Al presses the heels of his hands against his knees, breathing hard.

"Sit." The young man gestures toward a wooden chair and Al slides into it.

A side door opens, a few words are spoken to an old man, and in minutes a pot of tea and two small cups are set carefully onto a packing crate. His friend scrapes a wooden chair over the uneven cement floor and sits across from him, his face large for such a thin man, his skin stretched tightly across his cheeks.

Friend. What else to call him? He's a stranger, and yet he has saved Al's life — stopped him, at least, from taking the life of another.

"My name is Henry." The young man extends his hand, but cautions, "No last names. The less I know, the better."

Al nods, still breathless from running. He reaches forward and watches his white fingers disappear inside the brown hand. But where is he? What is this place? His ear pounds, his head aches.

"Al," he says, and quickly pulls his hand back. He looks around as he picks up a cup. "It's so dark."

"Try over here," the man named Henry says, and he stands to move the crate and his chair into the beams of light.

Al stands and toes his chair over, then sits in the halo's flush. He can feel his skin tightening under a layer of dried blood.

As he looks up he recalls how thick and frosted the bricks appear from the street, impossible to see into. From below they capture light and diffuse it, each slightly different, each a lozenge of lavender light that conjures up the silks and scents of the normal life that has eluded him, the shades of childhood, too — the pink glow cast by his mother's cranberry glass onto the dining-room floor, a blade of mauve from the stained-glass window that makes him think of castles and dragons, the childhood certainty of a life full of adventure.

"They'll be searching for you," Henry says. "It's best if you stay down here."

How long? Al wants to ask, but is afraid of the answer. Beyond the beams of light the walls are dark as dirt — old brick and stone stained black from soot and smoke and dust. Not like the old buildings above, swept by wind and washed by rain — no, darker. Darker than the mines. He looks down the long, black corridors with not even a headlamp to light them. He hasn't been in a place like this since —

Slowly, deliberately, he sets down his cup, tucks both hands between his knees and tries not to rock as waves of panic sweep over him.

Wisps of steam curl like smoke from the spout of the teapot as Henry leans over, offering more. Al shakes his head, then looks up.

Boot heels spill in clusters across the glass. He shifts his legs as though to spring to his feet. That should be him up there, too. But he sags back, his head throbbing.

He fills his lungs, aiming for composure. "That's really a dragon dance, isn't it? That's what they told us."

Henry sets the teapot down and raises his hands helplessly. "I'll ask the old ones."

He produces a lamp, steps far back into the shadows and strikes a match. Pale light glows from behind the grime-frosted glass. He beckons Al to follow him.

Al gropes along the blackened stone walls until he catches up to Henry, who steps into a small room. A bedroll has been laid out on a wooden pallet on the cement floor.

"Someone will bring you food. Your wound needs cleaning, too. And there is a bucket if you need it." He indicates the corner.

"You're leaving?"

Henry takes his hand again and shakes it firmly. "It will be night soon. You should rest. I'll see you in the morning." He steps around Al and into the darkness.

Henry has left the lamp glowing in a corner of the room. Beyond that glow the air looms like a black curtain.

Al lies on his mat, blinking back the thoughts that snake through his mind. A field of mud, barbed wire snagging at his leggings as he crawled forward. He thrashes back and forth, limbs tangling in the blankets. Nerves run like bugs beneath his skin, stinging. He claws at his thighs, digs a heel against each shin bone. He doesn't want to think about Artie. If he can fall asleep thinking of something else, anything else.

He scans the cracked ceiling, then down the brick walls and back up again, over the faces of soldiers who sleep standing up and sometimes die standing up.

Not them, either.

He had fought those images, fought hard, and he'd found a job and he was good at it — and then it was gone. So none of it mattered, not even the marches and the songs that kept the dark thoughts away.

Here he is, in a bleak cell, the lonely sound of water dripping far off down the hall.

He is exhausted. His eyelids flutter. He tries to stop the slide into darkness, puts out his hands and his feet to brace himself, but down he goes anyway, limbs flapping for something secure, a wall, a branch, a hand to hold onto. But there is nothing, only a cold breeze rushing through his fingers as he falls, trousers whipping about his legs until they wrap tight as bandages, guts pressing into his backbone. A tunnel leading into a tunnel leading into another tunnel as he plunges. All of it brown, then black. The sides brushing his cheeks, smearing them with filth, gouging them with bits of grit.

TINY CLICKING SOUNDS. CLUMPS OF soil tapping onto his cheeks. Stones tumbling over his collarbone. He lies on his back, a tide of earth rising, his limbs swimming slowly against the building weight. Then a wave of sand slaps over his nose. He gasps for air. Arms and legs shoot straight out, then churn against the tumbling clay.

His hands fly to his face, fingers dig into his nostrils. He flips over onto hands and knees, heaves and sprays black spit and snot until finally he can breathe.

But he can't see. Crouched on all fours, he pads forward on his hands. Two steps and his forehead nudges dirt. He sits back and slaps about in the darkness, frantic, feeling a damp, shallow cave that glistens with wet. A tomb.

His head pounds. His chest hurts. There's not enough air.

Think! Slow down. Ease back.

With fingers splayed, he combs carefully through the rubble of earth and human settlement — a metal cup, a solid boot, the broken handle of a shovel. He holds each item in his hands before carefully placing them beside his hip and continues his search.

Fear flutters with each trickle of dirt from above, each threat of cave-in. At last his fingers hook onto something flat, long. The board he wedged above his bunk. The board marks *up*, the route to fresh air, a precaution he'd learned in the mines. But it's behind his back, not above him.

He presses his fists against his forehead. Think. The board — what about the board? He squeezes his eyes, tries to picture it. Yes. There it is. But what if it had blown free in the explosion, twisted sideways? What if he's landed far from his bunk? This might not be his board. Half the trenches were lined with duckboard. If he digs the wrong way he'll come up on the wrong side.

He drops his arms. Flops his head against the wall. Licks his lips. He's thirsty. There was a miner's trick — spit to find *up*. He works his mouth, purses his lips. Nothing. He thinks of food, of mouth-watering meals like his mother's roast lamb, mint sauce and plump peas; desserts — apple cobbler and plum pudding. Still nothing. He was hungry before. Not now.

Christ, he has to piss, though. He works a hand downward, fumbles with the fly, pisses somewhere off into the dark.

That's it! He rolls forward, feels up the sides, along the ground, until his palms touch the sopping dirt. He squirms around and feels in the opposite direction. The board marks *up*.

He should start digging. But his arms ache. His lungs ache. He claws feebly at the air, the dirt.

Drowsy from lack of oxygen, he sleeps. And then sleeps again.

How long has he been down here? He fumbles for his pocket watch. But the crystal is smashed, he can hear the slivers rattling in the brass case even before he opens it. His thumb prods the face of the watch, but the brass hands are gone.

One hour, one day. Two. It's all the same.

He's been left for dead.

Each awakening is another nightmare as he realizes anew that he's buried alive. He curls up into a ball, hugs his ribs, rocks. *Not me,* he sobs. *God no, not me.*

Then his hand is brushed by something warm. Another soldier?

The warmth scurries over his neck and his hands fly to his eyes. Fear stabs at his guts, a blade from asshole to navel. A rat!

It knows he's dying. It's waiting.

He jackknifes in half, knees to throat, where a scream begins to build. And then his hands, clawing mad circles in the black air around him, hit the metal cup he'd set aside, and the handle of what had been a shovel.

His fist closes around the handle. One last breath. Slams the broken end into the upper wall, leans on it, releasing an avalanche of dirt. Tries to scoop with the cup, then with his bare hands. It pours all over him, packing his nostrils in dirt. He shakes his head, coughs and snorts. No good. Dirt falls into his mouth, rising to his chest, then to his shoulders, only one arm free. Head ready to explode. Stars. Gunfire. Falling and spinning in the air, tumbling. Then the whiplash lightning of a rat tail over his knuckles. Fuck! He swings out and up with his fist, punches right through the surface and then falls back, exhausted, a bolt of light burning his eyes. Then boots pounding. Voices shouting. *This bloke's alive!* Someone grasping his hand. His fingertips fluttering within the firm grip, his lips working to answer them. *No, I'm not.*

Twelve

AT DAWN HE WHIPS BACK the cotton covers, yanks up each trouser leg and searches in the pale light for shadows of rising metal, runs his fingers along each shin bone, probing. Nothing. If any bits were stirred up by his restless limbs and crawling nerves, they've gone under again.

Each time he drifted into sleep last night he had another rotten dream, and each time he awakened, in a prickly sweat, he felt himself immediately sliding down again. It's this place. All darkness and foreign sounds and smells. Even the food brought to him by a man in a filthy white apron swirled strangely in the bowl. He pushed it away.

Now he grabs his jacket and cap and heads for the purple glow at the end of the narrow tunnel. There he paces, waiting for Henry.

When at last Henry emerges from one of the side tunnels, he is holding a paper bag.

"I'm all set," Al tells him. "I'll be on my way now."

"Breakfast," Henry replies, opening the bag. "English food."

Again the old man appears from a side door, shuffling toward them with a teapot and cups. His hair swims wild and white about his shoulders as he sets out the tea things. He works so quickly that Al finds himself thanking his retreating back.

Henry takes a copy of the morning paper from his pocket and

hands it to Al, who flips pages of the *News-Herald* with greasy fingers as he nibbles at buttered toast.

As long as there's no news of a wounded policeman, Henry says, they can be certain he's alive. Only if he dies would the police admit that an officer was beaten.

"Then I can leave," Al announces, satisfied. Estimates place the previous day's Snake Parade between seven thousand to eight thousand participants. But there is nothing about a policeman. He brushes the crumbs from his trousers as he stands.

"Too soon," Henry cautions. "And if he was only wounded — did he see your face? Would he recognize you again?"

Al drops back into his chair. The cop has his name, too.

"There's talk of a march to Ottawa. When everyone leaves town the police will think you've left with them. Then it'll be safe to go."

Al looks from one end of the long, dark space to the other. "I can't stay down here. It's like a dungeon —"

Henry smiles. "Look." He points up at the purple bricks. "Move to the side. What do you see?"

Al shoves his chair over and looks up. The slats from a wagon wheel flicker across the bricks, the elongated blades of shadow taking the shape of a lady's fan, then a pleated skirt, narrowing into a strip of black. A cat's tail.

"Each brick is a window," Henry explains. "Each has its own view. Step to the side, another view."

The door opens again and the old man shuffles back in to collect the tea things.

Al watches him shamble away. "He's been down here a long time?"

"They're all illegals of some sort down here." Henry smiles. He means Al, too.

BUT AT NIGHT THERE IS no lavender light, no looking up through the glass. With the setting of the sun, blackness slams down upon the bricks and they blink in the dark like rows of eyes. Al has nowhere to look but down the bleak tunnel of damp cement and stone. He can smell the dank odour of clammy walls, of dirt leeching in from the seams. Nausea climbs his throat and he closes his eyes to calm himself. But eyes open or closed, the images that have been assaulting him since his arrival in this place continue to rush in. The brown sky ballooning and collapsing, hurtling everything back to the ground. The sides of the trench imploding, sliding in on him. The Australians digging him out. Still the dirt continues to rise, from behind his eyes, from inside him, darkening the thoughts that had always hovered, as he painted, as he marched, as he sang. Now his scalp twitches as they loom closer.

FOR THE NEXT FEW DAYS Henry brings him newspapers and they sit in the flush of the light, searching the columns of type for news of the constable.

Outside these pale beams the hallways remain darker than an alley at midnight, but the only creatures to emerge from the inky depths are the old ones, careful as night dwellers, their skins slick as mud, their fingernails curved like claws. Their eyes narrow as they approach, never meet his gaze. Their movements are slow, shoulders hunched, voices subdued, although he can't understand them anyway.

They cluck softly to him as they clean the wound and change the bandage above his ear. He shakes his head and lifts his shoulders — he can't understand them. But the clucking only increases, often accompanied by facial gestures and grand sweeps of their arms.

After a while, the meaning of their words doesn't even matter. He finds the rhythm of them soothing.

They give him broth in small bowls that he spoons to his lips in thin ceramic scoops. To the broth they gradually add slices of pork, then something green like spinach, and finally, no longer so strange looking, strings of noodles, even pinched pouches of dough filled with pork: won ton.

There is tea by the potful. Green and musty smelling. They lead him down the halls to a latrine where he must have pissed gallons already, then sweated a few more in the nearby baths. His skin glows blue under the glass bricks.

He is the only white man down here, but they don't seem to mind.

One day on the way back from the baths he spots a broken glass brick winking at him from a pile of rubble. How many years has it lain there, unnoticed, abandoned? Al pockets it, and that night slides it onto a shelf that faces his cot. *Step to the side*, Henry said. Al stares at it as he falls asleep, feels his body lift from the cot and step through the warped glass, float up into the sky with miles of ocean sliding below. For the first time since his arrival here, he doesn't dream about the creeping dirt.

The old ones continue to watch him without looking, to talk to him without speaking, their hands a ballet of gestures. One man plays a violin that is a box with a stick, the bow sailing across the strings. Its sound fills Al's eyes with tears.

"So many old men," he notes to Henry. "Except you. And your English, it's so good. Almost perfect."

For a long time Henry says nothing. "I was born here," he says at last. "You?"

HENRY STANDS NOT MUCH TALLER than Al's chin, but he steers him firmly by the elbow to a chair and turns him around.

"Listen," he says. "You need work, something to do until it's time to go."

Go. Al feels his features move at once. Grief. Fear. Anger.

Henry leans closer. "You were anxious to leave before."

He was. But the nightmares have eased. He's feeling better. And what if leaving is worse than this? He closes his eyes for a moment and sees Joe's coal-blackened face again, his pink lips telling him that being in a mine is like being a baby in a womb. Nothing can touch you from the outside. That's what this is like. A hidden world. Safe.

He opens his eyes. Mauve light washes the floor, their skin. "I have money. A little. Here."

But Henry shakes his head and studies his face. "A man needs a job, a purpose, or he goes crazy."

Al nods. Yes, he has heard that before.

"The others don't stay down here all the time. Is that what you think? They have to work or they'd go crazy, too."

Too. Al notes the emphasis, but says nothing.

Then Henry holds out a bundle of shirts and jackets in one hand, a slotted tray of buttons, spools of thread, scissors and needles in the other. Mending from a tailor above ground.

AL SPENDS CAREFUL HOURS MATCHING the right sort of button to the weave, the right fit for the buttonhole, the right colour. He's aware of the play of light and shadow overhead, sometimes dancing right over the tweed or serge he stitches. The marchers continue without him. Fine. He isn't one of them anymore.

He punches the needle through the fabric, pulls the thread through the button, punches again. Henry tells him the old ones climb above ground to stitch all night in the tailor's back shop. Together they can make a man's suit in just a day or two. Al nods deeply. Is the tailor the same one who made that extravagant summer getup of linen and silk? That Al no longer exists, either.

He could have burrowed into a bank of mud and slept through the next season if they let him. He's tired of trying. He's exhausted.

"Do you have family?" Henry asks.

Al looks up from the tray of buttons.

Henry places a copy of the *News-Herald* neatly across his knees. The headline leaps up at him. The strikers have left for Ottawa.

"Who else can I contact for you?"

Al can't go to Jack and Agnes. He sees his brother striding across the dance floor, Agnes with her crooked spectacles, her direct smile. He was so full of life then.

Hendersen told him that if they had any trouble he should stay away from known locations, from family and friends. He gave Al a name, Johnson, from Whitehorse. But Al doesn't want to go there. Land of blue ice and blinding white snow.

THEY APPROACH HIM THAT EVENING, surround him with their liquid eyes, their hands folded resolutely before them.

"Time to go," Henry says.

Al rears up onto his feet. "I can do more work for you," he sweeps the air with an arm, then sees that the mending has fallen to the concrete floor. He reaches down, snatches it up. "I can go above at night with the others. I'll do whatever you want. Just let me stay."

He hears at once the Ingram boy's plea in his own voice, and he knows right then what Henry's answer will be.

"You must go. You know that." He takes the bundle from Al's arms.

The circle of men presses a satchel into his hands. He clutches it for several seconds before their silence forces him to look inside. A clean shirt, a jar of tea, a parcel of leaves tied with twine that he knows will contain a mound of sticky rice with a centre of minced pork.

The circle unwinds and, single file with Al in the middle, weaves along a twisting hall and up stairs he did not know about, through a door, down more stairs and along another underground hall.

His back to Al, Henry says, "I asked the old ones about the dragon dance."

Al raises his head, weary. Does it matter now?

Henry's voice rolls softly in the dark tunnels. "They told me that the heavenly emperor was angry with the people and so he proclaimed a seven-year drought. The rice crops failed, fruit withered on the trees, lakes turned to mud. Millions died. They said the dragon princess could not bear it and, knowing that she was inviting her own death, she flew over the ocean and brought a cloud of water back to China. Other dragons saw her courage and joined her. Soon the sky filled and the people rejoiced. It had rained at last."

Henry stops to tie a blindfold around Al. He didn't need one when he arrived here, head bleeding, thoughts muddled. But Al is alert now, and Henry says the entrance to the tunnels must remain a secret.

They climb another stairway and he continues the story.

"The dragon princess had disobeyed him and so the heavenly emperor ordered her execution. She was chopped to pieces and thrown down to the earth. But the people sewed her back together with long pieces of silk and brought her back to life."

Al can feel cool rain on his cheek as they step through a door above ground — and then along an alley? He can hear the distant sounds of traffic, of tires slicing the wet pavement. He stands perfectly still as Henry unties the blindfold. Yes, an alley.

"The dance is held every new year to honour her and the rain she brought. Rain is a symbol of life and the new year is the start of new life."

"So," Al said. "That's it?"

Henry smiles. "That's what the old ones told me. I might have got it wrong." Then he holds his hands open, drops dancing on his palms. "A new start for you."

"No, I meant — I can't come back?"

Henry's silence is his answer.

Thirteen

MOTTLED PATCHES OF BLUE-BLACK SPACKLE the sides of the hills where the wind has scoured the rocks clean of ice. But the tops of the hills are the same cement grey as the wide river that has ground to a halt in the frigid temperatures. The signs through the frosted window tell Al that they are slowly approaching the town of White-horse. As the train shudders to a stop, Al slings a pack over his shoulder and steps out onto the platform.

A wall of arctic cold slams into his body and he staggers backwards, flings down his bag and claps a hand over his face, fearing a nosebleed. When he lowers his glove there is no blood at all, but the sudden blast of cold freezes his nostril hairs. He opens his mouth to breathe, and looks around for Johnson. Blast him for being late. Blast Hendersen for sending him here.

In the rest of the country they're still picking the last of the apples, raking up the leaves, lighting fires for children to poke at with sticks. The only good thing he can say about the temperature is that the colder it turned as he travelled northward — and he took his time, reluctant as he was to reach the north — the more absorbed he became with the task of keeping warm and making the next town in time to find a place to sleep. He didn't have time to wonder, *Who am I?* and *What am I?* "Cold" would have been his answer. Cold and bloody hungry. The last of Jack's money paid for a used parka and a seat on this train. He would have frozen to death riding in a boxcar.

Only a handful of people have met the train. One is an old Indian who approaches Al with his brown hand extended.

"Sorry, old man," Al says, stepping around him. He has no money for handouts.

The Indian smiles strangely and sits down on a frozen bench outside the ticket office. He rolls himself a cigarette and smokes it with all the pleasure of a man at a picnic. He doesn't even wear gloves.

Within two minutes the small gathering disperses until there is just the old man, sitting on the bench, and Al. Even the ticket office has closed.

As Al waits he considers that just a few more coins might have bought him a wool toque and gloves, some extra-thick socks. His eardrums ache each time he shoves the hood back to check the white road. Splinters of cold stab his fingertips. His toes throb.

Then thoughts begin to prickle across his brain. He swears to himself and marches over to the old man.

"You're not Johnson, are you?"

ON THE RIDE TO JOHNSON's home, Al is smarting inside. Hendersen should have said something. But Al figured, Hendersen and Johnson, must be Scandinavian of some sort. Hendersen said nothing about the man being Indian.

Quick glances to the side show a lean face, less grey in his hair than it seemed outside. Maybe that was frost.

The truck rattles up a steep hill, taking them away from the tiny town. At the top of the hill the land levels out, but soon the roadway of flattened snow cuts through high hills to the left, lower land to the right, with more hills off in the distance, all dotted with thin evergreens.

They roll up a side road.

Al expects another log cabin or rough wood shack like the ones he has been seeing along the way, but this one is finished in cedar shingles painted a cheery yellow, with white shutters that frame a multi-paned window.

They climb out of the cab, Al's limbs stiff with cold. A door of knotty pine opens and a woman's voice calls out, "That you? Did you find him?"

"I did!" Johnson slams the cab door. Then he looks at Al, who quickly looks down. "That's Jenny in there."

Al has to stoop to follow him through the door. When he straightens he comes to an abrupt halt. Inside, the English cottage has disappeared. The four main walls are made of peeled logs, studded with hooks and nails and, dangling from each, pairs of mitts, moccasins, rubber boots and coal-oil lanterns. Fishing poles and rifles lie horizontally across pairs of hooks. Al's eyes lift. An animal pelt complete with head and a mouth of fangs stretches across the rafters, from which also hang traps, netting and the broad underside of a rowboat.

"That's a lynx," Johnson says, pulling Al's gaze back down. "Have a seat."

Al scrapes his boots on the bristle mat and hangs his parka from one of the pegs. He chooses a wooden chair next to the wood stove and hunches his long frame over a mug of tea that Johnson hands him. An icy draft scores the back of his neck but his chest roasts against the oven's heat.

Sitting beside Al in a wing-backed chair, Johnson looks a lot less Indian. But he has the appearance of a man who works outdoors, a lean yet muscular build that seems younger than his years.

"Some time tomorrow," he says, "we need to fill those cracks around the door. They need filling each time the temperature drops."

Burning wood snaps in the stove.

"We'll check the snares for rabbits, too." Then he sighs. "Most wives do that, but mine's not Indian." He lifts his mug toward a separate room made from a grey blanket strung across a corner. "She's like you. She's from Outside — Nelson, British Columbia."

Al has never heard that expression before, but he likes it. Nelson. New York. It doesn't matter. They're Outside because they aren't here. It's a way of owning where you are, of making it yours.

What place would he call his?

Jenny emerges from behind the blanket, her red wool leggings flashing beneath a print dress. She lifts her head of russet hair and beams blue eyes at them. Al nods back. That's it for introductions. She crosses the floor to settle into an armchair with a book.

Johnson is watching her, too. "When I first met her," he says in a rough whisper meant to be heard across the room, "I said to myself, what kind of woman is this?"

She continues reading but a smile spreads slowly.

"I thought to myself, poor woman, who's going to marry her? What would their children look like?"

He must have told this story many times before, but Al knows today's telling is aimed particularly at him. Damn that Hendersen for not even a hint.

Johnson leans over so Al can hear him clearly, though his raw voice still reaches the pink ears of his wife. "I felt so sorry for her, I married her myself! And our boy, his colour came out halfway between. Handsome, though, wasn't he?"

She lifts her head from the book and contemplates him from across the room. The two of them must have been a good-looking couple when they were younger. Her husband's eyes meet hers and a hush falls over him.

At least Hendersen told Al that much. Their son died. Al assumed it happened a long time ago, but from their gentle way with each other, the long looks, he can tell that their grief is still new.

"You're so thin," Jenny cries suddenly, and closes her book. "Let me fix you something to eat."

Johnson gets up and pulls on a parka. She crosses the floor to the stove and hands Al the book as she passes.

"Ezra Pound," he says, reading the spine. He turns the first few pages and frowns. He can't make sense of it.

"Moose stew?" she asks. "Bannock with butter?"

"Whatever you can spare," he says. "Thank you."

Johnson squeezes through the doorway with an armload of wood and closes the door with his boot, sending a blast of cold air over Al.

"Still lots of caribou this year," he says. The split logs tumble loudly from his arms into the woodbox beside the stove. "And moose. Fish, too. I couldn't live in a city. All those people going hungry when you've got all this here."

He sweeps his arm toward the window. Navy pines etch themselves against the white hill. Already a pale moon crackles in a dark sky but it isn't yet four in the afternoon.

"I'll take you around tomorrow," he adds, "show you a few things."

Al noted when they pulled up that one of the sheds out back would make a suitable shelter, once the weather warmed. For now, as Johnson explains, his room is on a ledge up in the rafters, immediately above their room, and reached by a wooden ladder.

Jenny puts three bowls of stew on the table and they move over to eat.

Al picks up his spoon. "I guess Hendersen told you why I'm here."

Jenny smiles. "He said you might need our help for a while. Johnny and I don't need to know why."

So that's his name. Johnny. The man himself hasn't mentioned it, and in all the awkwardness at the train station Al has neglected to ask. He scoops a spoonful and tries to chew slowly.

"And it'll be longer than a while," Jenny adds, tapping her husband's arm. "Isn't that right?"

"It's going to turn cold," he says.

Al thinks about the frozen landscape they've just driven over. "Seems to me it already has."

Johnny Johnson winks at his wife, as though Al has said something particularly amusing.

THE NEXT DAY AL AND Johnny strap on snowshoes and wade into the bush to check the traps. He says that when they return they'll chop wood and fill the cracks around the door.

"Snares are for rabbits," he tells Al, "but for a marten you need a number one trap."

Just ahead, beneath a thin clump of evergreens, they see a circle of black.

"We check the traps every morning," Johnny says. "You don't want to leave them too long."

Al nods his head, warm now, under one of Johnny's woollen caps. Poor creatures.

"The leg freezes to the metal," Johnny explains, "and after a while they chew it off and get away."

As they approach, the marten unwinds from its tight circle, leaving its leg alone to prepare for attack. It's larger than Al has expected, about the size of a dachshund, though likely all skin and bones under that thick fur.

"Watch," Johnny says, "an old Indian taught me this."

He kneels down and reaches forward. The marten lunges and bites into his thick mitt. Al wears a pair just like them: leather lined with soft fur. Johnny reaches up from behind its head with his other hand and raps it across the snout with what looks like a small wrench, knocking the creature out. He puts the wrench in his pocket and reaches under the marten, between its front legs, feeling for the heart.

"Squeeze slowly until the heart stops. Hold it for another couple of minutes after that."

Reluctantly, Al moves closer.

"That old Indian used to chant something to show his appreciation to the animal. Right now I'm thanking it for being here and giving me a nice dark pelt that I can sell to the white man." He grins. "Even the light ones can bring twenty dollars."

Al whistles. "I only got twenty cents a day in the camps. This pelt is worth at least a hundred days' work."

Johnny seems to like that and laughs. He lets go of the animal and it falls softly into the snow. Then he retrieves his glove, pulls off his knapsack, opens the flap and stuffs the dead marten into it. They continue into the bush.

It takes Al all morning to adjust to the feel of showshoes. The wide-legged gait is awkward and Al knows that by night he will be waddling about the cabin like a woman nine months gone.

He is relieved when they stop to boil tea and warm up a pot of stew.

Johnny had made a couple of references earlier in the day to *our dead son*. Now, Al works up the nerve and asks, "What was your son's name?"

"Alex."

There are no photographs of him in the cabin, no mementos a boy in the north might have kept: a pair of ice skates or favourite hockey jersey. Al recalls how his own mother buried his clothes in her trunk, labelled the package as though it were his tombstone. He rubs his hands over the flame and tries again. "What happened?"

"He fell through the ice last spring. Jenny doesn't like to talk about it."

Al considers the deaths in his own family. His father's is the one he doesn't like talking about, but that's different. It followed so closely on his mother's that it was hard to tell how he felt. People always said how sorry they were. Al feels more sorry that the old man wasn't the kind of father a son could miss. He longed for a real father, had all his life. But if he says that out loud it will seem there's something wrong with him.

Using one of his thick mitts, Johnny lifts the handle and sets the pot of stew into the snow. "Alex was such a joy to us," he says. "And then he was gone. So many things I never had a chance to tell him."

AS EACH WEEK PULLS THEM further into winter the mercury continues to dip. Finally it plunges to forty-two degrees below zero and for two days they can't go far from the warmth of the cabin.

Al stamps his feet in the safe perimeter of the yard. From the dark tunnel of his hood, his breath a stiff plume of fog in the sharp air, he sees the world around him as a still life. Trees stand rigid, their limbs straight by their sides. Within the needles of the branches, lumps of ice have formed and sunlight glints painfully through the prisms of ice.

The brilliant light comes from a half sun that crests the horizon. In a few minutes that half will vanish, sending his world into twenty hours of night. Last night he saw northern lights undulating in the sky, tongues of green as pale as Chinese jade hissing and crackling against a black ceiling, and he recalled a poem about the soothing qualities of Chinese tones. He pictured misty greys and milky greens until he saw that sky with its waves of light.

He pivots stiffly, arms thick with the sleeves of his parka and two sweaters underneath. These are temperatures that overnight build ice as sturdy as concrete, kill all sound, square the truck tires where they've come to rest. How do the dogs manage? Each is chained to the base of its own tree, curled up with tail over nose, a heavy dusting of snow over its fur. Johnny assured him the huskies are fine. They have warm coats. If it gets really cold he'll bring them into one of the sheds. They aren't French poodles, he added.

But Al stops to pet each dog with a thick mitt. As always, the one with a crooked ear gives a low growl, and Al eases back, careful not to antagonize it. Then he clumps over to the two buckets he left by the steps. The pipe to the water pump has frozen, so they haul buckets of snow to melt for water. He stomps in them to compress the snow and adds another shovelful to each. Then he takes a bucket handle in each mitt and scrapes his boots on the mat before shoving the door open. He hangs his parka on a wall peg, then lifts the buckets onto the stovetop.

He turns and the walls close in. It might be cold outside, but at least there's space, light all around, he could stretch his arms, breathe. His mind lurches toward other thoughts.

Open a book, forget about the walls.

To fill the long, dark hours in the cramped cabin he has been mending snowshoes and reading through a stack of Jenny's books. The Shakespeare plays satisfied him for a while, especially those he'd read as a boy in school back in England. To his own surprise, though, he finds himself repeatedly turning to the puzzling poems in Ezra Pound's *Personae*.

Jenny is reading her own book and as he settles into his chair he says to her, "I don't really understand these. What do you think they're supposed to be about?"

She lowers her book. "What do they mean to you?"

He thumbs the pages. "I see pictures." He flushes hotly.

"Go on," she says.

"Pictures of things I've seen. Like this one about a metro station.

He writes about people's faces, here, then on the next line about blossoms on a tree branch." And he tells her about the tunnels below the purple bricks. "It turned everyone's faces pink, like petals."

Jenny studies him before speaking. "You were living down there."

Of course she must know that he was hiding down there. "Yes."

"They were friends," she says, changing the subject, "your poet and mine. I like this one because it describes heat so thick the fruit can't fall. It reminds me of home. We lived near an orchard and I see the orchard in August when I read this. You and I both read for the pictures up here." She taps two fingers to her temple.

They return to their own books. If there are lines in hers that remind her of Alex, she doesn't say so. There are poems that he doesn't mention, either: about weather turning cold in autumn and how the rain is full of sorrow. It makes Al think of the Somme, where every month looked like November. The letters on the page pull his thoughts down, wet and grey and brown, rain drumming more holes into the clay until the ground was a brown sponge filling with water. And his feet. He remembers that, too. He couldn't find his feet. He'd sunk up to the ankles.

He closes the book, closes his eyes, then forces them open and flips the pages, scanning the lines for a different picture.

NEWS FROM OUTSIDE SELDOM REACHES them, and when it does it arrives in bundles of old newspapers in the mail, often out of order. Reading yellowed sheets of news next to a crackling fire makes Mussolini's invasion of Ethiopia unfold like a well-told adventure story. Hitler seems like the child on the playground who grabs the ball and tells the others to go play somewhere else. It's all distant, unreal.

Sometimes they get mail along with newspapers. The latest bundle includes a letter from Jack dated January 10, 1936. With it are news clippings.

Things have quieted down around here. We aren't nearly as interesting to the local constabulary as we used to be. I told Agnes maybe she should go rob a bank, but she says the quiet is a pleasant break. We both miss you, but why not wait until summer? By then the roads will be clear and the weather fine and a certain incident long forgotten.

Al barely tastes his plate of meatloaf and potatoes. Summer. Five months! Maybe more. He didn't tell Jack he gave the cop his name. Would the man even remember it after that club to the head? Yes, perhaps especially after that. Al picks up the clippings, scans the headlines, frowning. It's all about Spain. Why would Jack send them? An upcoming election. A miners' uprising in a place called Asturias. Maybe because he's a miner. Or because of their aunt. The town she lived in had a peculiar name. Belle something. He can't recall.

"Jenny," he calls out, the clippings fanned around his plate, "do you have a map of Spain?"

He hears laughter and looks up. Johnny has grabbed her about the waist and is waltzing her around the cabin. Al missed what prompted this, but Jenny has thrown back her head of coppery silver hair as she twirls and dips, at complete ease in her husband's arms, her laughter rising up her throat, a catch to it that gives her a girlish sound, as they swoop past the hot stove, loop around Al's chair. There is no music playing but that doesn't seem to matter. They dance.

This is what Al wants one day. Exactly this.

WHEN THE TEMPERATURE WARMS BY twenty degrees he and Johnny set out again, and take the dogs. They're heading farther out to the larger traps and follow a route well-grooved from previous sled trips. The dogs run silently, mouths open, tongues dangling, their soft panting blending with the hiss of the sled's wooden treads in the snow as, tails curled up, they forge into wide-open spaces, long stretches of blinding white that dip and rise before them, the thin air brittle as glass. Al knows Johnny expects him to run, since Johnny himself steps onto the runners only to direct the team. "Gee!" he calls when he wants them to veer to the right. "Haw!" for left. But Al can't keep up. His lungs ache and he crumples to his knees after only a few minutes.

Johnny slams a foot onto the wooden brake, throwing up a plume of white powder. But the team only stops pulling when he flips the sled onto its side and wedges an ice hook into the packed snow.

"You sick?" he calls back.

Al gathers himself up and slogs forward. "The war," he huffs when he catches up. "My lungs."

"That was a long time ago." When Al doesn't reply Johnny adds, "Maybe you're just not used to running."

Al considers his comment. He climbed scaffolding and hiked and hopped trains and marched in demonstrations. Even so, his lungs haven't been the same since the war. Hell. He doesn't want Johnny to think he's an idler, not then, not now. He takes a deep breath, straightens and says, "I know how to use a rifle."

Johnny reaches into the basket of the dogsled and hands him a rifle. "Alex's twenty-two." So there is that reminder of their son, though Johnny kept it, not Jenny.

The snow has softened in the sunlight. Rifle in his arms, boots sloshing as though he were in mud, Al stares straight ahead at the expanse of white punctured by charcoal pines. Sunlight flashes through the trees, each waving branch triggering an explosion of light. From the corner of his eye he sees the long barrels of fallen poplar and birch. The sky flickers white and then black, the ground ripples beneath his boots and he trips over tangled deadfall, ducks and dodges the slap and rifle crack of breaking branches. He blinks and shakes his head, feels the mud suck at his boots. With each tread, bits of metal bite into his flesh, pinpricks of pain that rise toward the surface, his shins throbbing with the need to let the shards burst through.

He clasps the rifle to his chest. Despite the cool temperature, sweat trickles down his ribs.

Darkness is descending and he hasn't fired once.

At the cabin Al takes one look at Jenny's expectant face and Johnny's downcast eyes and he goes back outside to chop wood. He raises the axe high and lets gravity pull it down, feeling as well as hearing the wood split in two. He gulps one mouthful of air after another, the crystals of ice piercing the back of his throat, needling his lungs.

The smell of wood. The splintered end of a board. From his dugout? He was blown up into the air — but no, not from his dugout.

A metal cup, a solid boot, the broken handle of a shovel.

No, because, he now realizes, he wasn't in his bunk when the shell hit. No. He was —

He doesn't need to close his eyes. Faces leap out at him. Blue-eyed boys like Ingram, old men greyer than Johnny.

Germans.

By the time Al and Tubbs and Kirk reached their bunks an attack had begun. It must have been a raiding party caught by sudden daylight. He never found out.

His unit raced back out to take up positions. He must have fired a dozen times, stuck in that trench, mud gluing his boots to the ground, tearing one boot free, then the other, all the while trying to take aim at whatever fell in or ran past. Then his rifle jammed.

That's as clear to him now as this day. The wave of sickening fear, the cold sweat, the trembling as he realized he could not shoot back.

But he had the bayonet. When a German appeared out of the mud and mist from a bend in the trench, Al lunged and knocked the soldier down, sending his Mauser into the mud. Al grabbed at his leg, fell on top, stabbed him. They rolled, pulled, punched, wrestled. Al could smell him, the shit stink of fear. He plunged the bayonet again and again, long past the need for it, when the soldier's foreign pleas had thinned into one long animal wail and then choked to nothing, past any signs of life, until even his own mother wouldn't have recognized him.

Al stares at the axe in his hand, the split wood glittering at his feet.

The German soldier, he meant: unrecognizable. Mouth open, eyes open, jacket in shreds and red guts steaming, the rotten meat stench all over Al's hands, spattered on his own face and uniform.

The shell must have hit seconds later.

There was no need to kill the German after all. Not like that. No need to go down into that dark place, to awaken such evil in himself. The shell had blown the German to bits. The metal cup, the broken shovel handle — his. The solid boot — all that was left of him. The remaining bits landed in the dirt. And that dirt was blown into Al. Shrapnel in his legs, sand down his throat, grinding through his guts.

What power enables the mind to forget such a thing and then bring it back up? The memory is so strong in him now he puts down the axe, leans over and vomits into the snow, again, and then again, as his body tries one last time to purge itself of all that filth and darkness.

HE HAS TO CONQUER THE bad memories if he's to be of any use to Johnny. He needs to relearn how to fire a rifle cleanly, no shaking, no sweats. But more than that, he needs to know what to think of himself. What kind of man does such a thing?

A young one, yes, and a frightened one. But then, what about the cop? Al would have kept hitting him, he is certain of that. He's in this frozen place because of those actions.

Al hasn't seen a Lee-Enfield since the war, but he noted Johnny's two hanging from the log wall the first time he stepped through the door. They're supposed to be magnificent rifles. Al wouldn't know. His group was issued Ross rifles — accurate aim but with a tendency to jam. In the hospital he heard that the last of them had been collected and replaced with Enfields. What if he'd had one of those, instead, been able to simply shoot that German, a single shot to the heart? He pictures Johnny rapping that marten across the snout, squeezing its heart to a stop. A gentle kill.

SPRING STILL LOOKS LIKE WINTER to Al but each day the sun rises earlier and sets later and the extended days lift his spirits. The air is sharp with the scent of budding branches and warm enough that Al works in his shirt sleeves, though the land and the rivers are still frozen. At noon they plant their chairs into the snow, kick off their shoes and roll up their pant legs.

The hint of spring rejuvenates the nights, too. In the cabin Al hears sounds he hadn't noticed in the winter, a soft sound like the intake of a breath, a small rush of air, the swish of crisp cotton over a bare arm or back. He's half-awake, then sits bolt upright. Slowly, he lies back down again. He considers the novelty of the sound that has roused him from sleep. Unlike the frantic movements he was used to with strange women, or the total silence that shrouded his parents, these were the slow, comfortable movements of older lovers. Al is so struck by the beauty of this, and the possibility — if he can change, that is, and find someone to love — that he is careless in his movements, runs a hand through his hair and lets his palm fall to the bed with a smack. The soft sounds stop abruptly.

The next morning they send Al outside early to chop wood.

"How much do we need?" he asks, calling through the open door.

"An hour's worth," Johnny replies, and shuts the door.

Al begins clearing the shed that day.

ON ONE PARTICULARLY SUNNY DAY in early May, the temperature hovering around freezing, he and Johnny tramp the slushy banks of the river, the recent melt exposing bleached tufts of grass, piles of rock, fallen logs.

Johnny has been talking but Al can't quite hear over the sounds of cracking ice. Breakup has begun. Summer will follow, and then he can leave.

Great slabs of ice shift and grind together as they jam at bends in the river, scouring the banks into a filthy froth, some pieces slipping free and rising tall as houses, other chunks roaring into a side channel with the force of an avalanche running sideways. Al thinks of his own veins twisting and turning along his shins, frustrating the metal bits that try to emerge. Several times he has lifted a trouser leg and searched for the familiar bumpy trail of grey, and found nothing. But maybe he has removed them all, at last, and is troubled only by a phantom itch.

A few feet ahead, on a patch of snowy ground, branches of poplars begin to sway and snap, and Al wonders if the breaking ice has sent tremors into the ground.

Johnny notices, too. But he crouches, rifle raised, mitts scattered at his feet, just as a young moose crashes out of the bush and heads straight toward them. Al spins around and the animal veers slightly, an enormous black beast, its head lowered, its fuzzy, brown nubs of newborn antlers aimed like a pair of knuckles at his jaw, its hooves churning with a force that could gut him in one flying charge.

Common sense tells Al it isn't charging but likely was startled by something, maybe the cracking ice, yet it also seems as though the dark thing he purged from himself has come to life in this creature. The sight of it bearing down on him triggers the familiar sweats and shakes, and he raises the Enfield and fires.

He misses.

Johnny's head snaps around. Al ruined his chance. The moose swings away from the report of the rifle and stumbles down the bank to the river. The mass of ice, its surface rucked like a dirt road and studded with branches and boulders, heaves and cracks in several places under the sudden weight of the animal.

There is no point in shooting the moose now, as it will simply go under and they will have killed it for nothing.

To Al's surprise, Johnny springs to his feet anyway and takes aim. Al runs over to him yelling, "No! It's my fault, let him swim away!"

Johnny's expression is murderous. He snatches up an icy mitt and smacks Al right across the forehead with it. Al freezes in place, stunned.

Johnny shouts at him, "Just like my son swam away?"

The high-pitched whine that follows is the sound of the bobbing plates of ice meeting and grinding. An entire tree that stood tall moments before now plunges down the bank and is shredded to splinters. The young moose stands splay-legged on another ragged slab, snorting like a nervous dog.

"My God!" Al says, realizing the animal's likely fate. A bullet would have been kinder.

The waters move swiftly, spinning the chunks of ice, each turn bringing them closer to each other, then farther, then closer again, thumping and slamming against each other with a force that could gut the animal live.

He and Johnny begin to run, losing their footing in the soft snow, sinking to their knees and turning their ankles in the slushy mess. Each time they stumble to a stop they fire and miss and the poor animal grows silent, eyes wide.

Al is tiring and his feet go out from under him. When Johnny stops to pull him up he gasps, "Maybe the ice will jam — into the bank — he can jump."

Johnny studies the tree tops and doesn't answer.

Al knows what he has to do now. As he catches his breath he takes up his rifle, works the bolt up and flips out the spent cartridge. Then he reloads, snapping the bolt forward and down to lock it. He slings the rifle over his shoulder and begins a slow trot, picking up speed gradually.

His lungs burn. The muscles in his thighs are stretched taut. He breathes through his mouth. Sweat collects under his hood, matting his hair, and he shoves it back, icy air dancing through the wet strands. But he has to keep going. With each agonizing lope he pictures himself slowly squeezing the animal's heart until it stops.

Finally, Al slaps a hand against a tree trunk and, panting, looks down. He has outrun the chunk of ice. It turns slowly toward a bend while a mass of floating ice, branches and boulders finds the channel and closes in behind it. The stranded animal is so still now a miss would be impossible. Al braces himself against the thin pine to stop his shakes, then aims and fires.

The moose crumples to its knees, then its hind end collapses and it slumps over. Johnny catches up to Al and sags to the ground beside him.

One slab rams against another and then another. The impact tips the ice sheet heavenward and the young moose slides lifeless between the plates. A monstrous sound follows as the moving blocks of ice grind against each other.

Johnny's chest huffs, his eyes squeeze shut. "Forgive me," he asks Al.

Gasping too heavily to answer, Al drops a hand onto his shoulder.

In the six months he has lived with Johnny and Jenny, Al assumed their son had drowned. He never considered the ice.

That was it of course — the reason for Johnny's angry outburst just now, his intense grief. He kept the truth to himself. Jenny never knew.

Fourteen

IN THE BLUE OF AUGUST twilight, Al stands on the shore watching clusters of glowing lanterns hover above the water. Soon, he'll be leaving this place. Already in the cool hues he can see Pender and Hastings streets: the shadows between the buildings and the drizzle of winter rain over the glass bricks.

A dozen yellow moons flicker back from the water's surface. A dark oblong of boat or canoe noses between lantern and moon. Ringing the lake are the distinctly rounded tops of northern mountains. The far shore is ragged with the tips of pine and fir trees.

Jenny brushes past him, plucks up the legs of her trousers like they're skirts and steps into the boat, its bow grinding into the coarse sand. Johnny's young cousin Frank has sloshed into the water ahead of her to steady the boat, his thin, dark hands on the wooden rim until Jenny is settled near the prow. Then he climbs over the side, flipping back a ragged fringe of black bangs with a jerk of his head that makes Al think of Jack, before Jack went bald. Under the bangs are close-set eyes, a hawk nose that dominates his small face. Frank is maybe five years younger than Al. Johnny says he and Alex used to be best friends.

Al wades in next carrying nets and oars that he hands to Frank before he steps in, too. Each time they sink another couple of inches and the glossy water rises closer to the rim. Johnny sticks one of his legs into the vessel and pushes off, then sits heavily on the bench. The boat sinks lower once more.

Frank uses one oar to push them farther into the water and then he rows toward the centre of the lake to join the others. Johnny lights a wick, his dark eyes caught by the glow until he passes the coal-oil lamp to Al.

"Hold it high for now," he says, and Al leans over the side, watching his own distorted face recede and advance in the water next to the throbbing light.

Up ahead in the boats are more cousins, a few friends, some neighbours. Al has met most of the Johnson acquaintances. Some are Indian and some not. Together they cleared land at Willie Tom's in late spring, choppcd what was useful for firewood and burned off the scrap brush in a bonfire that the children danced around. Now Al squints at the boats, searching for familiar faces.

"Right over here," Frank says, and Al lowers the lamp and waits. He glances up as another boat closes in. From the halo of gold emerges a girl with a face so smooth it looks as though it had been carved from clay.

Al flashes a smile. She giggles and covers her mouth with splayed fingers.

"Hey!" He jerks his hand as a fish jumps, nudging his wrist. The others laugh.

"They think it's the sun," Johnny says. "Lower it again."

He does and Johnny leans over the side with the net. As two more fish surface he scoops them up. Jenny clubs them and slaps them into a basket.

When Al looks up again, the boat with the girl has disappeared into the dark.

EVERYONE CAMPS ON THE BEACH for the week. Jenny works along-side the other women, her movements quick as they slice and gut and hang the strips to dry. You'd never know she's from Outside. But she isn't any more. At what point, he wonders, would a person be from here?

The men haul over heavy baskets, some repair nets, sitting on the ground with their hooks and clips and ropes. Others pull out the oars and gaffs and clubs, then tip the boats over onto the sand to drain them. Al and Frank have just tipped their boat when Al spies the smooth-skinned face behind one of the racks.

He asks Frank, "Who is she?"

Frank wrinkles his brow. "Lucy. You remember her. She brought us lunch at Willie Tom's."

Al shrugs. That was a month or two after breakup and the smoke from the fire helped keep the mosquitoes and black flies away. He'd been covered in bites.

"Maybe I couldn't see her in all the smoke." He sees something pass over Frank's face. "She your girlfriend?"

Frank shakes his head quickly, and they draw the boat up from the shore. Al walks past the drying racks toward the truck, his eyes following her movements. Lucy works on the opposite side of one rack, separated from him by two rows of fish strips drying rankly in the sun. On her hip is a basket, and from it her hand digs in to hang more slippery pieces onto the racks. Her fingers glisten and rouse such unexpected thoughts that he hasn't noticed she's stepped into his path, ready to begin hanging strips from the other side.

Startled, he says a quick hello. She smiles, small teeth disappearing beneath wide lips. Her eyes, so black he can't see the pupils, remain focused on the wooden racks.

"I'm Al," he tells her.

"Al!" Johnny calls, as if to confirm his statement.

THAT NIGHT THEY RETURN TO the water.

Al has never seen anything like this lake in the cobalt light of summer evening, the navy surface flat but for the dipping of oars, the lanterns wobbling brightly against it, and the fish rising to them. Lake trout, bigger, but not as pretty as rainbow. Grayling with its own rainbow belly of yellow and purple. Pike with a mouth of teeth like a cat's.

And he has never seen anyone like her. Sculpted features and smooth, dark skin. Now he scans the lake for another glimpse, and finds her just a few feet away.

She calls to him, "Al," tongue curling against small teeth, the sound more like *Ull*.

He smiles at her with his eyes and feels the hoop of the net slap firmly against his arm. "Watch the light," Johnny says.

Al looks over the edge but concludes he's holding it just fine. He raises his eyes and this time meets the stern face of an older man riding in the boat with Lucy, then another girl, her face expressionless, and finally an older woman, grim and narrow-eyed. Her family, probably. Al nods but the three sail past, their boat heading toward the stream that empties into the lake. Only Lucy twists around to smile.

In the commotion of beaching numerous boats later that night, and then unloading baskets of fish in the dark, Al finds himself taking Lucy's hand to help her step onto the shore. His skin from knuckles to scrotum tightens as her thumb rubs against his. They step into the shadows.

He shouldn't. She's the daughter of one of Johnny's friends. But the feel of her fingers captivates him. They leave a trail of translucent scales along his bare arms, tiny discs that flash in the moonlight.

There is none of the false modesty of the girls he met at dances, who offered and withdrew, or who offered expecting something in return, the promise of a date the following Saturday. Lucy doesn't hesitate, says not one single word as her fingertips inch under his shirt. His sense of taste, touch and smell are heightened by the loss of light. He runs his tongue over her teeth, gathers in his hands her full head of hair, erotic with the smell of fish. His palms slide down her shoulders and over her breasts, pressing against her nipples, and he hardens against the pressure of her belly that rubs repeatedly against him, would have taken her right there had a deep voice not called out, "Lucy!"

FISHING IS OVER, JOHNNY AND Jenny tell him the next day.

"Too bad," he says. "I was enjoying myself."

He flushes at the unintended meaning of his words, and he sees them exchange looks before asking him to help haul up the boat.

"The others are still fishing." Al shades his eyes. Boats bristle with fishing poles on the sparkling water. In the bright sunlight he can't make out which one is hers.

"Have you changed your mind?" Johnny asks him. Al crouches beside him to turn the boat over. "You could stay for the winter."

"Winter?"

He has grown to like the north in summer. The days are long, and once, when the sun was shining brightly, he checked his watch to see that it was eleven o'clock at night. The sun dipped, then began to rise again at two o'clock. Even at midnight the screeches of children at play floated across the river. He caught a ride into town with Willie Tom just so he could wander around and have a drink at the Whitehorse Inn. Later he marvelled to Johnny and Jenny that people paraded about the streets at all hours, just like they did in Paris.

But another year here?

In his pocket is a recent letter from Jack, one that filled him with a desire to move again.

I don't know if you've heard yet, but civil war has broken out in Spain. The Popular Front won the election, so the army marched in last month to try to overthrow it. They're Fascists, of course, and no doubt are afraid this new republican government will push for land reform for the peasants. And so they should be afraid! The poor in Spain have nothing. We know how that is. But any reform is on hold, now. They have a civil war to fight.

Everything I read in the New Frontier *and the* New Commonwealth, *and every meeting I go to is about Spain. Agnes and I have been to the coast twice and are helping to raise funds and organize rallies for the Vancouver branch of the Committee to Aid Spanish Democracy. All of which goes to say that these are exciting times, Bertie. We can't wait for you to join us.*

Al sent a letter back asking whether Jack thought it was safe yet to return. Al thinks it is, and any day now he expects a reply confirming it.

Waves slosh onto the shore as Johnny grabs the side of the boat. "Frank says maybe you've changed your mind."

"Frank?" Al doesn't recall saying anything to him.

"Would you take her?" Johnny asks.

Together they flip the boat. Lake water rushes over the rocky sand.

"Who?" Al brushes his hands and stands. Johnny shakes his head slightly as he pushes himself up from the boat. Al's neck grows hot. "Oh. Lucy."

Johnny levels a firm stare at Al. "What did you think you were doing?"

It isn't really a question. The heat climbs to Al's face and ears as he counters, "It's her business. And mine. Isn't it?"

"She thinks you want to be like us."

Married! Al looks at the ground and then swiftly up at Johnny. "I never promised — never said anything of the kind." This is exactly what made him hesitate. She's the daughter of Johnny's friend. He knew he shouldn't have.

Johnny lifts one end of the boat and Al collects himself, grabs the other end and they huff it onto the back of the truck, loop ropes over it, pulling hard before knotting the ends.

"Up here, you do that," Johnny jerks his head toward the bushes, "it means something."

Like them. Jenny brought her lace doilies and wing-back chair into Johnny's world and he built her an English cottage. Their lives meshed and they danced past the wood stove and it all fit, just like that. But Al and Lucy? Just a few days ago he stood on this shore looking at the lanterns, telling himself that soon he will be leaving. He wanted to sit at the table with Jack and Agnes and hear more about these rallies, maybe take in one of them and see what it was all about. Maybe help out somehow as he had done in the snake parades. But Lucy? He tries to picture her in Agnes's drawing room. The scent of fish fouls the image. Her rough hands leave trails of silver scales over the chintz curtains.

THE NEXT DAY JENNY AND Johnny knock at the door of his shack. Jenny holds a thick, yellowed sheet of paper that has been folded many times. She sits in his only chair. Johnny sits on the edge of his bed. Al stands.

Slowly she unfolds the paper until it reveals a government crest and several lines of type indicating a hunting licence. The hand-written name is *Alex Johnson*.

"I birthed him at home," she tells Al, her blue eyes glowing. "I schooled him at home, too. The only piece of paper that states he ever lived is this," she lifts the document. "No birth certificate," she says, "so no death certificate, either. According to this, he's still alive."

When Al says nothing she continues. "Take it. Hank said you might need a new name."

"Hank?"

"Hendersen."

"You knew him?"

"His sister. We went to school together in Nelson."

So she's his contact, not Johnson. Of course. She's from Outside.

His eyes can't hold their focus. He tries to smile. "I didn't think Alex needed a licence."

Johnny says, "He didn't. He was my son." Then he looks at Jenny. "But he was hers, too, and he said it was only right."

Alex knew who he was, what he was. It was something to envy.

Al reaches for the document, holds it in his hands.

Fraser is the name recorded on relief camp documents, and it's the name he gave the cop.

But a new name. Alex. He could shorten it to Al and it wouldn't make a difference. Alex *Johnson* will take some getting used to, though.

Before he came north he had no home, no job, no woman. If only he could find a job, he used to think, then he could find a woman to marry, build a home. Now here he is, with Johnny and Jenny who've given him a home, with all the work he needs and Lucy. Yet he doesn't want any of it. Why? His answer had been clear and undeniable, even though he hadn't said a word. Well. They've given him a new name so that he can leave. Their name.

Jenny couldn't bear to lose a second son, so it was Johnny who had allowed himself to get close to Al, Johnny who, even now as they sit in his little house, can summon only one word.

"Son," he says.

Al nods, can't look up, eyes stinging as he folds the evidence of their son's existence and tucks it into his wallet. Jenny had kept something of Alex after all.

Fraser was the old man's name, so Al should be glad to be rid of it. But Fraser is Jack's name, too. It's one of the few things that bind him to the only living relative he knows, and the loss of it makes him feel as though he is disappearing. And yet, with a new name he could start all over. Alex Johnson had no darkness inside him. Alex Johnson had never been to war.

NOM DE GUERRE

Fifteen

THEY'VE BEEN AT SEA FOR over a week.

Al has grown to depend on the constant rhythm of the ship's engine. He can feel it pumping through the floor and into his feet as he walks, or rumbling along his ribs as he lies on his side in bed. If he grabs the bed frame he can feel the steady thumping right into his hand. His heart tries to keep time. One night, he was plucked from a sound sleep when the engine shut down. For a moment, he thought his heart had stopped.

Now he leans on the deck railing and feels the steady, reassuring thud of the engine reverberating along his arms. In his pocket is a passport issued to Alex Johnson of Whitehorse, Yukon Territory, with a small likeness of himself on the inside page. He pulls it out and with his thumb flips open the front cover.

Each time he looks at it he feels a jolt of surprise. *Who is this man?* His thumbnail caresses the stamp, *Not Valid for Spain*, then he flicks it closed. Spain is exactly where he is heading.

He has lost another year. From Whitehorse he headed straight down to Princeton, where he sat at Jack and Agnes's kitchen table, September sunlight glancing off the branches of a newly planted apricot tree, listening to them talk about Spain. The apricot tree was the most luxuriant piece of greenery he'd seen in a year, and he couldn't stop staring — its promise of fruit even as the leaves turned orange and fell — while he heard how the military junta in Spain was flourishing, how its leader Franco got an early helping hand from Hitler, whose planes had ferried the general's Army of Africa from Morocco to southern Spain, how both Hitler and Mussolini continued to send supplies and troops.

Junta was the first Spanish word Al learned. They used it in a letter to their aunt, whose town, Jack discovered in old papers, was called Belchite. But their aunt did not write back. Perhaps she and her husband took Maggie to England to get away from the war.

During trips to town, Jack introduced Al as a friend of the family. Some of the old-timers knew better and their eyes twinkled when they shook his hand. Al found it easy to say, *Alex Johnson, pleased to meet you,* but whenever Jack called him Alex he felt himself wince. He kept waiting for Jack to slip and accidentally call him Bertie. But he never did.

Al tucks the passport back into his jacket pocket.

Most of the men in the ship's third class are bound for Spain, too, Hendersen among them, who sidles up next to Al now, and asks, "Got a smoke there, stranger?"

Then he hooks a long leg through the bottom rung of the ship's railing and leans back.

Al hands him a cigarette, then aims his own toward two men who wear cheap suits like theirs. The outfits are intended to help them blend in with regular passengers, but both the stiff fabric and ill fit set them apart.

"They communists?"

"Might be." Hendersen pauses to strike a match, cupping it in his hands as he bends to light his cigarette. "Why?"

He snaps his wrist to extinguish the match, and drops it over the rail. The black ocean slides alongside them like spilled oil. Al watches intently, as though the surface might ignite.

"Because," he says at last, "the communists seem to be running

the whole show. The money, the organizing, everything. I'm wondering now if that doctor in Vancouver was a communist. He signed
my passport application, and when I showed him the hunting licence
he never questioned if it was really mine. Never asked me about the
north. Not a thing." When Hendersen says nothing, Al asks, "Are
you a communist?"

"I suppose I could be. I certainly have no grievances with them.
Look what they did for us in the camps. It was them who got us
thinking. Them who got us here."

"Why exactly are you here?"

"To fight Fascism. Why else?"

"I mean really. Your own reasons."

Hendersen thinks for a minute. "It rankles me that the people
vote in who they want and then some rich bully comes along and
takes their votes back. The peasants and the workers, they might as
well have been non-existent. Dead. Just like we were in the camps."

Al nods. "Same for me. Partly."

"What's the other part? Because," Hendersen adds, "I remember
those nightmares."

"I haven't had one for some time." Al knocks the toe of his shoe
against the railing. "But my brother asked much the same thing. He
said, 'How do you know it won't be like last time?'"

That last time, Al was sick with apprehension and excitement as
he crossed the Atlantic to go to war in France. Every meal he ate
ended up over the side. This time his emotions swung in neither
direction. If anything, he felt determined, resolved.

Jack's reaction had surprised Al. He seemed all too willing to
bury Al's old name. So why not embrace a new role for him, especially one that had sprung from the cause for Spanish democracy?
That cause was the very reason they took the train down from
Princeton. The apricot tree had just come into leaf when they heard
on the radio that Hitler's Condor Legion had bombed the town of

Guernica. Agnes had wrapped her arms around her ribs as though it were still winter. *Market day*, she said. *The streets were full of people. Ordinary people.* Then she turned to them and said, *There will be meetings about this. How soon can we pack?*

"We were in Stanley Park," Al tells Hendersen, "at the May Day rally. Someone announced that a group of men had volunteered to go to Spain. The crowd started cheering and throwing red tulips and red ribbons into the air. I kept thinking about Guernica." Al pictured women filling their string bags with carrots and onions, maybe one of them stopping to hold a tomato in the palm of her hand, considering it, as though she had nothing to worry about except what to cook for dinner that night. And then her ordinary world exploded. "I turned to Jack and told him, 'I'm going too.'"

"He didn't like the idea."

"No. I said I wanted to make a difference and he said, 'By going to war? You've done that before.' And I said, 'Not as Alex Johnson, I haven't.'"

Al tosses his cigarette into the swirling water. His claim sounds more boastful than he intended, and the fact was, the argument hadn't ended there.

Jack had whirled around and shouted, *Are you completely mad?*

Al shouted back, *You mean you're not going?*

Jack waved his arms about. *Did you see us lay a wreath at the cenotaph, walk all the way here from Victory Square? We walked for peace! We are here to help Spain, to send clothes and money, not men.*

Al countered: *Then what about the others who just joined up? You didn't seem to mind that.*

That's their business, Jack said. *But you. After everything you went through.*

He clapped a hand on each hip and talked up at the sky, shaking his bald head the whole time. *I know why you're doing this. You did it before. Didn't like working at the mine and thought you'd go to war. Have a little adventure. You're doing the same thing now.*

Even then he didn't call him Bertie.

Al was furious. Jack and Agnes were doing good with their committee work, but he wasn't doing anything. He didn't have a job. *I gave it twenty years,* he told Jack, *and look at me. I lost the best job I ever had. There's got to be something grander than digging dirt for a living. I want to do something that matters.*

Jack's face was as limp as a disappointed father's. *There's nothing grander than what any man in this park has done every day of his working life.*

Agnes stepped between them, *Boys!*

But Al was fired up. *Working? They're not working. Don't you see? You and your cause. When it comes down to it you're all talk!*

All this they shouted at each other while a brass band played a farewell to the volunteers, banners and signs sailed above the heads of the crowd, people hugged and cheered.

"I headed east without his blessings. But I've done that before."

Then Al presses his chin into his shoulder to study the skinny friend beside him, his missing teeth and thinning hair. If this were like the last war he'd be considered too old to soldier. So might Al. But he'd been overjoyed at the sight of Hendersen in that recruitment room in the Seaman's Union Hall in Toronto. He must have crossed the floor in two strides. They shook hands and slapped backs and then Hendersen said in that soft, gentle voice of his, *Well, I'll be. Alex Johnson. Right?* Al didn't need to ask how he knew. Jenny must have sent word.

"Those two who ran the recruitment office. They were definitely communists."

Hendersen's eyes dance. "They weren't from the prime minister's office. But see here, they helped us out, didn't they? Set us on our way."

They told Al and Hendersen that the volunteers would be travelling as tourists or businessmen of vision bound for the Paris Exposition. From Le Havre they would board a train for Paris. If they wanted, they could attend the fair while they waited for travel instructions to Spain.

The *Exposition Internationale des Arts et Techniques dans la Vie Moderne.* Al and Hendersen practised saying it to each other as, dressed in suits and fedoras purchased for them from the Salvation Army, they headed out to see the sights of Toronto.

Hendersen recalls, "You know, I'd never seen anything in British Columbia like that Union Station and the Royal York Hotel. But you remember what you said to me? You said, 'Wait till you see Paris.'"

It amuses Al all over again to think of what had once constituted Hendersen's world. They boarded a train for New York City carrying blue cardboard suitcases. On Fifth Avenue, Hendersen took off his hat and held it over his heart as he looked up, trying to glimpse the top of the Empire State Building. That was all they got to see of the city before being hustled into rooms at the YMCA, where they waited for their orders to sail.

Now Hendersen grinds his cigarette under his shoe. "You're full of talk tonight, that's for sure." Then he drops his voice. "I don't recall my old friend Al Fraser being half so chatty."

A group of men stops to ask if they know when the ship will reach Le Havre. Tomorrow first thing, Hendersen tells them. Occasionally, through the mist, they glimpse clusters of lights from seaside villages. They're almost there.

Al sighs while the men rehash the lines he's been hearing the whole crossing.

"Art is for the rich. What about regular people? This exhibition's going to change all that. There's a whole exhibit on the history of the railway."

"A locomotive — now that's a work of art."

"A sculpture unto itself. Looks and function — *des Arts et Tech-niques*. Just like the brochures say."

"Architecture. That's where art and science come together."

"I see it this way. You can't eat art."

Ezra Pound might disagree. But it's unlikely these men have ever read his poems. Still, Al is of two minds. Art hung on the walls of every mansion he painted. Why, then, could he not recall even one of them? Instead, his thoughts linger over the snap of a crisp drop cloth, a smear of lemon frosting, the clean smell of paint.

IT'S BEEN TWENTY YEARS SINCE he was last here, and the Paris of his war years became, over time, the looming presence of the Eiffel Tower. As soon as they climb above ground from the metro, there it is, its sharp outline against the morning sky, the black mesh of iron legs that always reminded Al of gartered stockings, *la tour Eiffel*. He nudges Hendersen and points.

But there will be no nightclubs this time, no plump matron singing wearily on a smoke-filled stage.

Within moments of their arrival at the trade union complex on Mathurin Morcau, their orders arrive. They will move out the next morning at six for a train trip south and then a climb over the mountains into Spain. That means meetings and an early curfew. But they have the day to themselves and the chance to catch the metro again, this time to the exhibition grounds.

The station is crowded, the streets along the Seine are crowded. The first pavilion they enter, the *Palais de l'Air*, is immense and yet it is crowded, too.

Hendersen pushes past the shoulders of onlookers and into the main gallery of the *Palais de l'Air* as though he were an old hand at navigating in bustling world cities.

It's like the airplane hangars Al has seen in books, though he has never seen so much glass. All around the room are pillars supporting plane engines as though they are sculptures. Above them hover the silver bellies of aircraft suspended by wires from the ceiling.

Outside again, beside the froth of fountains on the concourse, Hendersen stops to unfold a map, his elbows knocked repeatedly by pedestrians. To their left is the river Seine, to their right *la tour Eiffel* and clustered around the tower's legs and hugging the banks of the Seine, the fair's pavilions.

The crowd isn't causing Al to sweat or panic. Neither had the crowds at the rally in Vancouver, or in the union hall in Toronto, or even on the streets of New York. When had that happened? What does it mean?

Perhaps he is right — this time won't be like the last.

He leans over and jabs a finger at the map. "This way."

No discussion is needed. Of course, they will see the Spanish pavilion. As they pass the German building and its rooftop sculpture of an eagle with spread talons, Hendersen shouts over his shoulder, "Who invited them?"

Brochures tell them the Spanish display has been put together by the republican government.

"Our side," Al notes.

Within the entranceway hang large black-and-white photographs of dead bodies, blasted buildings, little children starving. Inside the pavilion, an entire wall is covered by a painting in ashen tones showing twisted, distorted shapes. A horse's head, open-mouthed, eyeballs rolled back, objects toppled over, people falling backwards. It is such a jumble of shapes and lines that to take it all in Al has to walk its length, then step back, forward, then back again.

Of course. *Guernica.*

Al read that the painting was Picasso's plea to the world to look at Spain, look at what was happening to her. The longer Al looks, the more he sees. The jagged edges, the jumble of shapes, chaotic and disturbing. Gradually arms and legs emerge, heads thrown back, as though an explosion has left images of their shattered lives embedded in the canvas. Al thinks of the Somme. Fields of limbs. Artie on his back, twitching. The bayonet in his own hands. The German blown to bits, and those bits in him.

There seems to be no one solid thing in this painting, not man, woman, animal or building except the child, and it hangs from its mother's arms. No colour. It's about death, and yet somehow the images churn and pulse.

Al stands at the back while people, some puzzled, some awe-struck, mill in front. Hendersen wanders off, calling back that he'll meet up in twenty minutes. But Al remains perfectly still. This painting is unlike any painting he has ever seen before, and it is one he will not forget. He can't take his eyes from it, won't. Not until he has memorized every detail.

Sixteen

IN THE BRIGHT SUNLIGHT OF a large arena, Al strains to see past heads and arms and shoulders bearing packs. There must be a hundred of them, maybe more, plodding the dirt floor of Albacete's bullring as they are grouped and then regrouped. Just moments before, Hendersen was rounded up with a gang of Scandinavians. Al should be able to spot him, but he can't.

The drone of foreign voices is constant and disorienting, a cloud of sound in his head, until a single word rises from it, clear, and in the distinct pitch of a German accent. *Hallo.* Memory bristles at the back of his neck and Al pivots on one heel, scans the faces swimming past, straining to hear it, again. French, Spanish, Russian — Dutch, perhaps?

Yes. That must be it. His mind is playing tricks.

His gaze settles on the rows of seats rising tall and empty around the bullring. Normally they must be filled with yelling, jeering crowds. It has the look of a coliseum, more Rome than Spain, though nothing so far has been the Spain he'd imagined.

Agnes made him promise to write, and he's not sure how he will describe it.

The train that brought Hendersen and him here had chugged down the Mediterranean coast, plunging through tunnels, light splintering through slits where stones had loosened, then bursts of water-bright blue from ragged portholes where the cliffside had worn through — the turquoise of Greece, he imagined, but not Spain.

Barcelona was only what he had seen from the windows, soot-stained tracks and crowds on the platform raising their fists and shouting encouragement: *A la frente!* To the front! and, *No pasaran!* They shall not pass! He waved back and raised his fist and then the train shuddered and they were gone.

Before Barcelona they had bedded down in a castle as dark and dank as any in England.

The night before that was the climb through the Pyrenees, exhausting, slipping over slick rocks and mud in the dark, thigh muscles screaming, lungs aching, with only a guide leading the group of them away from cliff edges and ravines. Some men climbed with the added burden of suitcases. Al and Hendersen had already ditched theirs for canvas packs. Eventually they crossed the border and descended into the foothills, and the guide whistled sharply. Now that was something to write about, though it still didn't look like Spain. Men emerged from behind the evergreens, much as deer move in the Canadian bush, as shadows, inch by inch, each step so tentative it can be snatched back in a moment, melting against bark and branch until you aren't sure you really saw anything. The shadows hovered for a moment and then gathered together, gliding forward to greet the new arrivals. Al knew they were soldiers because they moved with precision, but instead of uniforms they wore street trousers, ponchos or leather jackets. They were the kind of soldiers his father would have dismissed because they hadn't made a display of themselves. Al liked them instantly. Jack might understand that.

Now Al thinks about holding a gun again, shooting, and tries to swallow against the sensation of gravel in his throat. He rubs it with thumb and forefinger.

A republican *coronel* shouts over the crowd, "*Inglés!*" and then points. Al weaves past the strange faces to the side of the arena sectioned off for English speakers. Finally, he is surrounded by voices he understands, though he doesn't recognize anyone from the ship or the climb.

They smile to each other and blurt greetings, then straggle forward for supplies. Boots. Knapsacks. Wine skins to use as canteens. In Paris they had been warned about the shortage of supplies and to expect mismatched outfits. Al is given a light shirt, sweater and black beret, with a slip of paper inside indicating his room number. For now, he will have to wear his own suit trousers.

Hallo. That sound again. Al's eyes dart over the men to his immediate left to find the source of the voice. There. A brown-haired man waves his arms and the coronel approaches. The officer points to where Al stands. Something in Spanish, then in English. Al can't make out what the problem is. The man says something else and the coronel shrugs and marches off.

The brown-haired man has a long, rubbery face that stretches into a wide smile as he walks over to the line with hand extended. Al should have looked away, but too late now.

"Heinrich Gunther. Pleased to meet you."

Al was right about the accent after all. He feels every inch of skin on his body snap to life. He isn't afraid of the man, but of himself, of what he did the last time he heard such an accent. He can think of only one response.

"German —" he says.

"Yes. I thought I'd be in one of the German battalions. But that officer asked if I speak English, and I said yes, because I do, and now he thinks that I am English. So here I am. Well, no matter. We are on the same side."

Al realizes he hasn't let go of the man's hand. "Al!" he offers, and then releases his hold.

He has a generous face, somewhat homely in its fleshiness, younger than Al's, the eyes a warm green-brown that make it easy to look at him and to believe that this time will be different. After all, as he says, they are on the same side.

A voice calls over to them, uncertain, like a child's. "Did either of you get boots?"

Al turns. It's a young man in riding breeches and high, lace-up boots. The youth pushes fawn-coloured bangs from his face and eyes Al's *alpargatas*, rope-soled sandals he bought on the other side of the border specifically for the mountain climb. Al nods. "But not like those."

"Well, I like higher boots. There'll be rain and maybe even snow farther on." The youth plucks at the four pockets of his khaki jacket. "I'd like a leather jacket to match the boots but they gave me this dreadful *cazadora*. I wish there was a mirror."

Al smiles. No he doesn't.

"I'm Daniels. Actually, it's Brian Daniels, but no one goes by first names in the army, do they? What about you two?"

"Inglés!" the officer calls.

Al shakes the boy's hand, but he is picturing an easy smile stretching ear to ear when the German voice, melodious, now that Al thinks of it, says from behind him, "We are the English. To the coronel that is the only name necessary."

"Inglés!" the officer repeats. "*Batallón* Mackenzie-Papineau!" They form into an uneven line and march raggedly behind him, out the arena doors and down the block.

Amidst more bellowed directions they cram into a villa that serves as barracks. Al angles into the throng, right arm raised, shoulder blade a shield against the greasy hair and dirty necks of his fellow travellers. Daniels ploughs in behind him and shouts in his ear, "There's a group of us going for drinks. Five minutes." Then he is swallowed up by the torrent of men. Al squeezes past elbows and bags of gear until finally he reaches his assigned sleeping quarters, a large room for a bedroom but jammed from one end to the other with cots. Al hefts his bag onto the bed closest to the door and heads outside, where several volunteers are gathering.

On the way to the villa, Al was preoccupied with the conflicting emotions of missing Hendersen and then meeting a German volunteer, so it's as though he is seeing the street for the first time. Previous bombings tore the tops off buildings and jaws of blackened stone and wood gape at the sky. Rubble litters the sidewalks. They walk in the road instead, which has been scraped clear for the movement of trucks.

There are signs of a once lively town — awnings that now hang in strips, steps that were probably washed down each morning, now indistinguishable from the rubble around them. He can see Daniels up ahead, and the German fellow — Goon-ter, he pronounced it — near the front of the group.

If it weren't for the boards over windows, Al suspects that Daniels would be standing in front of each to catch his reflection and study the effect of his breeches and boots. The young man looks like a child in costume. Nothing quite fit. Al returns his focus to the street, to the rows of buildings. Daniels reminds him of the Ingram boy. Al's eyes skip back to scrutinize him. That's all they need.

Townspeople pass them in the street. Thin, weak, their skeletal legs seem to click as they move, though Al knows it's really the tips of their walking sticks tapping the stones. Still, if there is no food for the Spanish, how could there be any for the foreigners?

Several times they are approached by other volunteers scouting for tobacco. Despite the shortage, the air inside the bar is thick with smoke. The volunteer who has led them here stands beside Al, studying the room and the row of backs at the bar. He has thick black brows matched by an equally thick moustache.

He aims ice blue eyes at Al. "Name's Kreibs," he says.

"Johnson," Al replies.

The name sounds like a yawn, all rounded vowels compared to the raspy edge of Fraser.

The man offers no hand to shake and Al notes the well-worn fit of his uniform, the leather jacket and boots and Sam Browne belt with holster. The very outfit Daniels wants. He's no recruit, this Kreibs.

"You were at the front?" Al asks.

A waiter swoops past with a tray and gives them each a full glass of brandy.

Kreibs nods. "Belchite. With the Lincoln Battalion, Number Two Company."

Belchite. Al breathes in sharply.

"Got our asses kicked. Blasted the place apart, but we won apparently." He pauses, then adds, "Most of the town cleared out by then, and a damned good thing, too. Where you from Johnson?"

"The Yukon."

Kreibs whistles. "Winnipeg," he says, and they clink glasses.

Then he jams a cigar into the corner of his mouth and digs in his pocket. "Number Two was mostly Canadian." Kreibs talks through teeth that clench his cigar. "But the internationals are all mixed in together. Cubans, Mexicans, Slavs, Poles, Germans — of course, you heard about that in Paris."

"No, but I met a German just now in the bullring. He's in here, somewhere."

"You must mean Grunter."

"Gunther, I think it was."

"Yeah, Grunt. From Bavaria or Berlin or some such fucking place. A bona fide Hun. Isn't that something? Germans and Italians on our side, fighting Hitler and Mussolini on the other side. Whole fucking battalions of them."

Hun. The word hangs in the air. But the German isn't old enough to have fought at the Somme, not even if he lied about his age. He doesn't move like a soldier, either. He's all elbows and knees and big smiling face.

Al's eyes drift over the barroom and then back, looking for him. He has given up trying to spot Hendersen, though he speaks as his friend might have. "It's like a worldwide civil war."

Kreibs smacks Al on the back and says, "You're all right, Johnson." Then he flicks a match with his thumbnail and lights the cigar. Smoke curls under his black moustache. "Once we formed the Mac-Paps I thought I'd switch over. Mostly Canadians, but you're right, like every other battalion they include every fucking nationality you can think of." He drops the dead match onto the floor. "The officers are all American, you know. They were going to make me an officer, too, but what kind of a commie would I be then?"

Al stiffens, uncertain of his humour.

"So I offered to come here instead and help with the training."

Offered. What does that really mean? Has he been busted down to private? It would make sense, the way he talks. "We train here?"

"Didn't they tell you anything in Paris?"

In Paris he saw a large map of Spain, the east-west divide between the two sides a line that wobbled and looped like paint spilled on a floor. West of the uneven line was Fascist-held territory. They called themselves nationalists, but Al has never heard anyone on his side use the term. They were simply Fascists, a word you could hiss between teeth. East of the line was their side, but if they'd been told the location of their training site, Al couldn't recall. It wouldn't have meant anything if they had.

Kreibs gulps from his glass. His face puckers. "This stuff is shit," he says, then explains, "Tarazona de la Mancha. Not too far from here. We train for about four months."

Four months. Al sips his brandy and pulls a face, too. Four months to get used to the idea of firing.

"Use of weapons, manoeuvres. Lectures on how to be a good commie." Kreibs grins and then winks. "Nothing they like better than talking."

"Yes," Al says, perhaps too emphatically.

Kreibs roars.

A group of volunteers leaves the counter to join them.

"Grunt, you German son of a bitch. We were just talking about you."

Al smiles sheepishly but the man slaps Kreibs on the back and laughs, seems to accept his new name — an English one, after all.

FLESH AND BLOOD

Seventeen

HOT SUN. BLISTERING HOT. THE air is twisting with it, the ground burnt. But the heat feels good on his lungs. And what colours. Reds and golds and baked brown clay.

He lies flat on his stomach in the scorched dirt of a rye field, squinting through stalks of grain, the salt sting of sweat in his eyes. He hears the shouts of peasants in the field. No machinery. No horses. Just mules and donkeys and peasants. And them.

He is in Spain at last, the Spain he's been waiting for, and the joy of it fills him with such agitation he can't lie still, but inches forward and parts the stalks with the tip of his rifle.

In a clearing immediately ahead, a peasant's blue shirt ripples like water in the heat waves. Al watches him unhitch a donkey from a wooden cart while three more men hang their jackets and their hats over the wooden sides, then roll up their sleeves, pull scythes from the wagon and spread out to give each other swinging room. Al can hear the whisper of blades cutting the grass as he turns his head. Two women wade through the russet field, shoulder blades and hip bones shifting beneath print dresses. When they reach the patch where the men work they gather their skirts about their hips and crouch, brown hands collecting the fallen stalks into bundles, tying each with a long straw.

To Al's right the tall rye begins to shake, and he remembers his rifle. Kreibs is hunkered next to him, his bristling jaw working a dead cigar. A soft whistle rises from the field and soon their platoon leader scuttles out of the grass in a half-crouch.

"Johnson!" he shouts. "Kreibs!"

"Eye-van!" Kreibs calls back. They boost themselves up and huddle to talk.

The sergeant's name is really John and he's from Seattle, not Russia, but Kreibs says Ivan better suits a good commie. Al doesn't know how Kreibs gets away with his remarks, but the name has stuck, as all his names do.

"Grab a scythe," Ivan says. "We're going to help them with the harvest."

Al springs to his feet and bounds through the tall rye to the very spot he has been watching, his movement sending up veils of ochre dust.

Grunt and Daniels are at the wagon already, leaning their rifles against the wheels, draping their khaki jackets over the snouts of the guns. Grunt takes off his black beret and tosses it spinning onto the jacket's hump.

Daniels already shucked his beret the day before and replaced it with a woman's pale blue cloche hat he'd found by a roadside. He called it his own private protest against their mismatched uniforms. *Take my picture and send it to Ottawa*, he said. *Sign it, Love and Kisses, the Mac-Paps*. He's still wearing it, adorned with a gleaming silver pin.

Kreibs moves in behind Al and rasps into his ear, "Strange little fucker."

Al ignores him. He doesn't care who wears what. He was happy enough to have his suit trousers replaced with khaki last week, but he's more concerned about getting decent weapons. For practise they use whatever broken or mismatched pieces of equipment the republican army can spare. He isn't surprised to see Ross rifles and not a single Lee-Enfield. Ivan assures them that when they go to battle they'll be issued real guns.

The man in the blue shirt stops swinging and wipes his hands on his trousers. The peasants lean their scythes next to the rifles and begin loading the bundled sheaves into the back of the wagon.

Al and the other soldiers grab up the scythes and take the places of the peasants in the field.

He's never used a scythe. The wooden handle, polished from years of toil, is as tall as he is, the blade a menacing curve of metal half its length. A false move would cleave the meat from his leg. He braces himself with feet spread wide, one hand on the long pole of the scythe and the other on the protruding handle, and swings carefully. The row of grass remains upright for an instant, then falls soundlessly.

They work on into the morning. Bits of straw and grain stick to their necks. Dust coats their eyelids and the scarves they wrap over their mouths. Sweat runs down their chests and backs, their hands blister, the backs of their necks burn. Al's pulse beats time with each swing and he thrills at the sight of swaths of tall grain falling at his touch. Immediately behind him, women bend and rake, bend and rake, their wide bottoms blocking his view of the mounds they are bundling into sheaves.

The war is just across that plain and over a few hills. Each time a cloud passes over the sun he is reminded of this and his hands tighten on the scythe. It would prove a better weapon than the empty, rusted gun, but he hopes he won't have to use it.

THEY BREAK FOR A MEAL OF chickpeas in olive oil, washed down with tart wine. The brown water that swirls past is undrinkable, and at least the wine cuts the taste of the peas. Al rolls his tongue around his mouth. Wallpaper paste. Overcooked porridge. Sometimes the garbanzos are supplemented with sardines or a stew of strange-tasting meat — almost like hair in that way that goat's milk seems to taste like goat hair — but always they are fed garbanzos.

By the banks of the river, under the shade of dry, rustling trees, they eat and drink and talk.

"A man from the Yukon's gotta be good with a rifle. You hunt lots?"

Al smiles at Kreibs, but it's a struggle. Several thoughts strike him at once. The trouble he had shooting the moose, the rifle that jammed at the Somme, the German soldier.

He's glad to be Alex Johnson right now, a man who is going to war for the first time.

"We trapped, mostly," he replies at last. "Fished a lot, too."

Two women have come down with the medics. Al leans back on his elbow and watches them, young and healthy, heads thrown back, laughing. They are the wives of a couple of volunteers called Red and Stump, visiting before their husbands leave for the front. Across from them is a peasant woman, perhaps as young as the wives but with heavy lines across her forehead. She bares her brown shoulder and breast to feed her child. The small mouth tugs vigorously for a while and then falls open in slumber, letting the long, dark nipple pop free. Al forces his gaze away.

The very presence of women in the war both pleases and alarms him. One of the wives sits with her skirts carefully spread around her, the other is cross-legged in olive-drab trousers. She looks prepared for life and he likes that. Her outfit makes him think of the leggings Jenny wore beneath her skirts, of her ability to adapt to the north.

A recent letter from the Yukon crinkles in his pocket. Supplies make it across the border only sporadically, but the postal system runs as though it's peacetime. The letter has stirred up mixed feelings in Al, envy and joy in all the wrong places. Usually Jenny writes, but this one is from Johnny, and the words have stayed with him.

Son

Frank and Lucy got married on Saturday. I know you liked her but I think Frank liked her more and that's the way it's turned out. Frank and me shot ourselves a moose just up Teslin River. We took it to English Tom's to butcher and then we took some around for everyone to have their share. It weighed over a thousand pounds so there was lots.

Al figures Frank would have brought the moose down in one shot. He wouldn't have missed the way Al had. He pictures Frank trudging along the riverbank with Johnny, heating up pots of stew and tea. Talking. Learning. It takes Al a whole evening to come up with a suitable response. *That's a big moose.* But he has no problem writing several sentences of congratulations about the marriage. This amuses him now as he looks at the women sitting by the river. He is more jealous of Frank hunting with Johnny than of Frank marrying Lucy.

Then he sees that Kreibs is watching him. It spooks him — like scanning the bush to find a wolf staring back.

"Women," Kreibs says. "They shouldn't be anywhere near soldiers. They could be shot. I saw enough of that in Barcelona."

Al tries to correct him. "You said you were at Belchite." The name of his aunt's town had buzzed in Al's ears ever since. "The front is nowhere near Barcelona. We came through it by train."

"So did we. Last May. I'm talking about the street fights. The communists and anarchists. The socialists and communists. Everyone was fighting everyone. Half the women in Barcelona were toting guns and they wore those *monos* like Lapinsky's there." He lifts his chin toward the big soldier whose Spanish coveralls give him the look of a garage mechanic. Kreibs's voice softens. "Women, fighting like that." He collects himself. "A fucking mess."

Daniels sits up. "But they're all on the same side, communists, anarchists, socialists."

"There's left," Kreibs says, "and then there's *left*."

Daniels leans closely as Kreibs draws a circle in the dirt with his cold cigar. Al finds himself leaning over, too.

"At the top you've got fascism. You follow? To the right, capitalism, further down, liberalism." He stabs each with the stogie, then moves his hand to the left half of the circle. "Straight across from liberalism: socialism. Across from capitalism: anarchism. And at the very top, communism."

Daniels cries out again, "Right next to fascism? That doesn't make sense. That's why we're all here. To fight fascism."

This was nothing like the daily lessons from their commissar, Solly. His were all about maps, his head of frizzy hair bouncing as the pointer in his hand smacked across sections of Spain, sections that they hold despite overwhelming odds, sections that need more help if they are to continue holding them.

Al leans back. "Which one of them are you, Kreibs?"

Kreibs doesn't answer. All that Al can determine from his glittering blue gaze is thorough enjoyment of the irony. If Al had to guess, he'd say Kreibs isn't any of them. He has all the loyalty of a hired gun.

"I'm here because I'm not German anymore," Grunt offers. "Not like them. I can never go back home. Not now."

Lapinsky looms over them, balancing a second plate of garbanzos. "We're sure not here for the food." He folds his legs under his hulking frame, and sits awkwardly. "You joined after Guernica?"

So it was that common a reason. Al hopes they won't ask him.

Grunt says, "I was a student of architecture in Barcelona. I sketched its beautiful buildings. Then bombs began dropping on us, too. And I thought, what if these buildings are destroyed? I couldn't bear that. So I joined. You?"

"He's a Jew," Kreibs blurts. "Reason enough."

Lapinsky lifts an arm to dig into his food, but pauses to confirm, "I have an aunt and uncle still in Berlin."

Pursing his thick lips mockingly, Kreibs looks up at the sky. "War is good. I'm here to kill."

Lapinsky laughs, his mouth full of chickpeas. "You asshole."

Kreibs grins, then his eyes snap to Daniels. "What about you, kid?"

Daniels has been studying his boots, turning his leg this way and that, leaning over to rub dust from the dark leather with the sleeve of his cazadora. Now he looks up. "I was in New York — and one night I was in this club."

Kreibs jabs Al in the ribs. "Club!" he snickers.

Daniels says, "There was a Spaniard reading poetry."

"Jesus Christ," Kreibs barks. "That kind of club! I thought you meant a whorehouse."

Al pulls clear of any more elbow jabs. "Let him talk. For Christ's sake."

Daniels stammers on. "I couldn't understand him. A woman stood up after him and read it in English, but I preferred the Spanish. It was about a waltz and in Spanish it sounded like waltzing." He flushes to the roots of his fair hair. "The poet came back to Spain. I read in the paper that he was executed by the Fascists. It seems they didn't like his type. You know."

Maybe he thinks the others will ask what he means, ask why that confirms his decision to fight in Spain. But now, to Al's surprise, each of the volunteers busies himself with pouches of tobacco or boot heels that need to be pried free of stones. Each has deliberately turned away from the question. Even Kreibs. Because if they ask, Daniels will have to answer, and then what?

Instead, Kreibs says, "You haven't said anything, Johnson."

He was hoping he'd been forgotten, and he thinks for a moment before answering. He can't tell them about the German soldier, not with Grunt sitting here. "Why not join? There was nothing to keep me back home. No job, no wife."

"But still," Grunt notes, "you call it home."

"Habit." The crispness of Al's reply stops him from saying what else he is thinking, that for all he knows he can do more good right here in this field, working, than he can picking up a gun.

Eighteen

IN DRIVING SLEET AND SNOW they belly up the base of a flat-topped hill. They clip the barbed wire that circles it and roll it aside. One skein curls back and snags Al's leg, triggering an instant and unexpected plunge into a Shaughnessy garden, his limbs raked by rose canes, his reasoning mired in mud. His breath catches as he braces for the memory that will surely follow. But icy air needles the tears in his trouser leg, wet snow seeps through, burning. Al gives a yank and clambers after the villager who leads them up the back of the hill. Another platoon crawls up behind them. Al hears the soldiers' boots slopping in slush, their soft curses as they skid and slide into each other. It's such a miserable night the Fascists can't expect anyone to be out. Al pictures the enemy sitting around drinking hot chocolate, feet propped up against the fire. Maybe at tables playing cards.

The hill lies to the north and east of Teruel, a mountain city that, Kreibs says, has Spain's worst winters. A brief look at Ivan's map showed Al why both sides have fought so long for it, why it has changed hands only to be grabbed back again. It's the tip of a finger of Fascist-held land that stabs into the republican side of Spain, a misfit begging to be lopped off or expanded into something more substantial. It mocks both sides at once. On that same map this hill sits at the base of that finger, right at amputation point.

Near the top they grab their shoulder straps and pull their rifles up and over. Al has a Lee-Enfield, and he hugs it to his ribs even though it will be of little use. Kreibs has his own pistol, but when he saw the pile of battered guns that the four of them were supposed to take to the front, he disappeared for an afternoon and came back with these, from where exactly he wouldn't say. The ammunition, he added, would have to come later.

And so it had, just moments ago, when Ivan dug into his pack and pulled out a wooden box. He thumbed the top off and rattled the mixture of cartridges. Then he poured them into his hand, double-checked to see who in the rest of the platoon had what kind of weapon, and began handing them out.

Al stared at the single cartridge that was dropped into his palm. One shot.

Now, they wait, melting slush seeping through their trousers, numb fingers poised to pull feeble triggers. Nerves dance in Al's guts.

Ivan studies his watch, then raises his arm and drops it. At once they skulk half-bent to the building, then Kreibs kicks in the door and they fall to the floor as another section comes up from behind and sweeps through the room, and then the next, spewing bullets.

They had ammunition.

Al has the gun he wished he'd had the last time, but it has come with a hitch: just one shot, just one chance to redeem himself.

Chairs topple and Fascists scramble, and Al seizes his chance. He springs up, grabs his rifle by the barrel and swings it like a bat, a solid, clean club to the head of one of the Fascists trying to run. Kreibs shoots a second with his pistol.

The room goes silent and several pairs of hands rise in surrender. A white handkerchief flutters from under a table.

Kreibs flicks his pistol at them, signalling them to get up. Those who aren't injured struggle to their feet. Then Kreibs looks at Al with his upside down rifle in his hands and says, "You crazy bastard."

Al laughs. He isn't crazy. He's a new man. Here's proof.

From the wounded they harvest what they can: boots, sweaters and hats. The clubbed soldier sits up, rubbing his head. He'll be fine for marching. He can keep his boots.

Al lifts a greatcoat from the back of a chair, pulls off his poncho and buttons up the coat, tugging the poncho over top. He'll be warm, now.

"Daniels!" Kreibs calls, and strides over to the corner where Daniels stands over a slumped form. "Your goddamn leather jacket is all you ever talk about. Take it."

Daniels remains standing, staring.

"I'll do it," Al says, coming up behind them and kneeling to yank a sleeve from an arm.

The instant he touches the wrist he knows the man has just died. How quickly life leaves a body, the man's skin as slack as the leather sleeve. Al's upper lip beads with sweat and he presses it against his raised shoulder, furtively, as though he is only turning to look around the room. What he sees is Grunt, equally uncomfortable, his face wobbling into an uncertain smile as he herds prisoners to the door.

Kreibs's voice crackles in his ear, "If Daniels wants it, he does it."

Al gladly drops the sleeve and leaps to his feet, then hates himself for it, and for obeying Kreibs. "For God's sake," he counters, "He's just a child!"

"You want a child watching your back?" Daniels has crouched and is blindly tugging at the leather sleeves, sniffing loudly as he fumbles to roll the dead weight over and pull the jacket the rest of the way off. "Stop babying him."

Finally Daniels stands and begins to stuff the leather jacket into his pack.

"Put it on," Kreibs says.

Daniels's eyes go swiftly to the body it came from. Al recalls the rats slipping out from Artie's sleeves, his panicked run all the way back to the trench. A boy shouldn't have to see such things. He does what he should have done sooner. He places himself between Daniels and Kreibs.

There is movement in the room, soldiers running in and out, voices shouting, but Al is mostly aware of Kreibs, his frozen eyes and the black stub of a cigar jammed into a corner of his mouth.

Then Kreibs glances at Al's rifle still held like a bat, and a shadow of a smile touches his lips. He shrugs as though he couldn't care less what either of them does, and bellows to the others, "All right, you bastards, let's move it!"

They gather up weapons and cartridges, too, and Al realizes that this is what Kreibs really meant when he said the ammunition would come later. They'll have plenty now.

Eventually, they find the storeroom. Al and Grunt load jars of olives, bags of grain, bars of chocolate and tins of octopus into large sacks and drag them outside.

Ivan clomps back along the path of slush. He spreads his map out in the snow and shows them where the majority of the troops will be heading, slightly eastward to help with another offensive. But their platoon is among those assigned to take prisoners on a march to the train.

This is a different map from the last, no longer showing Teruel but an area to the north and east. Al follows Ivan's gloved finger as it traces their route. Afterward, he says, they will rest up in the village of Letux along with Spanish recruits. Two other towns form a triangle of encampments for the internationals: the British to the southeast in Lécera, and the Lincolns to the northeast in Belchite. Al stares at where Ivan's hand has come to rest.

"Kreibs," Ivan says, "you take Daniels, Johnson and Lapinsky. And Grunt."

With the simple words "you take," Ivan makes it official. Kreibs is their leader. Well of course. He got them the guns. Who's better experienced than Kreibs? He's been barking orders at them all day. Still, Al thinks of his wolf eyes, his cruelty over the jacket. He doesn't like it.

BY NEXT MORNING THEY ARE plodding the sloppy roads eastward, each unit taking ten prisoners and spreading out, hiking different routes into the hills. Kreibs chooses Grunt as scout, and Al regrets downplaying his experience with guns. He has more than Grunt, at least.

When the light begins to fade they stop to camp for the night.

Kreibs pulls an army shovel from his pack and spears it into the snow. "Which one of you speaks English? No one? I can't even ask if they want a smoke or — Hey! I'll be!" He grins at Al. "I guess smoke must be *español* for cigarette. This one here understands me. Eh?" He digs out a cigarette. "Translate for me and it's yours. *¿Sí?*"

The man dips his head in agreement.

"Tell them we'll be digging in for the night. We eat when the kitchen truck gets here. Got it?" The Spaniard begins speaking softly, then takes up the offered cigarette. "Good. Johnson, watch them. I'll go check with Grunt."

Al and the others pull out their shovels. "Choose four men," Al tells him.

The man and three other Spaniards begin digging. Those without shovels use their hands to lift large rocks and gradually a large dugout takes shape in the grey snow. Al shrugs his rifle off his shoulder and braces his feet.

If he has to shoot someone he'd prefer it be from a distance, or in defence because the other man is shooting at him. So far he hadn't shot anyone. But if one of these prisoners runs he'll have to.

"*Terminado*," the Spaniard informs him, still squatting as he leans on the short shovel, his breath forming clumps in the cold air. His eyes, two black slits in a long, thin face, regard Al steadily. Daniels motions to the others to sit, then collects their shovels.

"What's your name?" Al knows he shouldn't ask. Kreibs wouldn't like it. But that makes Al want to ask all the more.

"Delgado."

"You have a wife, Delgado? Children?"

"Sí. A little girl, and two boys at once."

"Twins!"

Delgado dips his head in a half bow. "Anything can happen to me now, because I have children. I may die tomorrow, but I will be alive still in them, in my sons *especialmente*."

"Just do what we ask and no one dies." Al hasn't expected to come this close to a Fascist, to know that he has a wife and children. The more he knows, the more he wants to know. He regards the ten young men. None of them look like Fascists. "Where are all of you from?"

"Everywhere," Delgado says. "Me, not far from Durango. A place of cool air and wonderful streams. In the summer we are the envy of all *Las Españas*."

Al pictures the Yukon. Delgado draws a line in the snow with a finger. "The French border." He points near one end. "Barcelona." He points at the other end. "*Soy Vasco*. I am Basque." He raises his head a little when he says this, but not much.

The name Delgado doesn't sound Basque, and Al is about to ask him about that. Then he realizes something else and his face burns. "You sided with the Fascists — after what they did to Guernica?"

Delgado's voice is flat when he replies, "Durango, too."

"Then why —" Al is finally seeing him for what he is. The enemy. "Your planes bombed people, ordinary people!"

From his hunched position Delgado's low-slung eyelids seem to underscore his weariness with the subject. "We are neither of you. *Nacionales. Republicanos.* You think there is a difference? I tell you something, Mackpack."

Al draws himself up.

"They come to your village with guns. 'Pick a side,' they say, 'and pick it now because we will not ask you twice.' You know what that means, of course. You pick the side of the one who asks, the one with the gun, or you get shot.

"I tell you something else. When they ask, I not even sure what side they are." He hikes up one shoulder. "When I learn who they are I say to myself, fine. I pick the side of the one who asks, and I live for another day."

THIS NIGHT THE KITCHEN TRUCK is a cart drawn up the steep trails by a burro. Al spoons up a mouthful of stew and chews. The strange taste, he has learned, is burro meat and he wonders if the poor animal that has tugged the cart could smell it.

Daniels stands guard while the prisoners line up for their meals.

"Artillery!" he cries, his rifle aimed at distant mountaintops and the green light of gunfire flickering across the black horizon.

"No," Al says. "Those are northern lights." All of them, even the prisoners, gaze up. "Where I come from," he tells them, considering each word, the potential heft of the lie and yet how true it feels, "you see them all the time. But I didn't think I'd see them here."

"My brother said the same thing about gunfire."

Al doesn't need to look to know who is speaking. The voice is clearly Grunt's.

So, his brother was a soldier. That's almost worse. "Was he killed?" Al stares at the sky as he waits for the answer.

"No. He survived."

Al knows what that meant. "You must have hated the English." *Us*, he is thinking.

"The French, too. But you know, I was ten years old — and look at me now, in an English battalion."

The ice green bands of light undulate with the rhythms of

Grunt's voice, an arctic dance in a Spanish sky. It seems as if the lights have followed Al here and that everything he's experienced in the last few years has been leading to this moment.

He will die here. It strikes him at once. This is why he has come to Spain, this is how he'll make up for the past. It's just a matter of when, and where.

LATE IN THE AFTERNOON OF the next day a light snow falls over a field of battle-blackened soil, not enough to cover the ruptured ground that exposes a corpse and a chunk of rusting equipment.

A road skirts the edge of the field, then veers to the right around the base of a hill before climbing. On the right shoulder is a drop-off. From around the bend in this road Grunt staggers into sight, white-faced, holding his side. Al feels the breath go out of his own lungs. Grunt has been shot. This is all wrong. This is not what Al had envisioned just yesterday, and his guilt deepens as Grunt falls, leaving a dark stain in the snow. Grunt struggles back to his feet, his rubbery features taut with pain, his side soaked in blood.

Hope rushes through Al. The bullet missed his guts. It missed his lungs and heart. He'll live. What's more, he won't have to fight anymore. He'll be safe now.

Al leaps forward before Kreibs can order him back, runs out and catches Grunt as he collapses again. In a strained whisper he shouts into his face, "We'll get you fixed up. You hear me? You'll be all right!"

Then he puts a shoulder under Grunt's chest, half lifts him and staggers back.

Kreibs turns to Delgado. "You tell them, one sound and I blow your heads off. Every one of you."

As soon as Delgado translates, Kreibs takes Grunt's arm and loops it over his shoulder, then orders Al and Delgado to go back with a shovel each.

Together they dig into the dirt and snow. With each plunge of the blade Al turns the earth over and buries any sign of Grunt's blood, then he pats it down with more snow. As they work, the others roll over the edge of the road and disappear.

When the whine of truck engines sound, Al and Delgado slip over the edge, too, and huddle against the wall of mud, hidden by the overhang of the road. The others must have scooted further along the ridge, beyond the bend, taking turns carrying Grunt, because there is no sign of them. For now, he and Delgado have to stay put.

They hear the gears grinding down the sloping road, closer and closer. When the trucks shake the ground directly over them Al clenches his teeth. They're stopping.

Heavy boots slop through the slush above them. A cough. A sigh. Then a stream of urine spurts over Delgado's head and sizzles into a patch of snow. Delgado squeezes his eyes closed against the spray that the winds blow toward his face. Al keeps the rifle barrel resting across his left shoulder, pointing directly at Delgado.

Then they hear the zip of a heavy object being dragged over the snow. A body tumbles headfirst over them, landing like a crumpled tent a few feet away.

Within seconds the surrounding snow, inch by inch, turns dark. Al digs his feet into the ground and pushes himself backwards.

Delgado's eyes narrow until they seem to close, his lip lifts in a sneer. Al forces himself to stop moving.

The Fascists hear the movement, though, because footsteps return and a round is fired into the body to make sure it's dead. The hot lead lifts the body and, for a moment, it's alive again, arms and legs dancing, provoking laughter from above.

When the trucks roll out, Al pushes himself up with his rifle. Delgado is already standing.

"Let's go," Al says.

Delgado smiles. He says something in a foreign language, his Basque language, Al presumes.

"I'll shoot," Al adds.

Delgado sneers toward the crumpled body that had set Al scrambling backwards.

"Jesus Christ, Delgado." Al grips his rifle. "Don't make me do this. Because I will."

Delgado doesn't know him at all. He isn't afraid to kill — is that what he thinks? No, his fear had come from killing, from that other war, from going down into that dark place. Right now Al feels no hammering of the heart, no jolt of energy, just a sadness filling him as he sees this moment rushing toward its inevitable conclusion. He isn't shaking or even sweating. No bits of grit slide under his skin to grate at his nerves. If Al lets Delgado escape then he will be shot. Kreibs will have no choice.

"I cannot go to your prison," Delgado says in English. "If I do, I die."

"You'll die if you don't move." Al sighs as he mouths the empty words.

"I mean here," Delgado says, and touches his temple.

An all-clear whistle sounds from up ahead. "It's Kreibs. Let's go."

Delgado turns and walks away. Al stands with his rifle raised. How can he shoot a man in the back? Delgado picks his way among boulders and climbs up onto the road, convinced, perhaps, that Al won't.

The crack of the rifle shot must have echoed clear around the bend. Kreibs comes scrambling over the ridge.

Al springs onto the road. "I shot him in the leg," he cries, and runs to the heap of uniform in the snow. He crouches to turn the body over. Then he sits back heavily. A red circle blooms over Delgado's heart. A matching circle widens in the slush beneath him. "I shot him in the leg!" he repeats.

Kreibs elbows past Al and flops the body onto its side, feels around, finally pulls a long knife from inside Delgado's boot. The body slumps back against the road.

"From the kitchen truck. Can you believe it? Here. Want it?"

Al shakes his head and stands up unsteadily.

The whole time they were under that cliff Delgado could have pulled the knife. Why didn't he? What convinced him there was no need? Arrogance? Or friendship?

Nineteen

AL WADES THROUGH TALL ORCHARD grass on a bench of land above the town of Letux, trying to compose a letter. Yesterday he'd sat for an entire evening with a blank sheet in front of him, not knowing what to think of the war anymore, what to write to Jack.

The four of them haven't bothered learning the names of the Spanish recruits. They're all boys. Al glances at them now, laughing in the sunshine. How long will they last?

It has been raining and the weight of the water bends the boughs of the trees until droplets run off. Eventually the dark branches spring free, releasing a sudden stream that spurts outward. The remaining blossoms glisten and drip and the emerging sun cooks the air until it is sickeningly sweet.

Al breathes deeply, testing words from memory, "Faces, in a station."

No, that wasn't it.

Daniels's leather jacket creaks as he shifts around to regard Al. He wouldn't wear the jacket as long as they had the prisoners with them. *What if it belonged to one of their friends?* he asked. Now, even on the warmest spring days, he never takes it off.

"Ezra Pound," Al explains. "I was trying to remember one of his poems."

A rough voice calls out, "That Fascist bastard!"

Al stops and turns. Kreibs.

"You didn't know that? Christ, he's over in Italy right now kissing Mussolini's ass! Been there for five years."

The author of all that poetry a Fascist? It's too incredible to be a lie.

Al waits for the others to mention Delgado's name, as they have for two weeks, marvelling at his ability to befriend a Fascist, then shoot him. Al half-hoped to strike up a conversation about poetry with Daniels, who barely acknowledges him these days. Daniels also liked Delgado, who was a Basque, not a real Fascist, he said. More importantly, Delgado knew of Daniels's poet, a man named Lorca, and told him his favourite poem was about a bullfighter, and that he would try to recite some lines for him.

He never got the chance.

One time Daniels asked, *Why didn't you just shoot him in the leg?* Didn't he believe Al had tried? It was another chance to confirm that he had purged himself. But he botched it. Grunt might have understood how he felt, how the line between friend and enemy could shift like that, forcing him into an action he couldn't control. But Grunt had been trucked out to a hospital.

Now Al has given Daniels further reason to hate him. Al's poet is a Fascist, a real Fascist, who chose sides with no gun pointed at his head. Worse, the man allied himself with the same people who killed Lorca, who bombed Guernica.

Perhaps Pound has a core as dark as his own, a potential as hideous, and for a moment he wonders if this is the real bond between them.

But no. The name Pound no sooner settles on his brain than it conjures up Chinese colours of northern lights and sorrow like November rain. The only darkness comes from the sadness behind these lines. His compassion for others, rendered in haunting images, is what draws Al. If it's possible to separate the man from his words, and Al hopes it is, then it's possible to loathe one and love the other. Certainly, he's not about to abandon one because of the other. What would happen to him if he let go of such lines, such pictures? He'd be no different than those others on the ship who claimed you can't eat art. Of course you can. He saw it for himself in Paris. He devoured it the way he devoured the pages in Jenny's books, the images in both that seemed to be plucked from his own life.

Has he ever pulled out the book in front of Kreibs? He doesn't think so. There hasn't been time for any reading, they're too close to the action. Maybe back at Tarazona, though. He can't be sure. All he knows is that he must act now before someone discovers the book.

They march down, out of the orchard, and onto the road that runs through the village.

"I'll catch up with you," Al says, and while the others amble toward the bodega he climbs the steps, looking behind him, and closes the door to their room.

He fishes his pack from under the bed, then sits and pulls out *Personae*. He runs his thumb back and forth against the edge of the pages, a gambler getting ready to shuffle the deck, wondering how to leave himself the best hand. Jenny gave him this book. He hopes she'll forgive him.

Slowly, he tears the cover from the spine. Then the back cover. Threads pop, the spine bursts. The cantos spill from their bindings, page after page. He flips past his favourites, the Cathay poems, then begins tearing again.

He recalls his dismay once that someone would tear an entire story from a magazine. But here he is gutting this book of all that makes it a book, leaving himself just fragments.

He jams the covers and spine between the wall and bureau where no one will be cleaning any time soon. Then he gathers up the torn pages and begins shredding them into tiny flakes so small, no single line can be deciphered. To the top margins of the remaining middle pages he applies the sharp edge of his knife, pressing down until they give way like butter. He tears the thin strips of page numbers and poem titles into confetti, too.

All of these he scoops into his hands and carries to the open window. In the distance, far beyond the tiled rooftops and curved roads, are the flat-topped hills so peculiar to this land. They make him think of the flatiron building in Vancouver, the Europe Hotel, and at once his thoughts are back in that rainy city, walking up Pender Street, the carts, the steam from the kitchens, the medley of voices in his ears even as he leans out the window and opens his hands, letting the tiny pieces flutter down and settle onto the stones below like petals. He leans on the sill, watching, then turns back to the bed. He rolls the trimmed sheaves of favourite lines into his pack. They won't give him away. Who but he would recognize them now?

He clatters down the stairs and steps out onto the street, over the petals, to join his unit.

They're at a table close to the fire. Al settles into a chair, stretches out until his feet touch the hearth, taking pleasure in the warmth, until he spots a paper blossom stuck to one heel. Before he can pull his foot back Kreibs reaches forward, presses a finger against the heel and studies the single, dry petal. Al holds his breath.

But Kreibs simply rubs his thumb against his fingertips thoughtfully, rolling the scrap into a tiny ball that he flicks into the open fire.

TWO DAYS LATER AL IS in Belchite. On a map, the town looks like the Crescent, where he painted the ceilings of mansions: roads branch out from it like spokes on a wheel. The village itself bears no resemblance to that wealthy neighbourhood. It's set on a low hill surrounded by olive groves and farmland. While it must have been a pretty place once, the cathedrals and shops have been turned inside out from the last battle, the plaster blasted from the bricks, outer walls torn away and roofs lifted, reducing them to ragged pink frames of terracotta. Skeletal dogs slink past them up the narrow streets while rats swollen to the size of dogs waddle along the bricks.

There is a foul smell on the wind, latrines that need sprinkling with lime.

He'd rather not have the other three of his unit with him, Kreibs especially, but Ivan won't permit the trip otherwise. The Fascists might return at any time to try to take the town back. They hold the city of Zaragoza, only a short distance upriver.

The four of them pass trucks as well as troops from the Lincoln Battalion, but those numbers thin the closer they get to his aunt's house on the outskirts of town.

He wonders if she looks like his mother. Who is she to him, except a tiny out-of-focus figure in the picnic scene in his mother's photo album? Still, other than his brother, she is his only flesh-and-blood relative. He will have to be careful about revealing his real identity to her, if she has survived the attacks. Daniels and Lap might not care. But Kreibs? Hendersen said any protestor who clashed with police had to volunteer for the army under a false name. So Al knows he isn't the only one. But there are spies every-where. If communists don't trust the anarchists, and they're on the same side, what might happen if his false identity is discovered? For all Al knows, he might be accused of spying for the Fascists. What would they do to him then? He pictures a mob, drunk on his blood.

When they reach his aunt's house they find it intact, though the windows are boarded up and the garden wall pocked with bullet holes. Al knows that in a civil war, where towns have been taken and then retaken, only two possibilities exist behind any door: our side or theirs. His aunt's family may have fled. Anyone could be in there.

They slide along the wall, edge around the corner, two on each side of the door. They listen through the wood, hear nothing inside. Kreibs gives the nod. Al stands back and puts his boot to the door. They burst forward in the usual formation, Daniels to the right, Lapinsky to the left, Al on the ground and Kreibs immediately behind.

Then, against all training, they freeze in mute surrender.

In the seconds that pass Al is vaguely aware of tiny sounds in the room: the ticking of metal expanding in sunlight, the creaking of floorboards beneath them, the rhythm — he is sure he can hear it — of blood pumping in every man around him.

He is the first to move. With a push of the elbows he boosts himself up and shoulders the rifle. He tries to stop the smile pulling at his lips.

At the far end of the kitchen several elderly villagers huddle behind a young woman who stares defiantly at the soldiers, her head thrown back, her blouse thrown open, her bare breasts gleaming in the soft morning light.

Then several old women totter forward, clustering around her like a husk around tender fruit. The air in the kitchen comes alive with the sound of tearing cloth as, reeling in circles with the effort, they struggle to rip their dresses open too. The matrons seem determined to show their solidarity to a cause that remains a puzzle to Al. Their swollen knuckles fumble with buttonholes and clasps until, finally, their leathered breasts swing free from their garments like empty wine sacks.

Even Kreibs is speechless.

At last, Al pulls off his beret and blurts, "Alex Johnson! Mackenzie-Papineau Battalion." He has no idea if he salutes next. He hopes not.

"Inglés?" the young woman cries.

Al lifts a shoulder and looked helplessly at her small breasts that seem to have been pinched from the flesh around them, the chocolate nipple at the tip of each disproportionately large. He feels a tightening in the groin and clears his throat.

"¡Bastardes!" she swears. She slaps her blouse closed and buttons furiously. "Not Fascists?"

The old women are slower, their knotted fingers working the buttonholes.

"You crawl around the house!" she says. "You kick in the door! We think you are Fascists!"

She's tall for a woman, big-boned but lean. A tangle of dark hair frames sharp cheekbones and a thin throat. She folds one arm over another. "What do you want?"

Al replies slowly, as though his thoughts are wading in the sludge of a dream. "You speak English."

"What do you want?" she repeats.

"I'm looking for my aunt," and his hand snaps forward to shake hers, "mi tia."

She recoils from the offered hand as if the possibility still exists that he is a Fascist.

He pulls his hand back and stuffs it in a pocket. "Señora Ellen Montoya."

Her eyes narrow with suspicion. Then she looks away. "She is gone."

The dusty beam of sunlight from the dirty windows traces the edge of a long, ugly scar along her thin neck and chin. She glances back and sees him looking. But she doesn't try to hide the scar. She tucks her wild hair behind her ear, further exposing it.

"Muerto?" Al asks. "Dead?"

"Sí." She presses her palm over her left breast, now covered by the cotton blouse, indicating her heart.

The family affliction. "*Mi consolencio*. Regrets, you know? Sorry."

She stares at him until he looks around the room. The shelves that climb the walls are empty. No pots on the stove or dishes in the sink. Dust grizzles every surface. These people must be starving. Why else offer herself like that? He smells the faint onion whiff of fear on her and determines to offer help.

He reaches into his pack. At once the knot of old villagers, women and men, bristle with knives, old shotguns, a pitchfork. This is what they have been planning for the Fascist intruders. She wasn't offering herself; she was the distraction. He shakes his head slightly. They would have all been killed.

"Not Fascists." Al says it loudly. Surely the woman understood this already. She called him Inglés. He asked about his aunt. But he raises his empty palms anyway. "Okay." Then he repeats it, "o-kay." He tries to look serious. "*Momento*. I'll go slowly. Sí?"

The villagers study him, rustic weapons still drawn. The woman stands perfectly still, a bent table fork in her dangling hand. Its crooked tines point to bare legs beneath an uneven brown hem of a skirt. On her feet she wears men's workboots.

Al reaches into his pack again. When his hand appears with a tin of octopus, several in the room gasp. He produces an orange next, then chocolate.

Kreibs, Lapinsky and Daniels all do the same, emptying onto the wooden table their haversacks of cigarette packages, tins of octopus, more chocolate, loot from the Fascist storeroom. Then they step back.

She looks up, and for the first time Al notices the wide, impish mouth — how could he have missed that — and the hair. He expected a young girl, but, he adds up the years, is once again surprised at how time has overtaken him. It has been only a couple of years since that portrait was destroyed in the raid on the hobo camp, but it has been a dozen years, maybe more, since it was taken.

To be certain, Al asks, "What is your name?" Then he tries it in Spanish. "Your *nombre?*"

"Magdalena-Rose Montoya."

He knew it. The girl in the photograph. Little Maggie.

"Sit," she commands, and the four soldiers tumble into chairs. Then she glares at him. Has he been staring? Of course he has.

She sweeps the food and cigarettes aside and sits at the table, directly opposite Al. Two matrons step forward hugging wine skins to their chests, and for a moment Al thinks their blouses are still open. With a crimped smile he watches as they begin pouring wine into cups.

For the English, they must be thinking. He spies an old man in the corner beside the cold stove, drinking wine the Spanish way, from a wine skin held up in both hands, a stream spurting into the back of his throat.

Magdalena-Rose rests her narrow wrists on the table's edge, her hands together as though she is praying. There is grime under her nails but she has perfectly long, tapered fingers. She would have feet to match, long and slender, like a dancer's, the kind that look elegant in heels. He pictures her in a deep red dress, draped over his arm as they dance.

"How is it she is your tia?" she asks. "I know of no Johnson family."

She has probably heard of him, her mother's sister's son. He glances over at Kreibs. His guts tell him to keep quiet about that.

"My mother — they were distant cousins," he lies, "way back on the Clark side."

"Clark." She folds her arms. "Then we are cousins, too."

"Yes," he says. "Distant cousins." A small lie.

"Mi —" she searches for the English word, but settles on French, "—*grand-mère*. She was Rose Clark. I am named after her."

Yes, Al wants to say, so was his sister.

"I am sorry about your mother," he repeats. Then, carefully, he asks, "Why are all of you still here? Why didn't you leave?"

"We did. But the Fascists, they lost the battle. As soon as possible, I came back to get my things. What is left of them." She glances toward a trunk and he thinks of her dragging her possessions through the war as his mother dragged hers across an ocean and a continent.

Kreibs drains his cup, checks his watch. "Eleven hundred hours."

They stand, say awkward farewells and file out the door. Al is last, and when he turns to her, she looks evenly at him. Her eyes are chocolate, too.

"You must come back to see us," and then she adds, "Alejandro."

Alejandro. He likes the sound of that. He'd be willing to bury Albert Fraser for the pleasure of hearing her say that name, Alejandro

THEY RETURN THE NEXT DAY to bring more food. The same villagers are busy tearing sheets and tying up bundles, preparing to flee.

"We haven't heard of an attack," he tells her.

"We have."

"Where will you go?"

"Barcelona. Anywhere else," and she shrugs.

Lapinsky and Daniels drag the trunk across the floor. Outside the open door is a cart, and an old woman herds them toward it. Kreibs stands watch by the only window that isn't shattered and boarded up, pistol cradled in his arms.

"We need water for the trip," Magdalena says, and she picks up a chipped, white cup from the counter. It's full of grey dishwater. "The pipes are broken, but our neighbour has a pump."

Below the counter are two pails. She looks at him and then at Kreibs, who steps forward, ready to leave his post at the window, until Al glares at him. He steps back, grinning, and Al seizes both pails and follows her out the door, an empty bucket banging against each knee. Lapinsky and Daniels are already outside, hoisting the trunk into the cart.

The neighbour's home shares the same garden wall pitted with bullet holes. She pushes aside the wooden gate that hangs by only one hinge. The pump sits outside a wooden shed that might have housed burros or goats.

She primes the pump with the cup of grey water, holding it under the spout, cranking the handle vigorously until the suction draws the water up into the pipe. It sputters and coughs. She pulls the cup away and he shoves the pail forward, water gushing into it from the spout.

Water reaches the rim and while he slides one pail out and the other in, she lets the pump handle drop, sending water spurting forward. It lands like a wet rope around his boots.

Except for the rifle over his shoulder, they must look like any other village couple gone to fetch water, a domestic ritual that, day by day, must feel as binding as any piece of paper or church cere-mony. Certainly, he has never felt closer to a woman than he feels now, the same water that splurged onto her skin, running over his.

This would be the time to say so. If nothing else, he should offer to take her away, to bring her back to his country where she'd be safe.

War. It ignites concerns that have never occurred to him before yesterday, when his own well-being and that of his unit were all that mattered, and it comes out at once, "It will be dangerous on the road."

She continues pumping. "This is war. Everywhere is dangerous."

"How will I find you?"

She studies the flow until it dwindles to a trickle. He watches as well, hoping. "I'll send you word," she says at last.

"Good." An agreement has been reached, though of what sort he isn't sure. But he will see her again, and his thoughts race forward, imagining that moment and what might happen next, impatient to get there.

He closes his fist around the handle of one bucket. She insists on carrying the second bucket between them and he doesn't object, her hand brushing his and water sloshing over their skin all the way back to the kitchen.

Twenty

HIS BOOTS SLAM ONTO THE pavement as he dodges holes and pools of dark water. A shadow streaks across the road and he runs, the metal underbelly closer to his face than anything he'd seen in the *Palais de l'Air*. The German Stuka dives down and begins firing. Bullets pepper the soft dirt, raising puffs of orange smoke. Al spins on one foot, reverses direction mid-step, then back again, running amidst a swarm of bullets. He skirts buildings, leaps a fence, crab-walks across the yard. A shell whistles and he falls forward, digging his hands into the earth to try to hold on. But the ground ripples under him, lifting him high and then dropping him hard. To his right, shells slit the river with a sound like the tearing of silk. Then he is up again, despite Kreibs's shouted warning to stay, reeling along the shattered street until he comes to Magdalena's house once more.

The other three catch up and enter.

The room is empty.

Al creeps up the narrow stairs that lead to a tiny, low-ceilinged sleeping area. It's empty, too, but for a photograph. Magdalena, before the war, in a white dress and heels, her hair brushed neatly in place. She wears lipstick. He tips the photograph toward the grey light from the window. No scar.

With his thumbs he pops the cracked glass free, puts the picture in his pocket and buttons it. Then he drums down the stairs.

SHE WAS RIGHT ABOUT THE Fascists.

A few hours after he left her yesterday, orders came down from command to prepare for an attack. Al paced the barracks, the streets, the mess hall. Had she made it out? Was she safe?

They marched westward, and in the dark they scraped shallow trenches into the rocky soil along a ridge. His thoughts returned again and again to the sound of her voice telling him, *I'll send you word.* Then in the early hours this morning the countryside erupted. The ridge was blasted by shell fire and the air thickened with smoke and pulverized rock. The sound was in his teeth, knocking around inside his skull, vibrating through his bowels. There was no shooting back. Al couldn't see in the dust and smoke.

The walls of their trenches were hit next and the dirt sluiced down the hillsides, exposing them and forcing them to scutter around the ridge. Al crouched behind an outcropping of boulders and brush, black clouds rolling over him, and saw his chance. After each blast he swam with the falling earth and rock, around and down the side and around again until his feet touched the road behind the hill. The other three tumbled out after him. Kreibs attempted to tackle him, but Al shot out from under, his lungs suddenly strong, his legs stretching, running, running, along the road back to Magdalena's home. By the time the other three caught up to him they were all winded.

At any moment on the unauthorized run Kreibs could have turned back and reported him. Could have shot him, too. They were risking charges of desertion because of him. But they had followed him this far, and continued with him into Belchite to look for her.

Now, the four of them creep back out of Magdalena's yard and down the road.

Lapinsky walks backwards, Kreibs marches with eyes forward, Al and Daniels check the ditches. A family of refugees in a mule-drawn cart appears, heading away from the very town they seek.

"Azuara?" Kreibs asks, and the man makes a motion of slicing his throat with his fingers. The town has fallen.

Their troops would have pulled out already and headed straight for that triangle of encampments. That is where they must return, too.

Kreibs bites into his cigar and says, "Shortcut."

They plunge off the road and into the hillsides of brush and rock. The latrine stink Al smelled before wafts over them, stronger, this time familiar.

They dig into their pockets. Al pulls two cigarettes from a pack, taps the ends against his palm until each crinkles like an accordion, ensuring a better fit, and then he stuffs one up each nostril. The others do the same and then they climb over an embankment and drop down into a mass of bodies. Ruined faces stare at nothing. Arms are flung wide or folded tight around raised knees. Still others lie with limbs and trunks perfectly flat, like suits recently pressed.

Ours? Theirs? Both. Kreibs plugs enemy corpses with bullets, just to be sure, though the smell that permeates even their tobacco-bunged noses tells them there is no life here.

The harsh sunlight leaves little unexposed in this field. Here, unlike the Somme, rats are rats, not some unseen force that enlivens the sleeves of the fallen, but simply vermin feeding on the dead. Al looks quickly at Daniels. You can never guess how a man will react. He is mildly surprised that it isn't young Daniels but big Lapinsky who is bending double. The footing is precarious. Al thinks of loggers he once saw dancing on floating booms near Vancouver, though the men were more graceful and didn't vomit onto the slippery logs as Lapinsky is doing now. The sight triggers sympathy waves of sickness in Al's guts that, somehow, the stink and rotting corpses did not. He breathes deeply through the tobacco, taking in more of the foul smell along with the sweet, and calms himself by thinking of Magdalena. That tangle of hair. Tall, lean, striding confidently toward Barcelona, her possessions in a cart that couldn't possibly leave the smooth surface of the road, thereby encountering this. Al is equally glad Grunt never had to see this — and to know what his brother saw when he fought the English.

At the far side of the plain, they leave the bodies and the smell behind and pull the cigarettes from their nostrils. Al sees the road ahead already swarming with refugees, a continuous grey procession. Behind it, distant towns smouldering.

The air grows thick with smoke as they climb onto the road, and this smell makes him hungry. All he can think of is bacon.

From a side road, volunteer soldiers emerge, visible only from the chest down in the low-hanging haze, their hands filled with crystal goblets, a silver tea service, a live chicken, a lamp. It doesn't matter what battalion they're from. They're busy looting instead of fighting. They've gone mad with greed.

A woman sits on a crumbling wall and looks vacantly at the procession of people. As Al nears her, he sees a man tugging at a bundle in her lap. Her eyes come to life and her mouth forms an *O*. The man gives one yank and it unfurls like a grubby cocoon, spilling the small, lifeless form into the mud. The unravelled cloth falls from the woman's hands, piles over top. Al leaps to the side to avoid stepping on it.

"Jesus Christ," he snaps. "Are you crazy?" Has the man never seen a grieving mother before? Al scoops up the mess of swaddling, it weighs less than a cat, and drops it into the woman's arms. "We bury," he tells her, and brandishes his shovel.

Kreibs pushes forward. "Johnson. What the fuck are you doing?"

But Al has already taken the woman by the arm and is helping her along the edge of the road.

This is familiar, too. Back in Vancouver he discovered a crowd buzzing angrily outside a house on Union Street. The front lawn was littered with shirts and shoes and lamps and wooden boxes. On the veranda stood a pale-haired woman with a face just like this woman's, her lips a circle of silent grief as two men in tweed caps and suits grabbed everything that was precious to her, and hurled it over the railing. With each thud of a crate came the tinkling of breaking glass.

Al leapt up the steps two at a time. He couldn't stop the eviction but he could stop them from smashing her things. Women cared about their possessions. Men didn't, but they should know that women did. They had mothers.

He insisted on carrying the remainder of the woman's goods into the yard. Bone china, from the way it clinked inside the box. Stemware, from the ping of crystal hitting crystal. She would have little use for such things, wherever she was going. Still, he helped her repack some of the stemware, and then stack the crates neatly. A small gesture, but it seemed to make the moment bearable. Sometimes it's all you can do.

Now, along this crowded road in the Spanish Aragon, Al leads the mother straight to a heap of goods in the grass, most likely discarded by the more sane of the looters, who found the items too bulky to carry. Al scans the pile. A little crate would do, perhaps, or a suitcase. He lets go of her arm and picks up an oak sewing chest the size of a large jewellery box. His mother had one just like it. He shakes out the spools of thread, the gleaming silver hoops for embroidery, the needles and scissors, until there is nothing inside but the quilted satin pin cushion of the upper lid, a restful moss green. He plucks out the remaining pins. The harm they could do to small hands and eyes. The mother has been watching him the whole time, and when he holds the chest open she places the tiny bundle inside it.

LATER THAT DAY THE FOUR of them crawl up a hill to the edge of a town. Kreibs looks through the field glasses, then hands them over without a word to Al. Nazi officers in black, smoking cigarettes.

Panzer tanks draped in brilliant red flags with black swastikas. The composure of the Nazis in the midst of all this — the teeming masses of refugees, the fields of bodies, the burning towns. Al's guts fill with ice. The four of them slither backwards, back into the chaos of the roads.

In front of Al an old man staggers with the effort of keeping up, then disappears. The crowd lunges and Al trips over something, street rubble, he hopes. He looks down but can see nothing save necks and bundled goods. Then there is no ground. The crowd carries him as though he has no legs or feet.

Yet another side road veers sharply to the left, and Kreibs takes it. The three of them straggle after him.

The town ahead is perched atop a high hill. In the days before planes such a location would have made the town as safe as a fortress. But as they reach the empty streets, Al sees that most of the buildings had been blown up or burnt in aerial bombings. Somehow a short stretch of street in the village centre has been missed.

Daniels turns in slow circles, his rifle slung horizontally across the back of his shoulders. "This is worse," he says, "than if the whole place was destroyed."

He's right. This perfect street — swept stones, potted flowers, polished glass in shop windows — is out of place, offensive in the midst of all the rubble.

They find stale bread on the shelves of a bakery and carry the loaves outside, tearing into them as they drop down, backs against the fountain in the square. Only Daniels refuses the food. He sits to one side, arms around a raised knee, head leaning back against the fountain's bowl, staring up at the grey sky. Al stops chewing as he watches him, can still see his slow dance, rifle across his shoulders. Daniels doesn't look like a kid anymore. He has slept and marched in that jacket and it has taken on the contours of his body. Coated in dust, it appears as aged as his chalky face.

It's an unsettling sight and Al looks away. Directly across from him, a shop window displays delicate shoes with high heels that are lined up in a curve. He studies them, then gets to his feet and moves closer. He chooses a pair that looks the right size, that she would not think frivolous, but elegant all the same, open-toed, the glamour coming from the simple lines, the cool, creamy colour. If she wears these with her white dress she will look as though she is walking on heels of ice.

He jabs quickly with the butt of his rifle. The smooth plate shatters and the blades of glass skate across the pavement.

IN THE BROWN SMUDGE OF daylight the next morning, they return to the road.

North of Alcañiz, a convoy of their own trucks finds them and the bumpy ride takes them over hills and around several bends until at last the brakes squeak and they come to a stop. Al jumps out into the protective circle made by the trucks. They are on the outskirts of a town that appears to be deserted.

Kreibs pitches a stub of cigar onto the ground and crushes it with his heel. Then he looks up and his voice is almost cheery. "Solly!" he calls out. "Son of a bitch."

Solly is slumped against a tailgate until Kreibs gives him three quick slaps on the back.

He straightens and asks, "Any of you see Ivan? No?" Then he digs into his pocket and pulls out a letter. "The mail made it through. Alejandro Johnson!"

The three of them burst into laughter at once, and crank up their voices to mimic a woman's. "Alejandro!" they tease. "It's for yo-o-o-u!"

Al grabs the thin envelope and walks away, studying the feminine handwriting. Then he tears it open and pulls out a fragment of paper on which is written an address in Barcelona, nothing more.

As he reads it he can hear Daniels. "You think we'll lose this war?"

"War?" Kreibs spits on the ground. "We haven't fired a shot. This is a retreat."

Al memorizes the address in his hands, then tears the paper to shreds. The pieces settle into the mud, turning the colour of saw-dust. Then he calls out to Solly, "Anyone taking mail back?"

Al has a letter to Jack already sealed and addressed. Now he reaches into his pack for the shoes.

SMOKE FROM GUNFIRE DRIFTS ABOUT the town, obscuring all but the tallest buildings: the church, the train station, the town hall. All the towns have become the same town. Kreibs names this one Casket, and it fits.

They creep down a hill littered with tombstones, abandoned shovels, a rusted wheelbarrow, a bucket, while the group ahead of them runs then drops, runs then drops, all the way into the town.

The four of them wait until a single shot rings out and they know that the sniper in the church tower has fallen. But the shot gives away their location.

Al begins to crawl forward. Within seconds a reply shot strikes Daniels as he steps around a monument, hitting him in the shoulder and lifting him high. Another bullet strikes him, an upward shot this time, the force spinning him, arms hanging, legs dangling, against the grey sky until yet another shot slams him into the ground.

In the hail of bullets a whistle sounds. Al covers his head and a shell hits the dirt and then twangs against the old wheelbarrow. He lifts his head, laughing crazily, tears streaming as he feels his skull. It missed him.

But Daniels. He jerks his head to the left and only then sees that Kreibs is down too. Al lunges to his feet as the air snaps around his ears. He and Lapinsky fall into a new formation never planned out loud but always understood. Al shoulders Kreibs to the safety of a pile of rocks, Lapinsky rolls Daniels down a slope just to Al's right, out of range of gunfire.

Lapinsky crawls back for Daniels's blue hat with its silver pin and returns under a buzz of bullets to place it on his friend's head. Then he lifts rocks to cover him. Al can't bear to see the leather jacket disappearing. He turns back to Kreibs, whose hand paws at an inner pocket, then falls away empty.

Al opens Kreibs's jacket and finds a wound the size of a helmet, an angry red hole carved from his guts by a chunk of metal peeled from the rusted wheelbarrow. It's still embedded under his ribs. Blood streams steadily onto the ground.

Al slaps his hands over his own pockets, as though a remedy lies somewhere in them. Kreibs's pale eyes circle the air for a point of reason, a point on which to settle, and when they find it in the grey sky that boils above, they never move again.

For a moment Al simply stares down, then he digs into Kreibs's pocket for his last letters to send to his family. Instead, he feels something deep within an inner pocket and pulls out a leather booklet like a passport. They were supposed to leave them back at headquarters. He opens it, finds a letter tucked inside and unfolds it. A government crest, a letter of introduction. *To whom it may concern*. He scans it from top to bottom and then his arms drop to his sides.

Kreibs was an informant for the cops. The Royal Canadian Mounted cops. What else could this mean? Al tips his head back. He would laugh but he can barely swallow. He opens the booklet again, and the letter. Kreibs isn't his name, either.

All of them thought that Kreibs must be short for something else, Kreibelhoff, maybe, and that he'd have a first name like Karl. Kreibs never indulged them with an answer.

Well, it doesn't matter now. His name was Eugene Tremblay.

Anger blossoms like a red flower in his brain. Al reaches inside his pack and pulls out the tattered sheets of *Personae* that he kept hidden from Kreibs, that he destroyed because of him. For what? Kreibs wouldn't have cared about those poems. He was no hired gun spying for the communists. He was spying on the communists for the Canadian government.

Fresh troops pound past as Al flips through the clumps of pages. He thinks of reading them aloud, shouting them at Kreibs's corpse, because he was Kreibs no matter what the papers said.

It would be a bitter eulogy.

All he can summon is an accusation, suddenly clear, though it has scudded across his brain more than once before.

"You shot Delgado."

The sight of Delgado's crumpled body had so disturbed Al he didn't think to check his leg. Kreibs had. That was how he found the knife. Perhaps Al wounded Delgado after all. The echo he heard must have been a second shot. Kreibs's. At the time, all he saw was that a bullet had struck Delgado's heart and it burst like overripe fruit. Al stares down. He looked very much as Kreibs does now.

Al always thought Kreibs was just a son of a bitch, but it seems he was protecting Al. Somewhere along the journey from Tarazona to Casket he stopped spying and became one of them.

Now he had died fighting for them.

But what if Kreibs's real identity had been discovered? What would they have done to him? Al's concerns about his own false name, his volume of Pound, seem ridiculous now. Even a shooting would have been too gentle for Kreibs's sort of betrayal.

Al flings the leather booklet into the air, followed by the torn pages of poetry. He wants them dead, too. The silly name and silly poems he would read to a dead man out of spite. A spatter of bullets blasts the works to shreds. Al nods with satisfaction.

"Blossoms," he whispers. Something about blossoms falling. He had carried those shredded poems to the window and let the flakes sift through his fingers and settle onto the stones below. A petal stuck to his shoe and Kreibs found it. Did it contain a single letter? A *P* for Pound or an *O* like that woman's mouth? Kreibs never said. He rolled it thoughtfully and flicked it into the fire. Yes, he was protecting him. Al looks out at the ruined town now, blinking, his eyes dry and the lids dragging over them like paper.

IT TAKES MOST OF THE day for the exhausted troops to move a few miles. They stop to rest in a neglected grove, the grass meeting the low-hanging branches of olive and almond trees, still bearing black bullets of unpicked fruit from the fall. The trees have grown so close together that the space between each forms shadowy caves. Above, sunlight flickers over the satin leaves. Insects hum in the drowsy heat while birdsong rises from the trees. And there is a smell, a green perfume when trees come into leaf. The Yukon smelled like that. Princeton, too.

Lapinsky sits, and with hands thick as baseball mitts removes a size thirteen boot. His foot is red and cracked. Moisture has peeled the entire sole away, and so he has bound his sole to his foot with a strip of red silk torn from a scarf. He unties the ragged ribbon and inspects the rotted skin.

"It was Daniels's." Lapinsky lifts the strip of silk. "I don't think he'd mind."

Al doesn't answer. The birdsong has stopped. He squints through the jumbled branches. The recent battle seems distant and unreal, except for Kreibs's voice that comes to him now, warning him not to get too comfortable.

Al turns to Solly, who jerks his rifle to the left as a signal to disperse.

"Get up," Al whispers to Lapinsky. "After Solly. Move."

"My foot's killing me."

"I said, get up! Get that boot back on!"

Lapinsky unwinds his large frame until he is standing on one foot, the other raised like a claw. Al is in a crouched position ready to spring forward, eyes searching out a deep hollow, a foxhole. He can't see Solly. He hears the distinctive squeaking of rolling treads, sees the branches shake and dives into a hollow just as a hulking Russian tank bursts into the orchard, flying the Fascist colours of red and yellow.

"Lap!" he yells. "It's not ours!"

He has expected the sleek lines of a Panzer. That would have been just, to meet his end at the long barrel of a German machine gun. But this is a T-26, a tank like a stack of biscuit boxes, one of theirs, one the Fascists have commandeered.

"Lap!" he yells again. "There!"

There is room for two in the foxhole, but Lapinsky still stands on one foot and sways, then falls in front of the tank. He tries to crawl but the treads roll forward, chewing up the ground, the orchard grass the same grey-green as Lapinsky's uniform, dangling from the metal teeth. Al closes his eyes, bends his head, claps his hands over his ears.

Tank after tank, too many for Solly's group to outrun, and then the snapping of limbs, the shriek of metal, followed by blast after blast of shell fire, consuming all noise, the air, lifting Al's brain until his skull is ready to split open.

He huddles in his hole, hands over his ears. When the ground stops shaking he lowers his hands and listens for the sound of familiar voices. There are none.

He waits a long time before crawling out and standing in what used to be a field of orchard grass. He keeps his eyes level with the horizon and away from the immediate ground and the gory ruts left by the tanks.

Most of the trees have been flattened. The few left standing have been pruned by gunfire into pointed stumps, the unpicked fruit blasted from their branches and hammered into the dirt. Dead seeds. Nothing will sprout from them.

And what of his friends?

They will never see another seed take root, another tree flower. He will never see them again. How is it possible that in one day he has lost every member of his unit?

The last land they walked was this burnt and corrupted corner of Spain. They hadn't marched to a final and glorious battle but squirmed and sweated along roads choked with mules and refugees and lunatics — a seething mass that in the end was their funeral procession. And when they fell, they landed in earth that was already dead and full of death, the graveyard and the orchard now one and the same.

Twenty-one

IT HAS BEEN THREE DAYS since he's last eaten. A sausage with mar-
malade and bread, coffee and toast, a small scoop of stew from the
kitchen truck. He can smell it still, coffee and smoke in his nose and
on his tongue. He swallows, trying to contain the taste. Garbanzo
beans. Yes, always them. But nothing since arriving here except
crusts of bread. When the gates open and guards drag steaming pots
across the dusty yard, Al staggers over with the other prisoners.
The guards can club him. He doesn't care. Here is food at last.

A chain-link fence edged in barbed wire confines them, but he
can hear a river surging close by. For two days he wandered, hoping
to cross that water and then set out on the road to Barcelona. To
her. But he reached the water only to find that this particular bend
no longer cut through republican soil. And by that twist of fate, and
water, he was no longer a soldier.

There is no shade in the yard and the guards make them stand in
a long line for a long time, bare-headed, holding empty bowls.

Now, finally, they stumble forward, arms extended.

The soup smells wonderful. It isn't hot or even warm. It's fish
soup and has been sitting in open buckets, but Al gulps it down with
two hands on the bowl the way a child drinks from a cup.

For several hours he sits in the sun, eyes closed. It is good to feel
full again. But his stomach continues to swell. Sweat slicks his ribs.

He pitches forward with cramps that send ugly liquid spurting hotly down the backs of his legs. On hands and knees in the dusty yard, he writhes and shits, until, finally, he is wrung dry.

One by one, every man who drank the soup collapses.

Then a short guard struts into the yard, livid, holding a khaki sleeve over his nose. He is the one in charge, the *jefe*. He is not ill, none of the guards are. Al nods to himself. He has seen this before. They do not eat the same food. Why should they? The truth sharpens with each wave of cramps. In the relief camp, the foreman Potts was after a profit, only. Sickness was not his intention. As long as illness did not interfere with profit, he could watch from a distance, unmoved. But there is no profit for the jefe. Sickness is not his concern except that he has to run this prison, inspect this yard and breathe its air. There are too many prisoners, and now they are stinking up the place.

He points at the men, at the soup bowls, then at the guards. He screams in a language that needs no interpretation. This prison is beneath him. One day he will run a beautiful, modern facility, befitting of a man of his stature. Al shifts onto his hip, the grit grinding through his worn trousers and into his flesh. He watches the jefe shout, then snap both lapels and march out of the yard.

Each prisoner is given a bucket of cloudy water to wash away the stench.

Al rolls onto his feet, strips to his skin and splashes with handfuls scooped from the bucket. Then he plunges his foul rags into the bucket and washes them, too. He spreads them out on the ground where they will get dusty but at least be bleached of odour by the sun. Weak with sickness and hunger, he squats beside the wet remnants of his uniform, bare back against a rusted, metal wall, bare testicles dusting the dry ground, hands hanging casually between his thighs, shielding himself. He mustn't look nervous. No. Not fearful, or the guards will go for him.

His khakis dry quickly in the warm spring sun. He pulls the hot cotton over his skin, relieved to have its protection again, and follows the others through the gaping doors, past rows of tall, silent machines, their belts and wheels frozen in place.

A sudden gust of wind sets the walls of corrugated metal groaning and then they too fall silent. Al settles into his corner.

This prison is unlike any prison he's heard of. There are no locks on the doors, no bars on the windows. They are not handcuffed or chained. But guns are trained on every possible exit.

It's a silk factory, abandoned when the shells started falling. Al can imagine the workers running, the whistle of approaching doom in their ears as the machines buzzed untended, the lengths of fabric spilling onto the floor, the upper belts wrenching loose, and then flinging strips of silk into the iron rafters.

Above him now in the high ceiling, those pale strips float before the sloping windows. Grey-white, blue-white, pink-white. They drift in the air like waves of snow in a Yukon sky.

Each day his eyes seek the solace of this high corner as he waits for the trucks that will transport them to a real prisoner-of-war camp.

His eyes seek that corner whenever the prisoners are dragged out for routine beatings. They are dragged back, unrecognizable, their faces pulpy, their bodies folded at the knees, their feet useless. This is what his side would have done to Kreibs.

Here in the *factoria*, the foreign prisoners are beaten for any number of small offences, he sees that right away. The republicans are punished for the simple fact that they're Spanish, like their jailers. And while the foreigners can check their behaviour, can learn from the mistakes of others, the Spanish can never be anything but Spanish — the wrong Spanish, the ones who chose left instead of right. So they are beaten frequently and more violently than the others. It makes perfect sense to Al. In that other war the enemy had been from another country, spoke another language. He was a stranger. But in a civil war there is no enemy more threatening than the one who used to be your neighbour, the one who knows you best. This is what the Germans will do to Grunt, if they ever capture him.

His eyes seek the pastel strips and his thoughts place them against his cheek, against hers, when the daily selection of a dozen men is followed by a dozen shots fired somewhere on the banks of the river.

He has his answer at last. He will die here.

"HENDERSEN! HE CALLS OUT, BUT the man scuffing past insists he is not Hendersen. "You look like him," Al tells the new prisoner. He describes his tall, thin friend with the missing teeth.

"I had teeth before prison." The fair-haired man speaks with an accent. He squats on his heels beside Al.

"Are you Scandinavian?" Al runs his tongue over his own solid teeth. "My friend was."

The man nods and leans back against the wall. "I'm a Finn. Maybe your friend signed on with the Edgar André."

A thought fires in Al's brain. "The German battalion."

"Yes. I believe there were many from Denmark in that one."

There is no point asking the man's name. He could be one of tomorrow's dozen. But what he says — Al's thoughts grope for its significance. Hendersen with the Germans. Grunt with the English. There is something satisfying in that. A neatness. But the ability to reason slips in and out of his brain, until it vanishes.

Al raises his eyes. Henry's soft voice reaches him from the tunnels below Chinatown. *Step to the side*, he says. *What do you see?* Al sees streams of silk running through the clouds. He flops his head to the side and through another pane sees ribbons coiling like snakes. Henry told him something about a dragon. He tries, but he can't remember. All he can think of is Magdalena, who is in Barcelona where bombs drop from the sky.

Each night before falling asleep he describes to her trees so thick they block the sun, winters so cold they turn rivers to concrete. Each night she whispers back to him, *I would like to see your country.*

AL HAS NEVER KNOWN SUCH thirst. He can't stop thinking of water. Clear blue, ice cold. Rivers and lakes of it. If kind villagers didn't press oranges through the fence he would go mad with thirst. If he ever gets out, he begins to think ... and then stops. How many times has he begun such a promise to himself? Under the mud of the Somme. Back in the coal mine when he was a kid. In Belchite, too. The water that ran over her skin and then his, promising a future.

In his corner, Al rubs his teeth one by one with a green twig. Johnny said if a man in the bush allowed his teeth to rot then eating would become painful. He would grow weak, and die. But if he's going to die, why bother? Al sets the stick down. Considers it. Without sound teeth he cannot tear into the tough crusts of rye bread. His death will be due to starvation, not execution. Slow, not quick.

He picks up the stick and continues rubbing.

The trucks fail to show and the men can only guess they're being used elsewhere in the war. The guards grow bored. They toss loaves of bread into the yard and take shots at any prisoners who run out to grab them. The jefe curls his lip in disgust, and turns his back.

Lapinsky would have been the first to brave the gunfire. His big hunger could not have resisted the loaves of bread. And Daniels. His fawn-coloured hair, his pale flesh. The guards would have gone for him. Neither of the two would have lasted here. It was just as well.

Al forgets what Magdalena looks like, except for her scar. It curls vivid and purple in his mind, reminding him that he meant to ask how she got it. Her photo is gone. He tore it up just as he had her address. Kreibs would have suggested that. Better destroyed than held by enemy hands, looked on by their eyes, used to torment him.

He presses his forehead into his hands and tries to recall lines of verse to fill his head. "Blossoms," he whispers, something about blossoms. He gets no further.

Al should have put a notch in the door frame for each day. He could have kept track of time. Instead, he scratches letters to Jack in the dust. *I am fine*, he writes, *just fine*.

The sky crackles like gunfire. A summer rainstorm rattles the walls and windows and drums on the tin roof. The Dragon Princess. That was it — she brings rain, and now she has brought it here, to the factoria. Al pulls himself to his feet and staggers to the window to watch. Heavy drops land on the hard-packed dirt like buckshot, then roll right off into the river. A fine, red mist of dust rises in the yard, and the storm ends as abruptly as it began.

Out of that dust appear two guards, marching between them a prisoner who wears the white silks and turban of a Moroccan prince. The factoria rumbles as though the machines have come to life. *A Moor*, the voices say, *from Franco's Army of Africa in a Fascist prison! What has he done to end up here?*

Al lifts his head. The guards will not be bored now.

The prisoners surge through the doors and out into the yard, Al among them. He is something to behold, this Moor, who sits cross-legged in a corner of the yard, his white turban gleaming in the sun, his white breeches ballooning like skirts, the hem of his white-lined cape settling in the red dust. If he understands English or even Spanish, he doesn't indicate it. Guards and prisoners call out. He refuses to speak.

The midday soup arrives. He refuses to eat.

Lunch. Supper. Breakfast. Lunch. Still he refuses.

He bears no resemblance to the murderous Moors who creep out at night to slit the throats of babies and rape their mothers. Al has seen the palatial mosques on distant purple hills, and that is where he places the Moor, strolling the long marble halls of an *alcázar*, cape billowing and curling.

The other prisoners have been taken from battlefields. They are underfed and filthy. The Moor's silks, and his pride, set him apart. He is a warrior prince, not a volunteer like each of them. He is a professional. His manner draws attention, but that is the first lesson Al learned in prison. Don't draw attention. Fade into the walls and the grounds, become part of the air.

He stares hard, trying to think these thoughts into the prince's head. *You make yourself a target. Get rid of the silk cape, the pantaloons, the turban.*

Yet if the Moor were to strip off his foreign uniform, prisoners and guards would be enraged by the sight of his naked, black flesh Worse to them than any Chinese. Darker. Evil. They would kill him.

Al chews his bottom lip.

His concern for the prince consumes him. He forgets about hunger. In the evenings the Moor is left in the yard while Al and the others are herded inside the factoria to sleep on the bare floor. Each morning, Al rushes outside on unsteady legs to make sure he is still there, sitting cross-legged, regal in the corner.

Dust flies in circles around him, rain falls on him, the sun beats down.

Lunch. Supper. Breakfast. Lunch.

One morning a crowd gathers around the prince, shouting, taunting. Two guards watch, and laugh. Al thinks they must be beating him, and he bursts into the circle, dizzy with fear.

But the Moor is sitting as still as stone. His turban is gone, and someone has torn his cape from his shoulders. Several prisoners dance around the cape like matadors and shout, "*Toro, toro!*" They clap and jeer, but the prince does not move.

The next day, at last, a truck arrives, and Al watches at the fence, fingers hooked through the mesh. It is here for the Moor. Weak with hunger, the prince's legs fold beneath him and they lug him out. Bare-footed, bare-headed and filthy, he looks just like the other prisoners.

Al returns to his corner where the silk billows above him in the last breath of summer. Someone has thrown the turban up into the rafters. It ripples and snaps, repeatedly drawing Al's thoughts to the Moor.

As he rubs his teeth he considers that the Moor offered no resistance to the crowd, made no attempt to eat or fight. He did something wrong to land in prison, and he accepted his fate. More than that. He embraced it.

Al accepts his fate, but he does everything in his limited power to delay it. He drinks his soup, he picks the bread crumbs from his beard, he rubs his teeth with a twig.

Even now, he brushes so vigorously that he uproots a tooth. He plucks the bloody bit from his mouth and places it in his palm, stares at it as though it were a piece of shrapnel. It means only one thing. His body is giving up bits of itself. It's giving up. He's dying.

He clenches the tooth in his fist. Why should he die? He hasn't found her. He hasn't made sure that she is all right. Magdalena's face leaps back into his mind, not just the scar but her eyes, her mouth, that fury of dark hair grazing the tips of her breasts.

In that instant, he thinks he understands the prince completely. Be like the Moor, he tells himself. Don't show emotion. Don't give anything away.

For all he knows the Moor went quietly into the truck and later made his escape. Al would never know. He doesn't want to. He only knows what he must do, and soon.

When the next day's dozen names are called out and the man across from him begins to cry, Al has already formed his plan.

"I'll go," he whispers. "I'll take your place."

He struggles to his feet and joins the line of prisoners that reels to the river's edge.

Many times, Al has watched the jefe yawn as he passes the open doors of the factoria, weary with the monotony of his daily job. Al guesses that for each dozen men marched out here and shot, easily half fall into the river alive. Chances are most of them drown soon after. Still, it is his only chance.

Al stands on the ragged cliff edge, swaying slightly, the froth of churning water below him, golden hills in the distance, and awaits his turn with a surging sense of joy. The gun fires down the line and bodies fall. He can feel damp dirt between his toes, a silken mist on his face. When the jefe stops to reload, Al holds his breath, ducks his head and bends his knees as though he is about to dive into a swimming pool, and drops over the edge. The wind is already whipping through his hair and clothes when he hears the pistol fire again.

Twenty-two

THE OLD PRODUCE TRUCK CREAKS as it bounces along the streets above the docks. The driver taps his brown nails nervously on the steering wheel and cranes his neck to check the sky. Overhead, aircraft rumble in the dark.

Al leans forward, peering through the windshield. A slurry of vegetables slides beneath his feet and the rank smell fills the cab. He rolls the window down but the air outside reeks. Smoke. Street garbage. Rotting leaves. The smell of neglect. He squints but can see little in the darkness. Barcelona is under blackout. A car rolls down the lonely street, its headlights switched off. The street lamps are extinguished, as well.

The driver pulls the truck to the side of the road and salutes with a raised fist. Al clenches his fist as well, then opens the door and steps out into the gloom.

Clouds straggle across the sky, and in the broken moonlight Al sees the hump of grey road just ahead. He begins to walk. Windows in the surrounding rows of tall buildings have been lined with newspapers, it appears, cardboard, heavy curtains. No light leaks through. He thinks all the inhabitants must be outside because the farther he walks the more people he sees and feels as they brush past him in the dark. Strolling along the wide avenue, they don't seem bothered by the lack of light or threat of bombs. Their tone is animated, not anxious, as though they are discussing art or theatre or everyday politics. *What is the mayor doing about the garbage? Nothing. Look at this mess.*

Al can only guess at their words. He has picked up a little Spanish but knows none of the language spoken here: Catalan, the driver told him.

Gradually, his own eyes adjust to the dark. Vendors call out from magazine stalls and waiters hover about café tables set out on the black street. Couples sit holding hands. The sun will be up soon but these are not early risers. The men drink brandy with their coffee. The women wear heels and carry evening bags.

All the way up one section of the street he has been hearing a continuous rasping sound like metal on rock and he imagines butchers sharpening knives on whetstones, but when he reaches the sound he discovers, instead, flower vendors dragging buckets of blooms across the bricks to their stalls. The flowers are all colours, petals pale as moonlight or dark as blood, and sunflowers, brilliant yellow even in this dark night. Once the sunlight strikes, the perfume will be staggering. He considers buying a spray of lilac, if they have it, or one of the brighter blooms. Will she consider that frivolous? He has already sent the shoes.

He pulls out a street map the driver sketched for him on a strip of newsprint. Once he steps into the narrow side streets he is immersed in complete darkness. The tightly packed buildings allow just a sliver of sky and throw the street into shadow, black on black.

All along the twisting streets people are crouched in the inky depths of doorways, hands cupping cigarettes to hide the red embers. Some of them talk, their soft voices rising up from the stoops and stairways, a constant hiss like rainfall. There is no need to whisper. The fighter pilots can't hear them. But the blackness encourages it and Al finds himself asking directions in a whisper, too.

Hands float upward, fingers pointing long and bony from coal-dark doorways. Al counts as he walks, his palm padding along the walls for guidance. At the place where the building should have been, his hand touches air and, groping lower, a jumble of stones. No number at all, no wall on which a number could be painted or engraved, no door.

He reels back then peers into the air, up the street, down, straight ahead. The street is only a block long. Moonlight shines briefly on the blasted buildings.

Has he got the address wrong? All these weeks. Months! He's had the wrong number or the wrong street? Lack of food, constant running — many things could have fogged his memory. Could this be the right address? She might have been killed in an air raid, crushed by falling debris.

He won't believe it.

He steps over the bricks, chucks his pack into a corner and slides down. With his back braced against the remains of the wall he listens to the drone of planes, the thunder of distant explosions.

An immense weariness envelopes him and he closes his eyes. As he falls asleep he sees again the little village just west of Tarragona, where the people burned what remained of his uniform and dressed him in a shapeless jacket and trousers, a worker's flat cap.

Brass instruments flash soundlessly in the sunlight of his dream. The villagers dance in slow motion while clouds of smoke build from the burning fabric. It is a confusing dream in black and white. Soldiers on horseback ride slowly into the gathering, the dancers no longer dancers but hobos who hobble out of the way, their limbs struggling as though they are hip high in ocean. Their shanties and flimsy tents fall under the horses' hooves. The cavalrymen cut casual figure eights, swinging clubs, knocking down the hobos whose mouths open, hands reaching for the sky, a jumble of sound-less agony. Smoke, so much smoke, as he tries to force his legs to move, to run. The musicians raise their instruments and then the soldiers raise their rifles.

He awakens with a kink in his neck and the faint warmth of winter sunlight on his face. The dream images crumble and the first sight to greet him is a pair of pale, elegant shoes, open-toed, with ankle straps.

He springs to his feet. "Where did you get those?"

A grey dress hangs over the old woman's bent frame. The hem grazes thin legs lumpy with veins.

"Those," he repeats, pointing at her feet, but she tilts her head, confused. "*Zapatos*. I gave them to her. I carried them everywhere and then I mailed them to Magdalena-Rose!"

The woman brightens and smiles. "Magdalena Rose," she says, "sí!" She points to the right.

"You know her?" Al asks. "Is she all right? Where is she? ¿*Dónde*?"

The woman beckons while he labours in a mixture of languages.

"No. Wait. Water. *Agua. Le agua maintenant* and then," he spins around. "*Razorio. Mi* —" he slaps his chin because he can't remember the words for skin, face, beard or shave in any language but English. He digs into his pack and produces a wine skin of water, a razor, a comb. "*Momento, s'il vous plaît*." He stuffs a dry toothbrush into his mouth.

"Sí, sí," she says and sits down on a ledge.

"*Solo, mio*," he tries, pulling out the toothbrush and hoping for privacy.

"Ah, sí," she replies and shakes her head sadly as if to say that she, too, is alone.

He gives up and takes a swig from the skin, swishes it around his mouth, spits onto the dusty bricks. Unbuttoning his shirt he pours a little water into his palms to wash. Then he shakes the bag. There might be enough for a shave.

"¿Agua?" he asks her. "More?"

"Sí," she says.

He smiles until she stands and takes the wine skin from his hands, expertly raises it and fires a last stream of water into the back of her throat.

Well. No shave, then. "Okay," he says. "Let's go. Magdalena-Rose, sí? *Vamoose.*"

She picks her way over the shattered pavement, tottering on the slender heels, Al two steps behind her.

He hasn't fully realized the damage until now, turning around to look behind him and seeing the street in full daylight. The fronts of the buildings have been peeled away and each floor gutted, leaving the stone-block framework empty, like stacks of apple crates.

They don't have far to walk. They round a corner, enter a lane and step through an unmarked, wooden door.

The inner space is a courtyard with several orange trees. Blankets and sheets have been strung up over the branches as tents. Water flows from a fountain and several tin pots sit around its edge, waiting to be filled. A small cooking fire burns where, once, elegant chairs must have been set. Two children race around the trees. Several old people, wrapped in sweaters, sit in the broken shade, watching. The old woman clatters over on Magdalena's shoes and sits with them.

The little girl screeches as she runs with the boy close behind her. The old people nod and mutter, smiling. Then the child comes to a halt in front of Al and raises her arm. "*Salut, senyor!*"

It's only half an arm, and Al tries to control the expression on his face. He salutes and says, "*Salud,*" but in a voice so quiet the girl snatches her limb from the air and hides it behind her back. Al smiles and feels the corners of his mouth stretch until they hurt.

Then he glimpses a sudden movement.

"Alejandro," she says, stepping out from behind a blanket. She wears a shimmering red skirt, snug across the hips and stomach and swirling about her legs, and those same ugly boots, even though Barcelona in early January is warm enough for the shoes he has sent her. After all, the old woman wears them.

He stands rooted to the spot. He is hoping for tears from her, an outburst of anger that he has taken so long to find her. He will tell her of his imprisonment and she will cry and throw her arms around him. He thinks of the water from the pump running over her skin, then his, linking them.

All she says is, "You received my note." She doesn't seem to notice the missing uniform, such as it was, or missing tooth.

"She's wearing your shoes." He wants it to sound like a casual statement of fact, has even intended to laugh at the end of it, but the accusatory tone is clear. They are far from the words he planned as he trudged along the dusty red roads that led to Barcelona. *I thought of nothing but you.*

Magdalena curls her lip. "They are the wrong colour." She offers no apology, nor thanks. It's not the truth, of course. Any colour would be better than the clumsy boots, and he might have said that, but she lifts a weary hand to her forehead and the movement reveals a fraying waistband, a small tear in her striped blouse. Al steps forward to touch her shoulder.

She jerks away. "You saw what happened to our other home. There is bombing and shelling all the time. From planes. From ships sitting right out there." She points behind him, but he finds himself looking for the wounded girl. Of course his concern about the shoes seems foolish.

She continues, "The rooms above are filled with refugees who arrived here before us. So we have this." Her hand sweeps over the courtyard. "All we have left is this."

She bends over the fire, keeping her eyes down as she stirs and bangs a large spoon. He wonders if she will cry.

"Well," she says at last, still looking down. "Will you stay?"

He crouches to help her. A pot of old stew, a bowl of unpeeled oranges and a length of stale bread. Lunch. There is wine, as always. The children race past, this time the girl chasing the boy, while the adults settle into the shade.

An old man turns to him. "You were an *internacional*?"

Al nods, noting the past tense.

"They left many weeks ago." The man raises his fist, saluting briefly. "There was a big procession in the streets, lots of speeches."

Maybe Hendersen was in that parade. Or Grunt, with bandages wrapped around his guts, following the Mac-Paps back to Canada.

The old man leans forward. "They left because the government asked them to. The war was to become a true *guerra civil*, they said. Spaniards fighting Spaniards. No foreign involvement. But —" he lifts his face to the sky "— bombs from *Italia* still fall."

Al asks him, "Is there a way to get through the border?"

The old man's eyes crinkle at the corners until they almost disappear. "They call me Pascal." He claps a large brown hand onto Al's knee. "You and I will talk some more."

"The others," Magdalena asks him, "the ones who came to the house with you —"

He lifts his face and she must know from his expression because she doesn't ask further.

IN THE AFTERNOON HE LIES on a pallet under one of the trees, close to Magdalena but surrounded by the others, who sleep. Pascal, with a cap pulled over his eyes. The old woman, still in the high heels. Both children in perfect repose, the girl with her arm tucked under her head. Al watches Magdalena as she falls deeper into sleep, how her face relaxes and her scar loses its angry colour. His own eyes close.

The snap of a sheet wakes him, and for a moment he thinks he is back in the silk factory.

She is bathing behind the sheet, sunlight angling into the court-yard, her body sharply defined in silhouette. Curve of hip, pinch of breast, a lifted foot, as long and slender as he'd imagined. The lux-urious sounds of water sloshing, fabric rustling. Then that same foot steps outside the curtain.

"You are waiting your turn?"

He rolls onto his feet, rakes at his tangled hair with his fingers.

"We have little firewood to heat the water. So we share. You don't mind?"

He could remind her of that moment by the pump, tell her how he felt when the water ran over both their skins. But he won't. It's one he keeps for himself as he strips behind the sheet and cups the water that was hers, still warm.

When he returns to his pallet she has coffee and an orange waiting for him. She is back in her boots and ready to go looking for day-old bread. "You can join me," she says.

He downs the coffee that tastes like boiled pencils and leaves the cup by the fire. He skins the orange with his thumbnail and follows her through the wooden door and down the narrow lane, leaving a trail of bright peelings.

Even in daylight the rows of ancient, dark buildings crowd out the sky and the narrow alleys angle in confusing directions. Al has to rely on Magdalena to navigate.

They pass her old street and he says, "It looks like Belchite."

"That's why we call it *Carrer Trencat*. That's Catalan for Broken Street."

"You speak Catalan, too?"

She squeezes his arm, amused. "Of course. And French. There is a saying: 'There are two kinds of speakers, those who speak several languages and those who speak English.' Here we are. *Las Ramblas*."

They round the corner onto the wide promenade he had walked along in the night. It is filled with people strolling and sitting at the café tables, waiters buzzing. He wonders if the street ever empties, if people ever sleep.

They pass the buckets of flowers and head toward a narrow alley.

"For a time," she tells him, "everyone wore workers' outfits. Ugly, dark coveralls. Sometimes I bought a flower for the buttonhole. I wanted colour. I wanted someone to challenge me, but no one seemed to notice."

He regrets not buying her flowers.

"And then," she sighs, "there was the big fight."

"In the streets. I heard about that." He scans the streetscape and from the corner of his eye watches for her reaction. "So, are you a communist?"

She rolls her dark eyes, revolted.

In a quieter voice he asks, "*Anarquista?*"

She doesn't answer his question, but continues, "The fight has ended and now —" she lifts both hands, palms upward "— we can wear whatever we want, but we have nothing."

Al knows better than to mention the shoes.

Magdalena takes his arm. It isn't a loving gesture but one that says, *listen to me*. He doesn't mind. He is in Barcelona, with her.

"We still have magnificent buildings," she says. "I'll show you."

The alley branches off into another alley and then a square, and just as they enter it an air raid sounds, lifting softly at first in the golden air, then racking up to a higher pitch, scattering pedestrians.

Her nails bite into the heel of his hand and they run.

Ahead is an opening in the pavement like the mouth of a mineshaft and he aims for it, pulling her along. He jumps down into the hole first, then lifts his arms to help her down.

She pushes his hand away. "I can do it." She lands beside him, steady in her boots.

The ground shakes and they lurch along a wall to the far end of what looks like a basement, slither over a ledge into a deeper chamber.

He wedges her into a corner and flattens himself against her, arms over her head, bracing for the impact. He feels the sharpness of her ribs and hip bones, smells the salt of her scalp rising up through the scent of cologne, lilies. Has she done this for him? The explosion sends clouds of coppery dust rolling along the tunnel, grit raining on their heads. When the rumbling moves farther off she pulls away and he steps back, slapping the dust from his arms.

"We are not the first ones down here," she says.

In the gloom he can make out a cluster of half-burnt candles. He feels in his pockets for matches, then strikes one to light the candles. The room leaps to life. Rows of columns, some shattered, a stairway that leads to nowhere, its top step hanging mid-air, and a wide, tiled floor in blues and whites and gold, a naked child riding a whale, an octopus curling its tendrils, several fish snaking along the checkered border.

"The bombings last spring must have uncovered this." She sits on one of the steps while he leans his weight against the wall, facing her. "I wanted to show you Barcelona. Its beautiful buildings." She twists her neck to survey the room. The scar pulses. "But here you are under the streets instead."

"Spain has been full of surprises. When I was a kid, I thought Spain was all bullfights and flamenco dances." He drops his eyes. It was Magdalena's mother who sent the castanets the Christmas that he, Jack and Rose leapt about the kitchen, clacking them between thumb and fingers. "The only bullring I saw was at Albacete. The only dancing —" if she were still in his arms he could show her. Instead, he describes the villagers who hid him and then waltzed as a band played and soldiers gathered.

She touches his hand. "They danced a *cobla*, a traditional Catalan dance. The Fascists don't like it, and the people knew that. They were a distraction so you could escape."

He had been climbing into the hills as the soldiers arrived and he could hear the music playing. Then suddenly he couldn't. The music had stopped.

"Like this, yes?" She places one hand on his shoulder, the other hand in his, raises it high and twirls around underneath it, just as the dancers had. Al feels as though he is on the highest scaffold, nothing but air and glittering light. He has travelled across the ocean for this moment.

Distant guns rumble. She gathers him close, at first, he thinks, in fear. Her quick movement knocks the candles over, snuffs out the flames. In the darkness she pulls him to the floor and then her fingers dig below his waist, sending a button spinning along the stones. His mouth against her mouth, neck, scar, tip of breast. She tastes of oranges from his hands that now slip under her skirt to cup her hips. She's already skinned herself free of her undergarment, and he pushes, pushes, darkness and warmth folding over him.

SHE WRIGGLES TO ADJUST HER skirt. "Not the candle," she says, her voice rising. "I'm not dressed yet."

He ignores her and blows out the match, not the candle, letting the wick catch flame and grow. When she turns to tug at the crimson hem, all she reveals is a length of thigh, the back of a knee. He closes his eyes and savours the sight, longs for an end to this war, a chance to take her away, to see her whole, complete.

She stretches her arms and tells him about growing up in Valencia, orange and lemon trees outside her window, her youth in the hot, dry hills of the Aragon, summers in England, where it was cooler and her mother's family held lawn parties. He recalls the photograph of the family picnic when she was a young child. He should tell her his real name.

"What is this place?" he asks instead.

"Part of the old Roman city, Barcino."

"It must be two thousand years old."

She lifts a shoulder. "Everyone digs up a piece of Rome in their gardens."

"Not where I'm from."

He has responded like Alex Johnson, of course, not Albert Fraser, who was from England, a land with many Roman ruins.

"What is it like, your country?"

Her drowsy fingertips find his ribs. He would love to show her the cobalt blue of a lake, or the twisted limbs of a ponderosa pine.

"You'd never go hungry," he says. "Not with all that food waiting to be caught. The wilderness is full of game."

At last she says it. "I would like to see your wilderness."

"You could come with me, now."

She lets out a cry. "You were hit?" she asks. She raises herself up on an elbow. On her fingertip is a pinprick of blood and she pops it into her mouth.

"No." He sits up and feels his ribs. "Not this time." As he has many times before, he pushes at the bone with thumb and finger until he feels a sharp point, then he kneads it up through the skin, pinches his fingers together and plucks it free.

He places it in his palm for her to see, tells her about the blast and the mud that buried him.

Some day, he will tell her about the German soldier, how the shrapnel continues to rise, a constant reminder. He pauses, expecting his guts to churn as they do each time he digs out a piece. But he feels fine. There is no trail of grey on his shins. He has checked often enough. This must be the last of them.

A thought strikes him then. Could they stay here? Not go back to the encampment in the courtyard, but stay here, alone? The shuddering from explosions loses its impact this far underground. It would be like living below Chinatown, he realizes, in the purple glow of the bricks where voices were hushed and sounds from the street above were muffled. A half-life removed from the rest of the world. Like a baby in a womb, Joe said.

Like a tomb, Al thinks.

He gets to his feet and pulls her up after him.

The explosions have stopped. They climb back through the hole, onto the street.

Under a darkening sky they pick their way back toward the tents among the orange trees. Their route is lit by buildings engulfed in flames, drawing crowds despite the fear of enemy planes.

People around them begin shouting and pointing up between the buildings. "*Bombas!*" and then a word that sounds absurdly like chocolate.

"What do they mean?" he asks.

"You saw Hélène. There was a rumour that Fascist planes were dropping chocolate. We saw something lying on the ground and the children ran over to see if it was true. I ran after them. I pulled André back, but I couldn't reach Hélène in time —" She tucks her hair behind her ear and exposes the purple scar. "Maybe it was one of ours. No one knows."

She looks up at the sky and Al tears his gaze from the scar and looks up, too.

"This is something else," she says.

Flames light up a sky dotted with bulky, brown packages. As each falls, white ropes burst from their tops and these ropes balloon into parachutes, the sound of each opening like the snap of a lady's fan. Clouds of silk fill the sky, drift downward.

Magdalena interprets for Al as an old man claims he has lived enough years already, and can risk opening a package. He steps forward as the silk settles onto the pavement, picks up a parcel and tears it open. There is no explosion, but his face falls. In his wrinkled hands he holds a bundle of papers. The outer sheets spill to the ground.

Al bends to retrieve one. "Fascist propaganda," he says. The poster shows a series of hammer and sickle shapes that gradually transform into a skull.

The old man drops the bundle. Al knows what's inside it, he can smell it through the sheets of paper: a loaf of bread, still warm and fragrant. Rye.

The message is clear: *Surrender or you will starve.* The ground is littered with packages and the air has filled with more white parachutes, and the scent of bread.

Magdalena says, "They are preparing to seize Barcelona. With this," she toes the bundle, "they hope to walk in."

Al watches her. If she takes the bread, she is not coming with him to see his wilderness. She is giving up. This is exactly what the Fascists hope each citizen will do. Then they will round up and shoot any of them who seem a threat. The old man. Her.

She hesitates for only a moment, and then gathers her red skirts about her thighs and crouches. But before she can reach the bundle Al grabs her wrist and lifts her.

He thinks of the women who bundled the sheaves, the men who swung the scythes, the soldiers who took their places. Him, watching the stalks fall at his touch.

"Your own people grew that grain," he reminds her. "The Fascists marched in and took it."

"Then it's our bread," she says, "isn't it?"

She is right. But still he holds her arm.

"Come with me," he says.

Al will find work, maybe even go back to painting. The last letter he received from Jack said jobs were opening up again. He could earn money once more, buy them all the food they need. Jack and Agnes could take the train down to Vancouver to meet them. They'd be a family together.

He'd have to explain to Magdalena who they are, though, and why his brother has a different name.

He takes a deep breath. "My real name is Al," he tells her, still holding her wrist. "Albert Fraser."

Her eyes narrow for a moment, as though she is trying to place the familiar name. Then her nostrils flare. He has lied to her. She yanks her arm back and for a moment he thinks she will strike him.

"You tell me this now?"

Eventually, perhaps, she will forgive him. There will be time for questions, for explanations, too. But not now. They have at most a few hours to see Pascal and make arrangements, gather her things. He doesn't know where they will get the money for the trip, what route they will take. He knows she can't stay here.

He takes her by the elbow. This time she doesn't pull away, because she must know it as well as he does: tonight will be their last night in Barcelona.

He'll memorize every detail as they make their way back to the encampment among the orange trees. Who knows where they might find themselves tomorrow? But now, right now, they walk arm in arm under a navy sky, parachutes bursting free from the tops of packages, uncoiling their lengths of fabric and then snaking up into the darkness again, over and over, to the snap of ladies' fans and the hiss of blooming silk.

Lustrous as ball gowns, ropes dangling like ribbons, the parachutes drape over curbs and branches and lampposts. They glow in the reflected firelight and dip so low that one sheet ignites, dragging a tail of flames up into the night where it lashes and writhes spectacularly, sending a shower of sparks down into the street. The air smells like autumn in Vancouver, and as he fills his lungs he pictures a procession much larger than the two of them. He can almost feel the presence of others hovering like shadows, spilling out from alleys and doorways, lining the streets, merging into a ghost parade of men that winds through the ancient streets, shuffles among the fallen silk, joining them, for the journey home.

Vancouver, 1975

AT 5:30 A.M. THE SMALL patch of yard behind Jackson Avenue is still bathed in the inky tones of night. If Al squints he can make out the unpainted pickets of the side fence, the winter plum next door, the tangle of Magdalena's roses crawling up the wall.

A beam of light leaps across the fence. Old Wong is awake too, his balding head framed by his kitchen window, a square of sunlight against the mulberry night. He sees Al and raises a dish rag in greeting. The arthritic plum twists above him, framing the window. Al lifts his shaving mug in reply. Maybe he'll go over later. Return that shovel of his.

He runs water and puts the coffee on. Then he sets up the shaving mug and razor, the hanging mirror. Out of habit he looks down the hall to the bedroom. She would give him hell to find him shaving over the kitchen sink. But he likes to smell the coffee perking and watch the yard lightening as he shaves.

A thin dribble of water in the mug moistens the cake of soap. He whips the brush until a thick froth bubbles to the top. He lifts his chin, stretches his neck until the dim light from the dangling bulb throws the right side of his throat into harsh relief.

The lump looks twice as large as yesterday. He twists his neck from side to side, studying it.

Usually it's the lungs. Men who haven't been in the mines for years start showing signs of it. Al seems healthy enough, still thin, his hair a thick tangle of salt and pepper. But hadn't they all looked fine until they didn't?

His doctor will say it's the cigarettes. He's always after him to quit.

In ever broadening circles he soaps until the left side of his neck is covered. Then he works the brush upward to the chin, twirls it over his cheeks and above his lip. Then down the right side of his neck and over the lump.

He picks up the razor and begins on the left side of his throat, scraping upward to expose smooth skin below.

Outside the window the black sky is draining into grey. Old Wong is out in his garden already, stirring fish scraps into a com post that he'll later dig into his vegetable plot.

It was Old Wong who found Al wandering the yard last week, holding a newspaper folded around a single article: *Franco Dead At 82.*

When Magdalena left Spain with Al, it was under the condition that, one day, she would return. All they needed was money, and Franco's death.

He lowers the razor as he recalls that she was ill for the entire crossing. He thought it was seasickness. But her health did not improve on the train. Then her stomach bulged, her breasts plumped and he added up the months. Oh, he was mad.

Al reaches into the cupboard with his free hand, cup and saucer rattling as he sets them down on the counter.

Her explanation was simple. *I thought you were dead.*

Al pours a cup, and lets it cool while he continues shaving.

It had been March in Belchite when they first met. January in Barcelona when they saw each other again. Foolish, foolish, to think she would wait, but he had.

Does he know? Al asked her.

I'm here and he's there, she said. *What does it matter?* Then, to his utter bewilderment, she added, *It will look like you. Perhaps only a little. But some. We have the same blood.*

Well. He lied to her. She lied to him. He supposed that made them even. He didn't forgive her right away, but he felt it his duty to look after her. They found this house, not far from his old apartment above the shops, with room for a family, a yard for a child to play in.

Their son was born and Magdalena named him little Alexander, Sandy, after him, because she never did call him Albert.

Al pulls his lip over his teeth and scrapes at the bristles under his nose, musing.

Well-meaning strangers always said the boy must take after his mother's side of the family. He looked nothing like Al.

Shortly after he was born, Hitler invaded Poland and the world broke into war. Al was too old for soldiering, and he doubted the Canadian government wanted him after his involvement in Spain. Besides, he had a family to support.

He found steady work at the Boeing aircraft plant, with its metal-strung insides and dangling plane parts that looked remarkably, soothingly, like the *Palais de l'Air*.

A year later, as Sandy slept, Magdalena read in the newspaper that the former president of Catalunya had been arrested in France by the Gestapo. He was taken back to Spain for execution. The last request of Lluís Companys, the article stated, was to remove his shoes so that he could die with his feet touching Catalan soil.

Al remembers that day with particular clarity because he came home that evening to the sounds of their year-old son sobbing. He went straight to the kitchen, looking for Magdalena. Instead, he found the newspaper on the table and Magdalena standing barefoot in their backyard. He hurried to the bedroom and scooped up Sandy from the crib, bounced him until he stopped crying. He changed a diaper and fixed a bottle, then fed the child. He bathed him and got a better fit on the diaper the second time. He put him back to bed. On that October evening while Magdalena grieved for a man she never knew and a country she feared she would never see again, Al became a father.

When Magdalena came inside her feet were blue. *I have decided to plant roses against the house*, she said. That was all she said that night. Al watched her feet as she padded out of the room. She was planting herself, as well.

As soon as the war ended, he went back to painting houses. Each month they set aside what they could toward Spain. She took in sewing work — the neighbour women stood on kitchen chairs while she crouched, a measuring tape around her neck, a row of pins glittering between her lips. Neither mentioned the unlikeli hood of the trip, but each year part of the money meant for Spain found its way into other purchases. A tricycle. A bicycle. A suit for Sandy's high-school graduation.

Her roses thrived. Blood red, pepper-scented.

Often he awoke at night and watched her sleeping, shades of midnight spilling over her pillow. If he had been a man of talent he would have composed a poem.

Did they find love? One time he asked her, *Maggie, would you have come with me if Franco had lost the war?* She had been arranging cut roses in a vase. *What a question*, she said. *He won!* But her lips, as he recalls, pulled in as though they were full of pins, and to smile would mean losing them.

It has taken the dictator thirty-six years to oblige them and die — two weeks too late for Magdalena. Al looks down the hall again, razor dangling in his hand.

It is now three weeks since her heart gave out. She was on a stepladder putting up kitchen curtains, and her last breath was the sound of breaking glass. Each night he wakes up, startled, to find her half of the bed empty. The house is unbearably quiet.

When Old Wong found Al in the yard last week holding Franco's obituary, he didn't try to get him talking the way most people might have. He took the newspaper from him and nudged him over to the raspberry and bamboo canes.

Twice a year Old Wong climbs over the side fence between their yards and together he and Al dig out rogue shoots. It has become one of their rituals along with smoking pipes on the front steps and talking about the snake parades.

There would be little growth, if any, in November, but Old Wong knew the familiar task would occupy him. They set to shovelling. All that morning they worked, digging up old canes, containing the roots of the remaining plants with sheets of plastic and metal. Then Old Wong had Al help him haul over a bucket of fishy compost for Magdalena's roses. By then Al had been too intent on the work to weep at the sight of her favourite flowers stubbornly blooming into November.

He and Old Wong haven't been in each other's yards since. It's rained all week.

Old Wong is his oldest friend.

Out loud Al says to his soaped reflection, "Everyone else is dead." Johnny and Jenny, then Jack, long before Agnes, though she was older. His lungs, the doctor said, from working in those coal mines.

And then all the others, so many others, simply gone, lost.

He applies more foam.

There is more stubble on the lump than anywhere else and he presses firmly with the razor to compensate. It scratches harshly against the blade. Suddenly he yelps in pain. The razor slips from his hand and clatters into the sink.

His fingers go to the lump, touch a sharp edge like a tooth. He cups his hands under the tap, rinses his neck, blots it hurriedly with the towel.

It can't be.

The black point throbs as he applies thumb and forefinger, pressing until it pops up and then out, leaving behind a small opening that bleeds surprisingly little. Al holds the splinter up to the light.

Has it been in his throat this whole time; has it worked itself up or down from somewhere else? Each time he thinks he has dug out the last of them, another eventually appears. He runs a hand over his throat, twists his neck from side to side, swallows. Nothing. No more discomfort.

His heart hammers at the memories heaved up by the shrapnel. He needs air. He leaves his coffee untouched and the splinter in the sink and staggers onto the little porch, grabs the railing, breathes deeply, looks around. A lip of light to the east bulges, the sky is the colour of bruises.

On weak legs he steps into the garden where the cool air might calm his foolish heart. At once he is swamped by the smells of compost and rotting fish mixing perversely with the last of the roses, a stench that grows stronger as the ground swims up from under him.

"Bloody hell," he curses, and the ripe dirt smacks him in the face, the stink of it up his nose and the grit of it in his mouth. He coughs and snorts and rolls onto his back, gasping. Something is squeezing his lungs.

The purple sky swirls above him, drawing him up until he feels he is floating, the small yard below him a square of black stabbed by spilled light from an open door, the night silence cut by a voice calling, "Albert!"

Then the sky releases him and he falls back to the ground. More beams of light leap across the square. Faces. A row of lanterns bobbing along a coal tunnel. The green light of gunfire and the sound of bullets peppering the soil.

Streams of lavender light cross overhead. Liquid eyes gather over him. All around, the strains of a Chinese violin. Footsteps like ink blots on a plate of ice. The blinding white of snow.

"Albert!"

Alejandro. He prefers that. The flutter and snap of silk. Magdalena standing against a Spanish sun that burns bright for a moment then fades.

He blinks as the steady beam of a flashlight turns from his face and is extinguished. From the pale sky, grey light spills over the little yard, the fence, and Old Wong's face.

His friend's gnarled hand pockets the flashlight. Old Wong turns to another neighbour. "He's okay, Ollie."

On his back Al regards the metallic light of an overcast sky. He can hear the two neighbours discussing who to call first.

The ambulance.

Yes, then his son.

Al struggles to sit up.

"Easy, Old Man." Old Wong sits beside Al, pats his arm. "Lie still."

Spider-fine strands of wet drizzle over Al's face. "Rain." The threads form beads on his lips.

"Continued life, Old Man. A sign for you. Sandy will be here soon."

"My son."

In the grey sky, knots of darker grey churn and tumble, unfurl sinuously, then gather together thick as smoke. Old Wong drapes his jacket over Al's chest, props an umbrella over his head. But Al pushes them aside.

He scans the coiling clouds, waiting. *My son.* The words roll and tumble, too. Sandy is a man now, a father. As Al beholds each new-born grandchild, he is struck by the fantastic sight of Jack's chin or Rose's fair skin or Magdalena's hair, but mostly, by his own features appearing in their faces — his eyes, his nose, his mouth — as if he is watching himself be born, over and over again, though he can claim no direct kinship.

He claims it, anyway.

Drops fall faster now, pelting the leaves of nearby bushes, beating on the tin roof over the shed. Then the wind swells, the skies open, and sheets of rain billow and slap, a deluge that drums the ground to mud, that sends neighbours scurrying for shelter. Except for Old Wong, who remains crouched beside Al, shaking his head at his stubbornness.

Soon the storm drains will fill to overflowing. Al can picture it. Car tires will slice through the giant puddles with a sound like the tearing of silk, drenching nearby pedestrians. It's the kind of cloud-burst Magdalena cursed even while she marvelled at its intensity. The kind of rain that lasts for days and turns the land a jade green. West coast rainforest rain, the kind Al never saw in France, in the Yukon or in Spain. He opens his arms and lets it fall all over him.

End note

ESTIMATES HAVE PLACED OVER 1,600 Canadian volunteer soldiers in Spain between 1936 and 1939. One-quarter of them died there.

Barcelona fell to Franco's Fascist forces in January of 1939. Valencia and Madrid fell two months later, on March 30 and 31 of 1939, ending the Spanish Civil War. Five months later, in September of 1939, Hitler invaded Poland, an act of aggression that triggered the start of World War Two.

Acknowledgements

TO JEN SOOKFONG LEE and Mary Novik of the SPiN writing group for their feedback and support, in equal measures, over many years, and to my agent, John Pearce, for his guidance, patience and understanding. My gratitude as well to Jack Hodgins for his generous advice and to my husband, Tony Wanless, for believing in *Underground*. Also, thanks to Thomas Wharton and Grant Buday who saw *Underground* in its infancy, and encouraged me, anyway; to Terri Brandmueller for careful readings; to Booming Ground, where it all began. To the men who offered their insights: Ashley, Orest, Paul and James.

A special thank you to Marc Côté, publisher and editor of Cormorant Books, for sharing my vision and for taking a chance on *Underground*; to the rest of the Cormorant crew for their talent and enthusiasm: Tannice Goddard, Angel Guerra, Bryan Ibeas, Coralee Leroux, Laura Houlihan, and Blake Sproule.

To the Canada Council for the Arts for its generous support that made possible a research trip to the north.

This is a work of fiction and as such is not intended to be a historical record. But I have endeavoured to stay as closely within the facts as the story would allow, and to capture the spirit and passions of the times, particularly those that led almost 1,700 Canadians to fight in the Spanish Civil War.

My appreciation to those who answered my questions and in many other ways helped in the area of research. Any errors are my own. To my father, Robert Hutton, for his memories of his father, who fought at the Somme; Diann, whose father, Tom (Red) Gleadhill, was a Mac-Pap; James Rear for guiding me for six days on the Yukon and Teslin rivers; The Erlams and Weigands for their memories of the Yukon; Jordi, Vicky and Laia Porta of Barcelona for their hospitality, Jordi as well for showing me the full-sized replica of Picasso's *Guernica*; Dan Posen, jazz trumpeter, of Barcelona, who invited me to see him play in a traditional *cobla*; my mother's twin, Henry Bacon, for recalling the shrapnel that emerged from their father's chin while he was shaving; my son, Garth Erlam, for the military facts; Margaret at the Metropole for allowing me to crawl through the hotel's basement to photograph the purple bricks; Cathy Lew, for arranging to have her uncle, Jack Chow, take me below the streets of Chinatown; the Eni family for many nurturing meals and stories; the late Henry Lahti who shared his knowledge about Scandinavians who fought in Spain.

Finally, my thanks to Arne Knudsen, now deceased, a Danish-born Canadian who fought in the Spanish Civil War with the Edgar André battalion. He sat through two interviews with me in the fall of 2005 and, at the age of 96, recalled the war of his youth in chilling detail.